Shane's Fire

Autumn Breeze Memories Collection

By Kat Pugh
Copyright©2019

Psalm 39:2-4

*2 I was dumb with silence, I held my peace, even
from good; and my sorrow was stirred.
3 My heart was hot within me, while I was musing
the fire burned: then spake I with my tongue,
4 Lord, make me to know mine end, and the measure
of my days, what it is: that I may know how frail I
am.*

King James Version

Table of Contents

DEDICATION 1
INTRODUCTION 2
CHAPTER 1... 5
CHAPTER 2... 11
CHAPTER 3... 18
CHAPTER 4... 23
CHAPTER 5... 28
CHAPTER 6... 34
CHAPTER 7... 40
CHAPTER 8... 47
CHAPTER 9... 52
CHAPTER 10... 58
CHAPTER 11... 63
CHAPTER 12... 70
CHAPTER 13... 80
CHAPTER 14... 89
CHAPTER 15... 99
CHAPTER 16...103
CHAPTER 17...107
CHAPTER 18...115
CHAPTER 19...118
CHAPTER 20...125
CHAPTER 21...134
CHAPTER 22...140
CHAPTER 23...150
CHAPTER 24...156
CHAPTER 25...163
CHAPTER 26...168
CHAPTER 27...177
CHAPTER 28...184
CHAPTER 29...191
CHAPTER 30...199

CHAPTER 31 206
CHAPTER 32 211
CHAPTER 33 218
CHAPTER 34 224
CHAPTER 35 229
CHAPTER 36 239
CHAPTER 37 247
CHAPTER 38 257
CHAPTER 39 263
CHAPTER 40 269
CHAPTER 41 275
CHAPTER 42 281
CHAPTER 43 287
CHAPTER 44 293
CHAPTER 45 301
CHAPTER 46 307
CHAPTER 47 312
CHAPTER 48 319
BEFORE YOU GO... 322

All Scripture references are taken from the King James Version, Public Domain.

Dedication

First and foremost, I dedicate this book to my Lord
and Savior, Jesus Christ. Without Him this book
could not have been written. I am humbled.

To all the Shanes and Seans of this world.
The young women and men who don't realize how
valuable they are in the eyes of God. This fiction
could be anybody's true story. Every family has
their secrets, their pains, and their stories of
redemption and liberation.

To my Mom and my Dad.
Raising a writer wasn't easy, I'm sure, but you
taught me how to use my words while considering
other's feelings. There is a right way and a wrong
way to use our words. I love you so much and I hope
this makes you proud.

To my children, Faith and Benjamin.
For letting me hide away to write all those days and
through many nights. I'm so blessed to be your
Mama. You both inspire me on so many levels.
I love you both so much!

Introduction
NO MATTER WHAT

No matter how many mistakes I've made, I still believe I'm worth loving. I no longer beat myself down and walk under the burdens of guilt and shame. I guess I could beat myself down and say no one deserves someone who's made the mistakes I've made, but I'm not my mistakes, I've been forgiven. The devil no longer has that grip of shame on my life!

Who has given me power that makes me stand firm in my speech? Who stood in my place and took my punishment? Jesus Christ! I realize there are people in my world that will never forgive me for the things I've said and done. I have and can apologize until my tongue falls out of my mouth, but their forgiveness isn't guaranteed.

There has been an invitation of forgiveness and love…a prior 2,000+ year old guaranteed covenant. A commitment from God, it's called unconditional love! It's called redemption.

No matter how I've been disappointed, I still believe I'm worth loving. My vision refuses yesterday's mistakes, and embraces awesome possibilities for future success. Even if I fail along the way, I can't sit down and stop, I still must pursue the vision…God's vision for my life.

Disappointment is a part of life, but it shouldn't pound a nail in your coffin. It reminds us there are other factors in this world to consider. There is life beyond disappointment to be lived and celebrated. Don't fear love, it's far too lonely without it.

No matter what I've gone through, I still believe I'm worth loving and my love is worth giving. Each day I rise, the Lord commands me to love, no matter what. Is this easy? You tell me. Have you tried to live this way? Sometimes you have to look deep, real deep. You have to understand some people aren't easy to love because they've been hurt. Hurting people do hurtful things. You don't become their victim, but you can pray for their peace and healing. That takes love.

No matter what, life is worth living. You never know what tomorrow holds. Contemplating suicide denies God the opportunity to reveal His sovereignty. He holds better tomorrows in His hand! I've learned that the struggles we go through today build character, strength, and trust in Him and in our ability to see our rainbows. When you feel you can't go on, God can be trusted to get you there. So you hold on. As you get close to the end of the rope tie a knot and hold on and hold tight. Help is on the way my friend!

No matter what, dreams are worth dreaming. Think about your dreams. They can come to pass, maybe not today, but someday! Each day we wake, we have another chance to work toward that dream, even if it means just getting through the day with the bare necessities. Each day you're still moving closer, as long as you keep that dream and plan alongside. Prepare yourself, see yourself fulfilling that dream. Who says your dream is crazy? It's someone who hasn't fulfilled their own dream. Don't let them keep you from staring at the stars at night. Don't let them stop you from seeking the end of your rainbow after your storm! Storms do end, you know!

No matter what, I'll learn and get through my mistakes. No matter what disappointments I've experienced, I'll forgive, move on, and love again. No matter what, my life is worth living, my dreams are worth dreaming, and I am worth loving.

Chapter 1
Life's a Party, Right?

Shane: Hey, girl, what's up? Are we still hitting happy hour tonight or what?

Lynn: Yeah! What's the drink limit to get the free grub?

Shane: One...Hah! I know how that is! It's a bit tight on this end too!

Lynn: I'm sure we'll see our friends tonight to hook a sista up! Meet you there! Cool?

Shane: Cool!

CLICK!

Oh, hello there! Let me introduce myself. I am Shane Vanity. Since this is my story, I'll just go ahead and tell you I'm the star of this gig! Hah! I love to laugh, smoke weed, and get my groove on every weekend at The Club! That's where I'm on my way to right now. And we have a ball! I must say, the brotha's are very hot there! Clean! Ain't nothing more attractive than a fine man with a nice haircut, smelling all good, with cash to spend...on me! My, my, my! Well...enough of that! I can't wait to catch up with my sistas!

We're not blood-related, but we are all tight. I refer to them as the Sista's Club...because they're my best friends in all the world. There are four of us; myself, Lynn, Essence, and D.J. Each of us has diverse lives for the simple fact that we are very different people. Yet in each of us is that thread of common ground. We're sista's trying to get ahead in life, or at least trying to keep up! Hah! We're all beautiful in our own special way.

Now let me tell you about my family. My parents are divorced and we don't know where my Dad is. My Mom is remarried, retired, and relaxing. My brotha is a little over zealous with the booze, but has a heart of gold. Me...well, I'll tell you more about me as we go along. How's that sound for a story? It's my truth...the way I see it, anyway.

I guess you're wondering what all of this is about, huh? Well, to be honest with you I've just invited you along for the ride of my life. I'm not sure what's going to bring my story to an end. I pray, maybe it will bring us to my new beginning. No joke. I guess I'm having fun...as long as the party's going!

Well, here we are! This is The Club! I love the vibrant neon colors and the music...it's so loud, you can hear it out here! Oh my, my, my...there goes...who is that with him? Uh oh, somebody is going to be mad tonight! Oh excuse me. I'm just checking things out, sizing up the night. You know, there is this guy that just lights my fire every time I see him. I still haven't really sat down and talked with him yet, but I sure do enjoy the view! Mmhm! My girls call it eye tag! Hah!

Well, let's go inside and check out my friends and we'll get our groove on! The D.J. is straight crazy!

Shane: Hey Lynn. How long have you been here?

Lynn: Long enough to see some very interesting things!

Shane: Yeah! Like what?

Lynn: Didn't Glenda and Johnny get married last year?

Shane: Yeah…

Lynn: Well, Glenda is over there in a booth with someone that don't look a bit like Johnny. Maybe it didn't work out. But then, I was pretty surprised Johnny married her anyway. She's not what you would call marrying material. Take me for instance. Johnny could have worked it all the way out with me. I'm the faithful type.

Shane: Yeah, girl! Talk to me! The only thing is that Johnny was looking for a freak-for-life. Not a

7

wife! Ya know?! I guess he's about to have a reality check!

Lynn: Hah! Shane you come up with some of the craziest sayings! But you know you do have a point! That brotha was straight asking for craziness!

Essence: Hey ladies! What's up? Is that Glenda back at it? You know she and Johnny broke up. I heard he was starting to smack her around.

D.J.: Yeah, Johnny hurt her pretty bad. It's like her Daddy all over again. She doesn't know it yet, but she deserves better than what she's putting up with. We need to love ourselves first, before we try to love someone else!

Shane: D.J. you say some deep stuff. Hey, since the Sista's Club is all here, let's go outside and smoke a J! I'm feeling a need to be set free!

Lynn: Cool! Let's do this thing!

Essence: I'm with ya!

D.J.: I'm already there!

Well, I'm sure you're wondering what us beautiful ladies look like! Brilliant colors of the human rainbow! A full variety of shapes and sizes! I'll let you imagine what we might look like. Hey, maybe I'll have a contest and someone out there reading

this just might come up with our look! I'm sure we're very real to some of you who can relate to us.

I don't know if this is a good thing to say, but I love to get high! I guess it gets me away from my problems. Between you and me, this is kicking my tail in the finance and motivation departments. But to be honest with you, what am I working for if I can't get a little something for myself. Life's a party...right?

Shane: Ahh! The great outdoors! Uh oh, is that my dude Maverick I see? Ladies, put down your matches! That brotha gets me so hot I could fire it up with my finger! HAH!

Essence: Hey Shane, looks like you're lighting his fire too! You guys really do need to stop this eye tag thang and get the party started!

Shane: Oh believe me, eye tag is a whole lot of fun right now. When it's time, he will make the move. Maverick...what a name! What a guy...let's get high!

Okay, no need for the details about our buzz session. Let's go back inside and find out what we've missed.

Shane: Now I'm ready to dance.

Lynn: Me too...ooh hooh!

D.J.: I love this song. Listen to the bass line, man does this groove sound good!

Essence: Ladies, I'll be right back—my groove thang calls!

Lynn: Work it, girl...show him how it's done!

D.J.: Work it out!

Shane: I'll flutter my eyes at Maverick, maybe he'll ask me to dance tonight! Come on Maverick, come to mama!

FURTHER INTO THE NIGHT

We've been having a good ole time tonight! We've all had a chance to shake our groove thangs! We came out to the patio to get a bite to eat. Oh...I should just throw my shoe at the cook...the food was...the bomb! Now tell me how you gonna cook chicken wings like that? He just needs to patent that wing! I had to play it off! I was grubbing so hard I was getting greasy! Hah! I sure didn't want Maverick to say, "My name is Maverick, but dang she eats like a horse"! Mmm, the breeze feels real good out here tonight. I'm just gonna chill out here and listen to the music and let my food digest. Why don't you relax and flip the page, I'll get back to you in a few.

Chapter 2
Eye Tag and You're it!

So, are you enjoying yourself, hanging around with us silly sistas? This night isn't much different from your nights out, right? I just love to sit back and watch the action. Some of the funniest sights and conversations go on here. I saw this chick walk by with toilet paper on her heel and I couldn't keep a straight face! She just KNEW she was cute. Haha! Man that stuff is funny to me! Well...is what I've been waiting for about to happen?! Do I feel my fire flickering!? Yes, yes, help me somebody! He got my eye mail! Yes!

Maverick: Hello.

Shane: Hi.

Maverick: Are you having a nice time tonight?

Shane: Yes I am. Are you?

Maverick: As a matter of fact, I am. And I hope it gets better.

Shane: What do you mean? How could your evening get better?

Now I really need to stop right here and dance and

shout! Because I've been waiting a mighty long time for this conversation! I don't want marriage, I don't want sex...well uh I can't say that with full honesty! But just not right now! Just to hear this man's voice is curling my toes! Do you hear me! I'm really hoping I can make his evening better and still maintain my dignity!

Maverick: Well, I haven't had the opportunity to dance with you all night. Did you save at least one dance for me?

Shane: Uh, sure I think I could squeeze out another dance, just for you.

Okay! This brotha is straight smooth! We are walking out to the dance floor. It's the weirdest thing...I could walk in my high heels earlier! Somehow my ankles have become rubbery. Now it would be totally jacked if I twisted my ankle before I had a chance to get me groove on! Hmmm...I could fall back into his arms. Nah! Too much drama!

Now I really like the way this brotha moves! I could burn a hole right here in the dance floor. Wouldn't that be jacked?! Big turn off! Okay, I really need to collect myself. He can't know that I'm off balance. I must maintain control or at least look like I have it. Now why are my girls laughing at me? I probably have a nervous look all over my face. I lose the beat when I'm nervous. Oh no...what if I have toilet paper on my high heel too?! Okay, I caught the beat. Now they're giving me the thumbs up. I really hope he doesn't notice all this.

Have my ears deceived me...do I hear a slow jam?! I love this song! Please ask me to dance, please, please, please! If I passed out, I wonder if he'd give me CPR.

Maverick: Hmm, a slow jam? May I have this dance?

Shane: Uh-huh. Sure.

Good, good. Hands in the right place...around my waist! Close enough to tease, and enough distance to keep my options open! Very good rhythm...he hasn't stepped on my feet. I'm in heaven. I'm in heaven I tell you! Okay, why does he smell so good! Okay, Shane, girl, get yourself together. He's talking to me...yeah right...he's talking to me! I'm looking right at him, but I can't even hear him. I'm mesmerized by those beautiful eyes! We'll have to move in a little closer. God, please help me tonight. I'm for real!

Maverick: Shane, I hope I'm not invading on another man's territory.

I have to handle this cool. He can't know I'm readily available...even though I am!

Shane: Hmm? If I was seeing someone, I wouldn't be slow grooving with you, now would I? What about you?

Maverick: Uh, no, I'm not seeing anyone. I do have to say, you caught my attention from the moment I first saw you.

Shane: Really? How's that?

Maverick: I'm sure you've heard how beautiful you are. But there is something else about you that I find striking. You seem to love life.

Oh YES, honey, I'm really loving my life right now!

Shane: Now how can you see all of that?

Maverick: I've been watching you.

Shane: Oh really? I take it, you like what you've been seeing?

Maverick: Mmhm...

Okay my heart just stopped! Did you just hear what this gorgeous specimen of a man just said to me? Good thing he's holding me, I'm about to fall over! I love my life! Dang, the song is over!? Oh

come on, not a fast groove! NOOOOOO! I want him to hold me and continue to whisper wonderful words of inspiration to me! Stone the D.J.!

Maverick: Do you want to stay out for another dance?

Shane: Well, not right now. I need to go to the ladies room. I'll be right back. Cool?

Maverick: Cool.

Yeah cool...I got to cool my jets! I feel like cussing out the D.J.! Maverick! Maverick! Maverick! I would love to hang out and rap a while, but I can't tell this man I want to mother his children just yet! Hah! Of course my sistas are already waiting for me in the ladies room! Come on in, let's hear what they have to say!

D.J.: Queen Sista Shane! Rocking the beat!

Essence: You were working that thang Shane!

Lynn: Eye tag has moved to full body tag—hey!

Shane: My ankles got weak! Could you feel the heat from your seat? How did we look together ya'll? Talk to me!

Essence: You do the talking sista!

Shane: From what he whispered in my ear, as we held each other oh so close...he's been checking me out for some time. And that's all I'm saying!

Lynn: Say no more! I'm off to the dance floor!

D.J.: Queen Sista Shane! Until we meet again!

Essence: You guys really looked hot, Shane. I'm irritated though. Dillon is here.

Shane: For real? What's going on with you two? You look so sad...isn't Dillon good for you?

Essence: Let's go outside, I need a cig...I need to talk.

Shane: Okay. I need to smoke too, this time I'll use my finger to light it. Hah! That Maverick is so hot! Do we look good together Essence?

Essence: Yeah...hot, real hot!

Shane: Let me tell Maverick I'll be back. I'll meet you at the door. Cool?

Essence: Yeah...cool.

Shane: Maverick, listen, I need to step out and talk with my sista for a few. How long are you staying?

Maverick: The night is still young. I'll be here for

a while. Take your time, I'll wait.

Shane: Thanks.

Now I'm starting to think Maverick is too good to be true! I really hope he's not waiting for a booty call. I'm really trying to maintain my dignity. But, my goodness, he's smooth and oh so fine! God, please help me. I'm for real! Calm down and take deep breaths girl, deep breaths. Come on, let's go outside.

Chapter 3
Allergic to Love

Now Essence is my confidant sista! We share a lot of secrets. She and Dillon have kids together. For some reason, she won't give Dillon 100%. I'm not sure why. Her Mom and Dad had a tore up marriage, it broke her heart. Her Mom has been in and out of her life...it would have been better if she stayed away. What's with these folks? I don't know, but I'm all ears and shoulders.

Essence: Shane, Dillon asked me to marry him again. I'm getting tired of coming up with excuses.

Shane: Explain to me again why you keep making excuses.

Essence: Well, actually I haven't explained it to you.

Shane: Yeah, right! And I don't get it Essence, because we share everything. Don't pull me away from my future-husband-and-the-daddy-of-my-children for this! Tell me what's really going on!

Essence: Shane, I'm scared of commitment. What if he gets me and then treats me like crap?

Shane: What if he gets you and treats you good? He's good with those kids. And you've always said he was good to you!

Essence: Well, another problem is...his Mom and I don't get along! She is a trip, Shane! She tries to talk to me any old kind of way...I can't stand it. Then she tells my kids that she loves them more than I do, because she's their grandma. What kind of crap is that, totally disrespecting me and my Mom...their other grandma? I hate her Shane! She makes me feel like...crap!

Shane: Yeah, that's jacked up, girl! What does he say about that?

Essence: He said he'd walk away from his Mom to be with me and our kids, if that's what he had to do. Even she knows this.

Shane: Hold up! Not too many men will do that! Essence, we've been friends forever. Please tell me what's going on with you, for real.

Essence: Shane, I just found out that I have... A.R.T.M.

Shane: Huh? Did you say ARTM? What is that...some kind of form of phobia or something like that?

Essence: Yeah. Allergic Reaction to Marriage! Hahaha! I just don't love the man like I should. It's not the kind of love a woman should feel for a man…to spend the rest of her life with. And I feel so bad about it. But I guess I shouldn't have ever started making love with him. It's just so dang good, Shane! What a mess I've made for all of us.

Shane: Making love? Girl, ya'll been making babies. So are you still doing the stanky dank?

Essence: Must you call it "doing the stanky dank"? There's got to be a better choice of words...let's see…

Shane: Essence! You're silly! But this really is involving other hearts besides your own. Don't forget the kids. I mean, I'm not holier than thou, but you have daughters. Do you want them to think living like this is cool?

Essence: He said if I didn't marry him, he couldn't bear to continue seeing the kids knowing that he can't have me. So I engage him to stay and help me with the kids. Shane, you know what? I sound like a desperate prostitute! What the hell am I doing to myself? It's like my Mama all over again in me. I never did understand what that was all about. What should I do Shane?

Shane: Just think about my question…what about your daughters? Okay, Dillon just got out of his car. Essence, you'll do what's right...either way. Here comes Dillon now. Go tell him how you feel. Work from that point. Talk to your Mama. I don't know…pray.

Essence: Pray?! Girl, I haven't done that in a long time. I sure ain't talking to my Mama! She ain't got nothing for me. Sigh Well, thanks for the ear and shoulder Shane. Later!

Shane: Ciao! Hi Dillon, bye Dillon!

This is getting pretty deep. Kind of a buzz kill and this is more than I want to handle right now. I'd like to handle Maverick right about now. Maybe I should run and jump in my car and leave before I find myself somewhere I'm not trying to be right now!

Look, I'm going to touch base with Maverick real quick. I'll let him ask for my number, if that's his intention, and I will head for home. I think Essence just burst my party balloon! Come on. Back to my stallion, Maverick! Man this brotha is so fine. I hope he's not a stalker. I can't say I like being watched that closely.

Shane: Hello there!

Maverick: Hi. Did you forget about me?

Shane: No. The conversation was deeper than what I expected. So...did you miss me?

Maverick: Maybe. Girl, you have such beautiful eyes. Would you dance with me again? I think this is the last slow groove for the night.

Shane: Mmhm, I must say, Maverick, you are very smooth. Have you had a lot of practice with the ladies?

Maverick: Practice? It's not hard to tell someone the truth or is it? I call it like I see it, Shane. Come on.

Okay...I'm gonna hang out a little while longer. I know it's getting late, so you can run along and find something else to do if you want. You ain't got to go home, but you're not gonna read anything else in this chapter! Hahaha! I'll see you in the next chapter... in my world of drama! Ciao!

Chapter 4
The Night's Still Young

Okay, so I didn't rush home right away. But I did have a fun night with Maverick. He asked for my number and walked me to my car. We talked for a while. This guy talked a lot about the Lord. I noticed that he didn't drink the whole night. I felt like a wilted flower. I'm interested in Maverick beyond his gorgeousness. But what is this brotha really about? He's smooth, fine, and confident, not to mention he smells so oh oh good! What a provocative combination. I hope he doesn't abuse that kind of power. Well, I'm off to bed. I'll catch up with you in a few.

RING! RING!

What?! This better not be Tom...booty calls are the stupidity of the past! I can't believe the nerve of this jerk!

Shane: Hello?!

Maverick: Hi, it's Maverick...I just wanted to see if you made it home safe.

Shane: Uh...yes, I'm in safe, thank you.

Maverick: Okay, cool. I'll let you get your beauty

sleep. Sweet dreams.

Shane: Is that all you wanted or where you just checking to see if I gave you my real number?

You're too fine and I've been waiting too long to do that.

Maverick: Shane…don't you think I care enough to see you're in safely? Why would you say that?

Shane: No reason. Maverick, thanks for calling. Good night!

Maverick: Good night Shane. Sweet dreams.

CLICK!

Now that was a little embarrassing! Why on earth would I say that…even though I was thinking it, I could have kept that to myself. But I will have sweet dreams alright! Oh yes! Sweet Maverick dreams! Running with the horses and riding bareback…

RING! RING!

Shane: Hello?

Tom: Hey, baby…what are you doing?

Shane: Going to bed.

Tom: Would you like some company?

Shane: Nope. Tom, do me a favor.

Tom: Anything for you! What?

Shane: If you can't take the time out of your busy schedule to treat me like a lady in the day time, don't you dare set me up to be your late night booty call! Don't call here anymore!

Tom: Shane!? I...I...

CLICK!

Oh did that feel good! He better not call here again. The answering machine will have to take my calls from here on out. Tom is a big joke...I'm so tired of his bull! Dude has issues and he's a pathological liar. There's just no room in my world for his nonsense. He's one of those guys that I met when I was partying pretty hard and not paying attention. The worst mistake I made was letting him come home with me one night. Once I sobered up and got to know him, I realized he's everything I DON'T want in a man. Now I can't shake him! Geez!

RING! RING!

Hello you have reached Shane's world. Leave a

message if you want to! *BEEP!*

Tom: Shane? Hello? I'm sorry. I'm sorry. Hello? Hello? I told you things had been pretty rough. I just wanted to stop by and make things right. You don't have to be with me tonight. I really wanted to hold you. Is that so wrong? Can't we work things...? *BEEP!*

RING! RING!

Hello you have reached Shane's world. Leave a message if you want to! *BEEP!*

Leo: Hey Shane, baby, this is Leo. Listen I've been trying to reach you all evening. I wanted to take you out to dinner and a movie. You can check your messages if you don't believe me. Girl you are so busy. I know you are sitting there listening to my message because I'm parked outside your apartment leaning on your warm car.

BEEP!

Oh boy Leo! Dang how do you get around that!? All in ya face...right? Let me throw some clothes on. Oh man, he IS leaning on my car. That's a dang shame, he's waving at me. Hahaha! I think Leo is so sweet, but he's always busy...talking about me. Let me get this man in here. So maybe I want to spend a little time with this hunk of man, I still

26

have my eye on Maverick though. I'm not tied down you know. Well, I guess I'll see you in the next chapter. We're gonna hang out for a while. Ciao!

Chapter 5
Mom and Daughter Play Date

BUZZ! BUZZ! BUZZ!

Oh man, I'm not feeling it this morning! I want to stay in bed for the rest of the day. Once Leo finally left the sun was coming up! I hate when he does that. That man knows he's fine though...we had a good old time and...that's all you need to know. Hah!

RING! RING! RING!

This better not be Mr. Tom Stankman!

Shane: Hello?

Mom: Hello darling! Are you up and on your way?

Shane: Huh? On my way to where? Did I forget something Mommy?

Mom: Baby, remember you promised you'd take me to the Inspirational Baptist Buffet, Fellowship, and Fashion Show today! Have you forgotten? I don't believe it Shane! Come on, baby, shake a leg!

Shane: Mom, hold up...let me catch my bearings! I'll call you right back...okay?

Mom: No, baby, I'll call you back. Listen Shane, I know you love to run the streets, but I really want us to spend some time together every once in a while. I hoped that this would be a good day to do that! Shake yourself and wake up. I can smell your stinky lips through the phone! Hahah!

Shane: What?! Whatever! Hah! Okay Mom, that's not nice, I just need to get going here. I'll talk to you in about a half hour silly lady...okay?

Mom: In a half hour! Bye, baby!

Shane: Bye Mom.

Stinky lips? Wow, okay. She's got jokes...she cracks me up. I know I'll get a good laugh today! Hmmm, where is my purse?! Let me get a joint ready before I take my shower. I really am not ready to be around Brotha Where-You-Been-Shane? And Deacon Girl-You-Still-A-Pretty-Thang! I get hit on more by these married men at church than the men in the clubs...I just ain't feeling it. I don't believe this is how it is everywhere, but it sure has put a bad taste in my mouth all together about this church thing! Let me get in the shower and get started...Mom will call me in a half hour on the nose.

I need to find something good to think about...oh yeah...Leo AND Maverick! Yummy yum! I just might have to take a cold shower! Between the two, I really am digging Maverick the most. What is it about that brotha that floats my dag on boat? He's so much more. What's a good word? He's more tantalizing...than Leo! Yeah, tantalizing! And Tom has no place on the list! Yuk!

I'll be with you in a moment. I'm sure my stinky lips are the last thing you want to imagine right now. Go peek on Maverick and find out what he's doing. I know you can't tell me, but I'm sure it would make the story more interesting!

MAVERICK'S WORLD

Maverick: So Man, when does this gig start?

Rico: Soon Man, help me with this speaker. I really appreciate you taking the time to help me out...I tried to call you last night. Where were you?

Maverick: I stepped out for a minute.

Rico: Yeah? I know about "stepping" out for a minute. Listen Mav, are you serious about what we discussed? Do you really feel like the Lord is calling you into the ministry?

Maverick: Yeah, I am. I mean look at what we do...it's already ministry, right.

Rico: Yes and no. "We" is different than "me". You dig, man? So, for real Mav, what took you out last night? What's all of that about Man? Are you in or just blowing smoke?

Maverick: Listen Man, I'm in, but I need to do this in my time. I don't want to jump in blind...I need to take my time.

Rico: Yeah, whatever. I guess when I was ready I jumped in with all my heart. Something or someone has a grip on your heart that's holding you back. What's her name?

Maverick: What? Now you're tripping man! Alright, is there anything else you need me to do?

Rico: Not at the moment. But I sure could use your help through this thing. They got me playing some booty shaking secular music. What are they thinking? They better be lucky my Mom begged me, because I sure didn't want to do this gig! I'm gonna slip in some gangster gospel jams and blow their minds! Can you hang out and help for a while? This is going to be wild! Watch and see!

Maverick: Okay. Listen, I see my Aunt. I'll be right back, I want to talk to her real quick.

BACK TO SHANE

Okay, good your back! I'm showered and feeling refreshed! I could do a commercial! Hey! So, did you peek in on Maverick? You did?! And what did you find out? I know you can't tell me, but you can't blame a girl for asking! Hah!

RING! RING! RING!

Shane: Hello?

Mom: Are you ready? I want to get a good seat!

Shane: Yes Ma'am! I'm on my way.

Mom: Wonderful Shane, we'll have a good time!

Shane: See you in fifteen minutes.

Mom: Okay! Be careful! Love you, bye.

Shane: Love you too, bye Mom.

Dang! My weed is getting low. I'll save this for later.
I really hope Brother Lee isn't there today. I guess he
has a crush on me. If I felt like I fit in, he'd be the
perfect choice. He plays the "game". It just seems
like some church folk are so fake. My Mom is in
church, but she can't wait to go smoke a cigarette and
have a beer after morning service. She's always
listening to her Isley Brother CDs. She's sweet, but
since she married my step-Dad, she's changed so
much. I guess I have too...who knows. Maybe she's
mad at God. Only He knows.

Sometimes my heart just hurts! My Dad just went on
with another woman and left us. How can you just
take up with another woman and leave your family?
He met this old trifling trick at church. I tell you, it
seems to me the devil likes to go to church too!
What's the difference between going to the club and
going to church?! They both are social activities, with
some folks lying and trying! I guess anywhere there
are people...there's always drama somewhere in the
mix. I don't know...that drama did a lot of damage to
our family.

Dad screwed up so bad that Sean had his friends
driving him around looking for him for years. It really
messed my brother up! Sean still wants to kick his
tail and we don't even know if he's still alive! It
messed us all up. Sean drinks pretty heavily now, but
he's a sweetheart when he's sober. Actually he's a
sweetheart when he's drunk too, he just cries a lot.
But it's totally jacked to see him drunk, he seems so

lost. I haven't heard from him in about a week.
Maybe I'll call him later today. Yeah, I will.

Well, I'm at my Mom's house. Listen, I'll meet up
with you at the Inspirational Baptist Buffet,
Fellowship, and Fashion Show...I really don't want to
subject you to this crazy conversation. I'll catch you
in the next chapter! Ciao!

Chapter 6

Just Keep It Real

AT THE FELLOWSHIP AND FASHION SHOW

Mom: Well, baby, let's go up toward the front! Oh! There goes Sister Gladys, she said her husband just passed a kidney stone…oh could you imagine!? They thought he had a real bad case of gas for the longest…I know that had to hurt! Anyway, I want to talk to her. Go get us a seat up front Shane!

Shane: T.M.I, Mom! Too much information!

And once again folks, she shews me away to chat with her buds. Oh well…gas pain and kidney stones is not what I want to hear about today or any other day.

D.J.: Hi Shane!

Shane: D.J. is that you? What the..? Who did your make-up? I told you about smoking that weed before you put it on! Hahaha!

D.J.: Real funny Shane! Believe me, I really hope no one recognizes me in my clown make-up! Hah! Girl, why did my Mom sign me up to be in this fashion show? She waited until this morning to tell me! What makes it so bad is I had a few too many drinks last night and I feel like crap!

Shane: Yeah, I know! But it was a good time…I think! So what time did you finally make it in?

D.J.: Four a.m.! Me and Lynn went over to that after hours joint on the west side. We met Frankie and Jeff. We had a blast… Frankie is getting ready to go to the Army. It's too bad though, I'd give him the time of day if we had the time.

Shane: Yeah…I feel you. It's hard to hold a long-distance relationship together. Remember when I was trying to keep up with Leo when he was out of town? Girl, now it's more like he's trying to keep up with…

Maverick: Hi Shane!

Shane: Huh?! Oh! Maverick!? Hi. **Okay, is he stalking me?**

D.J.: Hah! Busted. I need to get back and get ready. I'll talk to you later Shane! Hi Maverick! Bye Maverick!

Maverick: Hello…so Shane, what brings you out here? You look good in red! I'm really surprised to see you.

Shane: My Mom, thank you, and I'm really surprised to see you too! **I really was not expecting to see you here.**

Maverick: Uhm, yeah! I'm sorry for staring…it's just really good to see you. Have you found a seat yet?

Shane: Not yet, my Mom sent me ahead to find a couple seats close to the front. To be honest with you, I'm very uncomfortable in this church. I went here as a child.

35

Maverick: Oh yeah? Hey, there are a couple of seats where I'm sitting. Come on…take my hand, it's real close to the platform.

Shane: Thank you Maverick.

Okay…do you feel the heat? I was doing fine, minding my own business and POW! Heaven drops in right on time! He looks so nice. And, yes, he smells wonderful! Maybe this will be a good time after all. Maybe I'll get a chance to learn a little more about him. I can see if my Mom thinks he's cool or not. He better not be a stalker.

Mom: There you are. Shane, baby, these seats are perfect. How did you get them?

Shane: My friend Maverick had a couple next to him.

Mom: Mav who?

Shane: Maverick! Uh…Maverick I'd like to introduce you to my Mom, Mrs. Sharmane Douglas.

Maverick: Nice to meet you Mrs. Douglas.

Mom: You too, Maverick.

Maverick: Excuse me Shane, I'm helping with the music and I think Rico needs me. I'll be back in a bit.

Shane: Oh, okay.

Okay, maybe he's not a stalker after all.

Mom: Maverick, huh? He's really good looking isn't

he, baby? And he has good manners. Where did you meet him at?

Shane: Oh really, I hadn't noticed. I met him a while back, I forget where. He finally got the courage to ask for my number last night.

Mom: That's nice…you got to make them work for it, then you know they're serious. Hmm, when is this thang gonna start? There's only so much sitting my backsides can take! And this better be nice as much as the tickets cost!

Shane: I'm feeling you, Mom! D.J. is modeling…tell me if you can pick her out! **She's the one in clown makeup! Haha!**

Maverick watched me the whole time. He almost messed up with the sound. I loved it! Hah! D. J. did pretty good, but I could tell a drink would have made her feel more comfortable. She was shaking her groove thang all over the place…Haha! I guess I would sound hypocritical if I was one of them church folk…but I'm not. I don't try to play about something like this. I love the Lord in my own special way…I just don't get the church thing.

Good, my step-Dad just walked in. He can take this beautiful woman I call Mom home!

Mom: That was nice, I guess. But…DJ? What and why - what and why? Hahah! Tell her don't do that anymore, okay Shane. Make sure you give me a call later. Okay? Give me a hug.

Shane: Mom you're so silly! I will. Love you too and tell Mister I said hi.

Lovely Mom and daughter time has come to an end for today. I'll just mosey on over and talk to D.J. for a spell. She had us cracking up!

Shane: Queen Sista D.J.!

D.J.: Was I working it, girl?

Shane: You worked it out! I thought I was at the club or a circus! DJ, you did a cartwheel though! What were you thinking!? Hahaha! I was cracking up.

D.J.: Hahaha! Yeah, well a couple Mothers told me I shook my behind entirely too much. I felt like it was a challenge, so... What do they expect? We were jamming like the club! Oops! They'll get over it. Girl, I'm ready to blow this scene. It seems like we can't do anything right. Hypocrites! If they'd give us a real role model, maybe we'd do better! They need to get real...can't nobody be as perfect as they pretend to be! I think it's all for show. I don't get them.

Shane: I know, sometimes I hear "Jesus is your role model", but that's not really helping me. He's perfect and I'm not. Ain't nobody really living like that, that I know of anyways. I don't know D.J. I'm so ready for the real deal. If I ever come across it, I'll dive in head first! So girl, are you gone?

D.J.: Yeah! I'll call you later. Ciao!

Shane: Ciao!

This is so jacked. It seems some of the Mothers of the church are so busy telling us what we do wrong, they can't hear us. They make us feel like steaming stanky poop on a hot summer day! You would think they stepped out of the womb old, holy, and without sin! I sure miss my Grandma though, she loved the Lord, but there was something about her that separated her from everyone else. She had something real. She could relate to struggle. She had the real love and compassion of Christ. So real, it's THAT that I'm looking for. Not this stuff I've been seeing. One day I'm going to take the time and try to read her old Bible. That was the only thing she left me. She gave it to me for a reason. Mom cried when she gave it to me. She said my Grandma made it very clear that I was to get her Bible and no one else. Hmmm. I wonder why. I need to look through it.

Chapter 7

Chewing on more than Dinner

Maverick: Hello? Earth to Shane. Are you okay? You seem deep in thought. Are you okay?

Shane: Yeah. Just sitting here waiting for folks to clear the parking lot. Sometimes they get to blowing horns and stuff. I guess I should be going. Everyone has just about left now.

Maverick: No, uh I mean, don't leave just yet. If you're not in a rush, I'd like to kick it with you for a while.

Shane: Kick it? What do you have in mind? **Lord, I need you on standby, for real!**

Maverick: Well, did you enjoy the tiny chicken wings and crunchy potato salad?

Shane: It wasn't that bad! Hah!

Maverick: Well, did you enjoy the meal?

Shane: Uh, well, I didn't eat. But my Mom had a few choice words for it. That's why I didn't eat.

Maverick: Listen, my Aunt was in the kitchen, and she said that the ladies who were supposed to cook didn't show up... so they had to do a quick take out at that little hole in the wall down the street.

Shane: Remind me NOT to go there! It looked a mess!

Maverick: For real! If you're hungry, I'd love to take you to this nice little spot across town.

Shane: I'd love to.

Maverick: Great! Let's take my car. I'd like to enjoy your company on the way, if that's all right with you?

Shane: That's fine. Let me roll my windows up and lock the doors.

Did I just hit the million dollar jackpot?! Well it's not THAT good, but it sure is close! Eye tag has been fun, but I never dreamed that my fantasy is becoming reality! This brother seems to be going for it. I wonder what is on his mind concerning me. How did he end up at this function? I guess I'll have the opportunity to learn more about him today.

Good Lord! What kind of job does this brother have? His car is sweet! Oh yeah! A very nice change of pace! The last guy I went out with had me smelling like gasoline by the time we got to the restaurant. He had to climb through to the passengers' side to get out of the car, and he had cushions taped down on the seats. From the outside it was cool, once I got in I went into shock. It was our first and last date...boy, bye! Ladies, what is really going on?

Maverick: Shane, hold tight, let me get the door for you.

Shane: Huh? Uh, okay.

This is what I'm talking about! Treat me like a lady...

that's how I want to be loved!

Maverick: Okay, are you settled?

Shane: Yes, thank you.

Maverick: Listen, it's been a while since I've wanted to spend time with anyone. I've had a great time with you since you've finally given me the time of day!

Shane: Yeah right! It hasn't been like I've been surrounded by admirers' non-stop! I don't know Maverick, I think you're a tease.

Maverick: Yeah, that's what you think. You'd be surprised at the brothas that would love to spend time with you.

Shane: Whatever! I guess you're the only one with enough courage to approach me. Or was it on a dare?

Maverick: Courage, huh? I saw you fluttering those beautiful brown eyes at me, girl, you just don't know! Shane, you have no idea how interested I am in you, not a clue.

Shane: What took you so long to approach me...even my sistas were teasing me about how we've been playing eye tag for so long! What's up with that?

Maverick: We're here. I'll answer that question once we get seated and settled. Cool?

Shane: Mmhm.

Okay! My heart is beating so fast. My palms are

sweaty. I'm loving my life! Who needs weed when I'm high on Maverick...I could wrap that man up and take a hit! I'm really shaken at the way he's being so open. Dang, I've been through too much for this to be some kind of game! Lord, let this be for real and help me to do the right thing through it all.

Waitress: Can I take your order?

Maverick: What would you like to drink?

Shane: What are you having?

Maverick: I'll take a strawberry lemonade.

Shane: Um, yeah I'll have the same. That sounds really good!

Maverick: Are you sure? You were looking at the alcoholic beverages.

Shane: No, actually strawberry lemonade sounds delicious.

Honestly, I'd really love to have a drink right now. I wonder if they can spike it! Just kidding...I have some weed for later. I wonder if he gets high...all of a sudden I feel secretive and ashamed of my indulgences. What is really going on?

Maverick: Shane, what are the qualities you seek in life?

Shane: Huh? Where did that come from? What do you mean, qualities of life? Meaning...?

43

Maverick: Meaning, what do you want in life? Where do you see yourself going? Do you feel you have a contribution to give to this world, as crazy as it may seem?

Shane: Outside of my job, I haven't really put much thought into it. Let me get back to you on that. What about you? It sounds like you must have dreams bursting at the seams! Do you?

Maverick: Well, yes I do. I don't want to scare you away though.

Shane: What makes you think you'd scare me away?

Maverick: Shane, I'm not one to play the field, especially at this time in my life. I've been through a lot as far as relationships go. I'm not interested in games. I'm interested in...Well, I'm interested in the condition of man. And I'd like a woman by my side that supports that. A woman who loves life...possibly ministry!

Shane: Maverick, what or who do you think I am? Do I look like Mom Teresa to you? I'm a far cry from a "good girl". **Ugh did I just say that out loud?** I'm not on the arm of every guy who gives me a moment of his time, but I'm not living the way you're thinking! I hate to disappoint you, but I think you have me mixed up with someone else or something.

Maverick: See, I knew you would freak. Listen, Shane, calm down, take a deep breath. I'm not saying I'm perfect by no means. I just wanted to put that out on the table. Shane, I'm interested in you. Since we've started talking, my interest has increased. I don't know

44

how you view yourself, but you are truly an incredible woman. Don't you know that?

Shane: I don't know. I guess it's been a while since I've taken inventory of myself. Maverick, I know the best move for us is to establish a good friendship first. From there I can support you without the pressure.

Did I just say that? These dang cold feet, girl, you got cold feet! Oh NO! I didn't mean to say that. I was thinking it and then boom it bursts right out of my mouth! What is he thinking? I could get up and run out of here right now. I'm crazy about this guy, but he's making me feel my inadequacies. I don't feel good enough for this man. Here he comes talking about the condition of man? Meaning of life? Now I need a joint, a drink or something! Ministry? He is straight tripping! I ain't the one.

Shane: I mean...well, I'm interested in you! God knows I am. I've been through a lot in relationships and I don't want to hurt you, or be hurt. Can you give it to me slow, and let me chew each bite? The truth is...I wasn't expecting this type of first date conversation.

Maverick: Shane, I'm sorry. I feel like an idiot about now. Shoe leather tastes real bad! Look, I'll bring it down and take it slow. I'll show you what I mean. I'm not about to scare you off.

Shane: Good, Maverick, I'm cool if you take it slow. It sounds like you're about something real and I'd like to find out more about your dreams. I'm just not used to a man with this much substance.

Maverick: Cool! Mmm! The food is here! Let's eat and go from there.

Shane: Cool!

Thank God the food has arrived. I'll have to eat slowly so I don't choke! Whoa...Maverick. You've got to slow that down my brotha! Is it me, or is he running like a race horse trying to win a soul for Jesus?! How would you handle these questions? See...you have time to think about it, but if it was all in your face like this you'd probably freak out too! Even if it's just a little bit.

I'll just say this...it's about time I had a challenge...even though he scares the mess out of me, he's what I need. I have a feeling you tuned in to my life at the right time. Things are definitely changing...I'll catch you in the next chapter.

Chapter 8

How did I get so shallow?

Finally, I'm alone. Free to smoke this J and think about my day! Maverick, Maverick, Maverick! What is really going on? This brotha is sea deep! Deep I tell you! Have I been wasting my time living a superficial life? Could there be more to this life than just getting up, going to work, getting high and going to bed?

My Mom and them used to talk about the blood, sweat and tears of the 60's. A time when folks stood for something and the people had a purpose to get up in the morning. It seems somewhere along the way, we stopped pressing on. I guess I've become a part of a smoked out generation, but I really don't know how to change yet. I want to though.

I believe God puts people in our lives for a season and a reason. I wonder what Maverick's purpose is for coming into my life. Regardless of what it might be...he sure is nice to look at! What do you think? Is there more to life than what I'm living? I really hope so.

RING! RING!

Shane: Hello?

Essence: Shane! What's up, girl!?

Shane: Not too much, what's going on?

Essence: Listen...do you hear it?

Shane: I don't hear anything.

Essence: Exactly! Dillon has the kids and I have a free night! Hallelujah! Are you free tonight? I already called Lynn and D.J.! We're thinking about going to The Club tonight...around 10! If you're free, meet us there...okay!?

Shane: Okay...I'll try.

Essence: Hold up sista! You sound down...is everything okay?

Shane: Yeah, I'm cool...just chillin', with a lot on my mind. I actually had an early dinner with Maverick today!

Essence: Say what?! How did that go? I don't feel no heat coming through the phone line...what happened?

Shane: Oh, no there is still heat...no doubt! But the brotha is so deep, girl. I'm not sure if I want deep right now. I guess I just need to think. This brotha had me walk away with much on my mind.

Essence: You know...that's not a bad thing! There are far too many shallow brothas in this world today. I think it's a good thang, personally. Shane, you used to be deep too, but you got to smoking on that weed, and you just seemed to flow, and let go. Ya know?

Shane: No, I don't know. What do you mean Essence? I used to be deep?

Essence: Girl, things were always on your mind. You always seemed to have an opinion about world affairs, fighting for a cause and stuff like that. Once we started hitting that weed real hard, you just eased off of it and got all party-fied. Not saying that it was bad or wrong...I just figured you couldn't change things, so you stopped talking about it. I guess we've been numbing the pain of life.

Shane: Wow...numb...that's just how I feel right now.

Essence: Well, Sista Deep, I'm getting ready. I want to take my time and do it right for tonight! If you can make it out, we'd love to have ya! We copped some weed earlier, so don't sweat it! Cool?

Shane: Yeah...cool. I just might see you out there...Ciao.

Essence: Tootles!

I would almost say this is a crazy dream or something. What do you think? This ride is getting kind of bumpy about now. I never realized that I was ever considered deep. I used to have these deep conversations with my Dad, before he left. Sometimes I hate him...when he left, it seems like he took a piece of my soul with him...a piece of myself. Even though it's been a lot of years...I still feel like something is missing... something important. I guess I am numbing the pain...like Sean.

RING! RING!

Shane: Hello?

Maverick: Hi Shane! Were you busy?

Shane: Hi Maverick! Well…I was thinking about going out for a while…

Maverick: I just wanted to let you know that I enjoyed our time together. I hope I didn't put you on Front Street too hard. Girl, I'm digging you and I…well I…um…well…

Shane: I can't believe it! You are at a loss for words?! You had a lot to say earlier. Hah!

Maverick: Yeah, I guess so. I'm truly at a loss for words! Shane, what are you doing to me…huh?

Shane: Whatever!

Maverick: Whatever? Oh so it's like that huh? You think I'm all talk…playing a game…don't you?

Shane: I didn't say that…are you?!

Maverick: Don't make me come over there, girl! I'll have you look in my eyes and see I'm for real! And I'll…

Shane: Maverick…I…I've been thinking about our conversation today. Actually, that's all I've been thinking about since dinner. You don't have to come and let me look in your eyes…I seen it earlier today.

Maverick: Yeah…I know. I feel like I've scared you away. Have I?

Shane: No, no, you just made me tap into a girl I once knew a long time ago. I used to be so involved…I had dreams of making a change, but no one around me ever

50

stepped up and wanted to go with me. I wanted to make a difference, even if it was in one person's life, but I guess I was too scared to do it alone...I don't know.

Maverick: Shane, can I come by and pick you up? I want to talk. I promise, I'll keep it light...let's just savor the moment...cool?

Shane: Uh...well...sure, I'd like that. About what time do you need me ready?

Maverick: How soon can you be ready?

Shane: Give me an hour.

Maverick: I'll be there in an hour and fifteen.

Shane: Okay.

I need some mellow time. I think I'll wear my new jeans and that new blouse I've been living to impress Maverick with. So what do you think about all of this? Ever since you opened this book into my life, all sorts of things have been going on. Do you have something to do with all of this? Hmm? Well, I'm gonna hit the showers once again...it's been a pretty hot day. We'll pick up the journey in a few. I'll be out quicker than you can turn this page. Hah!

Chapter 9
A Small World

A HALF HOUR LATER

Knock! Knock! Knock!

Uh oh, I'm so glad I took my shower when I did...I hope this is my brotha, Sean! We'll have a chance to talk!

Shane: Who is it?

Sean: Shane its Sean, open the door!

Shane: Sean, where have you been?! I left a message on...

Sean: Yeah, I got it. I need to talk little sister...do you have a minute?

Shane: I'll always have time for you Sean, what's up?

Sean: I was at the supermarket last night and ran into Carol. Do you remember Carol?

Shane: Let me think. Was she like the number one love of your life in high school...was it THAT Carol?

Sean: Oh man, Shane, she looked so good! I about fell out when I saw her.

Shane: Aww isn't that sweet?

Sean: Yeah...anyway, she saw me and I know I wasn't

looking too good. This alcohol is holding me down...so anyway I said hi to her, and asked how she was doing. When I looked her in her face, she had this kind of glow...she looked...shiny! I know this sounds weird!

Shane: Keep talking. I'm sure there was an explanation, right? Maybe it was her make-up or something like that.

Sean: Anyway, she told me that she got born-again and was attending that crazy church way out in the country. You know...near Route 650.

Shane: Yeah...did she call it crazy or is that your terminology?

Sean: Ahh...well that's mine. But anyway, she said that when she got born-again, it changed her life. She said she was real messed up when her Mom died and she got into drugs real heavy and from that she even lost a baby. Shane, she was real messed up.

Shane: Wow! I didn't know that!

Sean: Yeah, anyway she invited me to a fellowship earlier today, so I went. Shane, what she has is real! It blew my mind! I've never seen anything like it! People were...

Knock! Knock! Knock!

Sean: Who is it?! Interrupting me!

Shane: Sean, I'll do that...who is it?

Maverick: Shane, it's me...Maverick!

Sean: Maverick? This ain't no race track! Hahaha!

Shane: Shh Sean! Hi Maverick...come in. This is my brother Sean!

Sean: Maverick? What's up man...where do I know you from bro, the race track? Hahaha!

Maverick: Hey man, what's going on?! Nah, it couldn't be the race track. Oh, I see, you got jokes. Pretty funny...but you do look familiar man.

Sean: Yeah, hahaha, well anyway... listen Shane...like we were talking about...I'm going to go back. I really want to see what's really going on there! So I'm going tomorrow. Sis, I'd like you to come too. I was out when you called because I had to get my suit cleaned and get my old tired shoes cleaned up. I tried to get some new soles on them. The man didn't want to touch them! He told me I needed to just buy some new ones. Haha!

Shane: Wow, Sean, you're for real, huh? Excuse me gentlemen, I need to get my purse...don't leave yet Sean!

Sean: Yeah, okay Sis! Anyway, I'm ready to get my life back on track! Maverick! Now I remember where I know you from man!

Maverick: Yeah, I remember now too.

Sean: Listen man, don't tell Shane just yet, it would crush her!

Maverick: That's where we're going tonight...
Shane: What are you two talking about? I walk out

the room for one minute...and an alliance is formed between my men. Uh...I mean...

Sean: Oh yeah? Let me know how it goes, man! Since I know what you do, be sure my little sister is safe...cool!

Maverick: I promise!

Sean: Little sister, I'll call you in the a.m....cool?

Shane: Cool! Here Sean, you go and buy you a new pair of shoes and a nice shirt and tie for tomorrow. I expect to see you wearing them in the morning when you come and pick me up. I love you!

Sean: Ahh Shane (Choking up) I can't thank you enough, Lil Sis. I'll go straight to the store...I'll see you in the a.m. Later ya'll!

Oh man! I'm so proud of my big brotha! Lord, don't let him blow the money. I guess this is a good way to find out if he's for real. I really think he's for real...I NEED him to be for real. We need a good change in our lives.

Maverick: Well, Shane, you look great! How did you know purple was my favorite color?

Shane: Thank you Maverick, I didn't know, but now I know. So what were you and my brother talking about?

Maverick: You'll see!
Shane: If you've been anywhere my brother has been, I don't feel real good about that...I love him and all, but he's been known to be in some straight shady places. I

mean places the police won't even go! And I...

Maverick: Shane, baby girl, you're with me. I will make sure that you are safe. If I don't your brother would know where to find me. Ha ha...uh oh, I was just kind of playing, girl. Believe me, your brotha hasn't told you his whole story. I have a feeling he's on his way up!

Shane: Yeah...that wasn't funny. So you really do know him?

Maverick: I don't KNOW him, but I can say that where I have seen him...he'll be fine by and by!

Shane: I hope so! Maverick...I wonder about you! Okay, I'm ready!

Maverick: Great, come on.

Some things just blow my mind! Imagine Maverick having met my brother before! That is scary to me...my brother can be a trip! Still, I know how he used to be. He used to be involved in the youth ministry at the church. He could have easily been a youth pastor...but life smacks you so hard sometimes and makes it hard to get up. I know I don't talk a whole lot about prayer... but I pray for him. I pray for both of us! We have been through so much and we really need something to get us back on track!

For him to see Carol after all these years and seeing how her life has evolved, that's a wonderful thing. Sean had it bad for her...Carol was Sean's fire! Just like Maverick is trying to be mine! If Carol impressed

Sean enough to go to a fellowship and then be impressed enough to go back...something is really going on! He might even put on some cologne Hah!

I'm really going to take Sean up on that invitation...I know there is no perfect churches in this crazy world, but there has got to be something somewhere close to what Jesus tried to get going. I got to keep hope alive.

Chapter 10
Not Good With Surprises

Okay...where are we? I've only driven through this area...with my car doors locked, windows rolled up and looking straight ahead. I even ran a red light...I'm not trying to hang out here. And Maverick is looking for a parking spot?! Father God, what is really going on?!

Maverick: Shane, don't panic! You look terrified, baby... it's going to be okay! Believe me, you'll be safe with me.

Shane: Uh...Maverick...uh...what are we doing here?!

Maverick: Shane, this is my parents' Bed and Breakfast!

Shane: Maverick! Is this some kind of sick joke? What is this building? Hold up, this is that soup kitchen for the homeless! What are you talking about? That ain't funny!

Maverick: I know that, but we prefer to call it the Bed & Breakfast. It gives the place some dignity and the people who come here. Listen Shane, this is where I know your brother from.

Shane: What?! Hold up, Maverick! You saw Sean here?! Oh no, no...not here. This is the last place folks end up...

Maverick: Yes! And we were able to help him...really! I have the night off, but I told my Mom and Dad that I'd stop by. I told them I hoped I'd have company with me.

Shane: Maverick! Couldn't you have given me a hint! Jesus? **Sean? Oh wow!**

Maverick: Yes! JESUS has everything to do with this!

Shane: Oh.

Maverick: Let's go in through the back. Really Shane, it's okay.

Shane: I trust you, Maverick. Uh...yeah... let's go on in.

Okay, I sure wasn't expecting this to be a place to go and talk! But you better know I'll have plenty to say when this is over! I can't believe my brotha ended up in this place! Bed and breakfast? You've got to be kidding me! Oh God! The smell in this place isn't too pleasant. Oh, okay the dumpster is by the door. Okay...I really need to chill! Once I can breathe I'm going to take deep breaths, deep in, blow it out, deep breaths. I can't even play this off. My eyes feel like the size of quarters. Oh wow, you're reading my anxiety attack. Don't laugh at me. Thank God I'm a fictional character, I'd be ashamed to show my face if I were real. I'm doing the most.

Wow, this must be a horrible place to have to stay. How can someone fall to this level in their life? I could run and find a place to cry right now! I guess if you don't have anywhere to go, this is better than

being out on the streets. Who's in these pictures on the wall? These are nice. Is that Sean sitting down in the background? It sure is. Oh wow, he looks so raggedy and frail...beat down a bit. I can't cry. I can't cry right now!

I just changed my mind three times about Maverick! First I thought he was the future Daddy of my children and the husband of my old age, then I thought he was straight funky bringing me up in this place. But as we move in a little further, I now believe this brotha is cool...possibly beautiful. The pictures on the walls are incredible...really.

What a good looking couple...this must be Maverick's parents. Wow, the love shows in their eyes! Now I'm anxious to see what this night will hold. My heart is in my throat right now! Wow, this has to be the couple in the pictures. They have aged, but that safe love shows in their eyes. That kind of love that's warm and fuzzy... kind of like my favorite teddy bear...yeah I still have it and I sleep with him too!

Maverick: Hi Mom and Dad, how's it going tonight?

Mrs. Grace: It's been pretty busy tonight...you know how it is on the weekends! The women's area is full and the men are fighting a bit. I have a couple girls going cold turkey...so it's going to be a long night.

Mr. Grace: Yeah, I had to throw Freddie and Bingo out! I won't have that mess in here! They know the rules! Oh hello there. So, Maverick, are you going to introduce us? You know, young lady, you're the first young lady my son has ever brought here that didn't need our help. You must be something special! Hmm.

Shane: Hi, nice to meet you.

As I stand here in shock with a smile frozen on my face, hoping it's not real obvious.

Maverick: Uh yeah...This is a very special lady, her name is Shane Vanity! Shane these are my parents, Mr. and Mrs. Grace.

Mrs. Grace: Hi, baby, I'm sure this is overwhelming to walk in to! It's pretty busy on the weekends. Did Mav tell you what was going on here?

Shane: No, not in detail! You're right, I was a bit surprised when he pulled up here...uh, how long have you all been doing this?

Mrs. Grace: Doing this? Hmm…let's go sit in the Chapel... oh is my back hurting me! The hardest part is over...I think...anyway, come on in and have a pew, let's talk.

Shane: Uh...well. Are you coming, Maverick?

Maverick! Don't you leave me!

Maverick: I'll be close by, go ahead...it will be alright, I promise.

Shane: Uhm, okay.

Okay...I am EXTREMELY uncomfortable right now. Couldn't we have met at a nice dinner and later watched a little T.V. or sat out on the porch listening

61

to the sounds of the night at a nice little house in the suburbs? Now...I'm really trying to figure Maverick out! This is far deeper than I anticipated! But I really see the need here! My God, these folks need grant support...big time! Knowing my brother had to be here, I feel the need to do something more than just drive past like a brinks truck on lockdown. The walls need a fresh coat of paint. They could use new carpet in the hallways and replace some of the broken windows...ply wood is not the vision...

Well, I see I'm going to learn something new tonight. Don't you dare put this book down especially now. What do you think is getting ready to happen? If something jumps off, I know my way around this area to get out of here...so I hope there's no drama up in here. Come on, let's see what's going on here! Please don't leave me!

Chapter 11
A Girl Named Pearl

Maverick's Mom is incredible. She showed me a few of the rooms as we walked to the Chapel. It's set up pretty nice, it's just the outside looks so bad and there is still plenty of work that needs to be done inside. She said Maverick has been working hard to get it up to code and add improvements. I see where he was coming from when he talked about helping people. This is a ministry...for real. This is something I would consider being a part of. Once I can get through the fear! I heard someone moaning in one of the rooms...my hair stood up on the back of my neck! Jesus...are You with me?

Mrs. Grace: Shane, let me tell you about this girl name Pearl! Girl, this child Pearl was something else! Woo wee! She lived as if the world revolved around her! She was a trip...isn't that what they say...you young folks!

Yeah, her life was one big party! Pearl didn't care much about anything or anyone else. A lot of it had to do with watching her Mom and Dad fight and scream up until the day he beat her Mama so bad, the police had to carry him off to jail and then prison. Her Mama was never the same after that! I guess Pearl was a "good" girl and a dreamer up until that happened. Yes she was! But she decided, after all of that, staying numb and leaving her hellish conditions in any way she could was better than living in that life.

Her Mama started bringing all kinds of men to the

house. They'd get her real high and drunk until she passed out. Then they'd try to go after Pearl. She'd sleep with a knife under her pillow and lock her bedroom door. She stayed dressed, just in case she had to climb out the window and down the fire escape. There were times she had to do just that. She lived with fear every day.

So when Pearl got older and tired of all of that crazy living, she ran to the streets trying to find comfort! She started hanging out at the bars...until she was a regular. She was naïve at first, but then after a while...she wasn't so innocent anymore! She started selling her body for money to put food on the table. And then after a while it was for drugs and alcohol. Lord Jesus, she was a great big hot mess! Oh Jesus, she was a lost child!

One day, she ended up in some old crazy love triangle. Everyone was high on drugs and alcohol, and cussing and fighting...including her! They say one of those guys she was fooling with had a crazy gun-toting wife...and as Pearl was getting away she pulled out that gun and shot at her. The bullet grazed her back...I guess it was more than a graze...she ended up in a hospital, out of town for her protection, for months recovering from that nonsense! She had all kind of crazy nerve damage! She was in bad shape.

Shane: Oh...how awful!

Mrs. Grace: Mmhm! She had to go through physical therapy...and in those days, being a black woman, you weren't treated gentle...you know what I mean?! I guess it depended on who was on duty. But one night while she was in the hospital, Pearl made a promise to

64

God. She said, "God, if you give me a new life, I promise that I will make it count for something!" And that was that!

Shane: Uh...is that all to the story? What ever became of Pearl?

Mrs. Grace: Oh, plenty became of Pearl! When she got out of the hospital she had nowhere to go and didn't know anybody in that town. Her Mama ended up in a nursing home, she just couldn't take care of herself anymore! And her old Daddy was nowhere to be found. Not one family member wanted anything to do with her! Yeah, they visited her in the hospital...once or twice...but that was about it! She was nothing but trouble.

She knew she couldn't go back to the life she led before, because she promised God...and she meant it with all her heart! As she walked slowly, I mean slowly out of that hospital...this young taxi guy called out to her. He said, "Hey ma'am...do you need a ride?" She told him she didn't have no money and nowhere to go...so NO she didn't need no ride! But this taxi guy was persistent! She was in too much pain to argue, so she asked him "What exactly do you want?"

He told her, that just because he was a taxi driver didn't mean he can't be concerned. He asked Pearl was it true that she really didn't have nowhere to go! And she said "yes", so he told her he could help her. He brought Pearl here. She decided to change her name so she couldn't be traced. Here she recovered, cleaned up her life and she went back to school. She even got a college education. Ain't that something? That was that.

Mr. Grace: Pearl, that little girl Lola that's doing that cold turkey is awake and calling for you! Hurry up, baby! The nurse is with her, but she needs you!

PEARL?! What is really going on? So SHE is Pearl?! Whoa... I'm not real sure, but I think she just preached to me. Don't you think?! Maybe I've been going in a bad direction...like Sean. I'm not that bad, am I? Maybe that's not the lesson here. Hmm...

Mrs. Grace: Oh, this Lola girl is something else! Maverick talked her into coming back for help. Let me go take care of this girl. You and Maverick go on and leave now... we'll be fine. It was nice meeting you Shane, baby!

Shane: Uh, yes ma'am! Are you sure I can't help?!

Now I want to see you in action Ms. Pearl!

Mrs. Grace: Oh, I have plenty of help...but I'll take a rain check! Go on now, you and Mav have a nice evening...I'm sure I'll see you again...real soon! We'll talk again!

Shane: Yes ma'am. Okay...it was real nice talking to you!

Maverick: Are you ready?

Shane: It seems I have no choice...yeah, I guess.

Maverick: Shane, are you okay?

Shane: How long has this place been in existence?

Maverick: Wow, this place is older than us! It's been around a long time! But it needs a whole lot of work now!

Shane: Who owns it? Do your parents own this place!

Maverick: Yeah, my Mom and Dad were very close to the previous owners. As a matter of fact...my Dad used to drive a taxi cab back when he was young...he brought people here who needed help sometimes...that's how my parents met.

Shane: So, your Mom's name is Pearl?

Maverick: Yes, it is! How did you know?

Shane: Your Dad called her Pearl…

Maverick: Oh yeah. Did she by chance share a story with you about Pearl?

Shane: Maverick, I'm speechless about now. Excuse my tears...I'm just... jacked up right now.

Maverick: Shane, I...I'm...uh...here for you. Let me hold you close. We're almost to the car. I'll go ahead and take you home. I laid it on too heavy...I'm sorry.

I can't believe how this night is going. I'm so blown away! Let me get myself together right now! Jesus, what is really going on here?

Shane: Maverick, um...can I ask you a question?

Maverick: Sure, Shane.

Shane: Why did you bring me here?

Maverick: Well, at first I wasn't...I mean this wasn't the original plan. I mean, this wasn't the first step for tonight, but when I saw your brother Sean...I realized that God was bringing us together for a reason. I brought you to B&B to see what impact it would have on you and I needed to be up front with who I am and where I come from. Does that make any sense?

Shane: Yeah, I understand especially after earlier today. I guess I'm wondering why it's so important to you that I know this.

Maverick: Shane...do you remember where you first met me?

Shane: Yeah, well I saw you first at that little pizza joint down from The Club. But we met officially at The Club.

Maverick: Uh...no. You met me long before that!

Shane: If I would have met you long before that I'd remember believe me when I tell you! So what are you talking about?

Maverick: Camp Genesis.

Shane: Camp Genesis?! I haven't heard that name in years. You went to Camp Genesis? Shut up! So how come I don't remember you?

Maverick: That's what I'm trying to figure out! I remember you were very quiet. You had to be talked into doing everything. I overheard some of the camp

counselors talking about how homesick you were.
They said you cried a lot.

Shane: Camp Genesis...huh. My Mom sent me there
after our Dad left...I wouldn't say I was
homesick...more like heartbroken. Yeah...that summer
was a crazy blur. Well Mav, I hate to end this lovely
conversation, but I need to take my tired self into my
house and get some sleep. I really had a good
time...very interesting. I hope you don't mind if I
don't invite you in.

Maverick: Shane, uh, that's fine. I'll talk with you
later.

**Well, Maverick brought me home, safe and sound!
How could I ever be the same after tonight! I'm glad
he brought me home though...I'm not sure how I'm
feeling about now. I need some time to chew on this
here! I'm tired. It must be from all the tension at the
B&B. I always hear about shootings out that way.
Dang! I was straight scared. Well I'm home safe now.**

**I've got a just little weed...I got to get me some more!
I'm going to go to church with my brother tomorrow.
It's time to find that missing link to Jesus! Listen, I
don't know what's going through your mind about
now, but I'm blown away! I'm so tired I don't know if
I can sleep or not, I might still slip out to The Club. I'll
see you in the next chapter.**

Chapter 12
Can People Really Change?

KNOCK! KNOCK! KNOCK!

Shane: I'll be right there! Who is it?

Sean: It's me Sis, hurry up...open the door!

Shane: Okay...sorry, I was in the bathroom getting my face on! Okay...I'm ready. How do I look?

Sean: Cool. Listen, Carol is in the car...Shane...wow! She looks so good, she smells good too, and she...

Shane: I get it Sean! Lord, help the brotha! Hah! Let's go!

Well, we are on our way to this "holy roller" church. I think the name is Holy Tabernacle of the Pre-Raptured...I could be mistaken. Anyway, Carol does look great! Seeing her brings back a lot of memories...some good and some sad. And Sean looks so handsome in his new shirt and tie and those shoes are sharp! He could have stayed out all night and got drunk...but he actually did the right thing! My big brotha is serious this time...I'm gonna keep watching him. If he can change, I know I have a shot!

Carol: Hi Shane!

Shane: Hi Carol! How are you?!

Carol: Blessed, girl! It's been a long time! You look

great!

Shane: Yes, a long time…you look great too!

Carol: I'm so glad you two are coming to church with me! I couldn't think of anyone else I'd want to share this experience with more! We've all been through hell…and I found out there is a way out…with a whole lot of peace!

Sean: Yeah, that's what I've been looking for! Peace! Hey Shane, did you and your race horse have a good time last night?

Shane: It blew my mind! Sean, how come you never told me?

Sean: Because I didn't want you to know how bad I had gotten. I've been in some pretty crazy places…but I never thought I'd end up there! That broke something in me, Shane. And your friend stayed and talked with me for a while. He really helped me…him and his parents. I told him when I get myself together, I might just come back and help them out. That boy can pray too! He's a good man, don't let him get away…even if you're scared.

Shane: Uh huh…well they could use the help. We'll talk more.

Scared…that ain't the half of it! I'm not ready for all of this!

Carol: Are you talking about the B&B?

Sean: Yeah.

Carol: Now let me tell you, Mrs. Grace ain't no joke! Her husband and her son...oh now I get the "race horse"...real funny Sean! Haha! Maverick is real cool!

Shane: Oh? Have you been there too?

Carol: Yeah...more than once! When I started messing around with those drugs...my mind was totally jacked. My Mom shut me down...I couldn't go to anyone...no one trusted me. I was in really bad shape, Shane!

Mrs. Grace took me in a few times. She told me the last time I was there that if I wasn't going to at least ask Jesus for help, I would just end up coming back over and over again...or worse. I thought she was nuts! Huh. Then one day...my Dr. Feel Good wasn't giving me any more drugs. He said I wasn't paying by cash anymore and he wasn't interested in my body anymore, because I had gotten so skinny and sickly looking. Just like that it stopped. I couldn't cop anything from anywhere! Mrs. Grace said she would pray for every door for my destruction to be closed tight, and they did...she ain't no joke!

Sean: Man, that's hard to believe you were living like that Carol!

Carol: I know. Pain can cause a person to do crazy things to escape it! I didn't go straight into the heavy drugs...I started out with beer and weed...for me after a while it just wasn't enough. I could still feel the pain.

Sean: Well, we're here! Where is a good place to park?

Carol: As close as you can get to those doors right there.

Sean: Cool!

All righty then! This is tripping me out! See, Carol was one of those girls who didn't party or have sex and didn't hang around those who did. She seemed to have her head on. I guess you never really know what's going on inside of folks!

This church is huge! It's absolutely beautiful! I really don't know what to expect, but I'm really excited!

Carol: Do you like it Shane?

Shane: So far, so good! There are a lot of people in here!

Carol: Yeah, but once you become a regular…you don't even notice it, people for the most part are friendly here. The ones that aren't I figure are hurting and that's why they're here.

Sean: Carol, can we sit up near the front? I don't want to miss anything!

Carol: Sure, let's see what we can find! Yaay Sean! You're really serious. Come on.

Well, that was an experience! I've never felt such peace in one place with SO many people! Usually there is mass confusion. Sean messed me all the way up! I've seen Sean cry, but I never seen him cry like that. And when he came back from the altar, he

looked so...so different! He tried to explain to me what happened to him, but he kept crying. I drove me home, and Carol took over from there. I'll call him later to see how he's doing.

RING! RING!

Shane: Hello?

Maverick: Hi Beautiful!

Shane: Well, hello handsome!

Maverick: Huh? You think I'm handsome, Shane?

Shane: Sure I do!

Maverick: Mmhm...how has your day been so far? I tried to call you earlier.

Shane: Incredible! I went to church!

Maverick: I'd love to hear about it...in person. Is that possible today?

Shane: Yeah, but I need to run an errand before we get together. Its two now, can I meet you somewhere about 3:30 p.m.?

Maverick: That's cool. Meet me at the Lion's Park at 3:30, okay?!

Shane: Okay...handsome!

Maverick: Mmhm I hear you, girl!

Cool, now it's time to cop a little something. D.J. told me to meet her at her crib about 2ish. I'll change real quick and head over to her house. Anyway, I have to tell her who I saw at the church today. I'll meet you at her house in a flash.

Ding! Ding!

D.J.: Who is it?

Shane: Me. Shane!

D.J.: Hey girl, come on in. Have a seat.

Shane: Oh this jam is sweet! You've got to let me borrow this!

D.J.: In time…I just got it! I love it!

Shane: Well, girl, what's up?

D.J.: You tell me…didn't you tell me you went to church with Sean and Carol?

Shane: Girl, yes!

D.J.: How did it go?

Shane: D.J. I'm going to be for real with you, it was so deep, I'm not sure what I saw. I'd love to have my Grandma back to talk to. She could explain more to me of what I experienced today.

D.J.: Experience? Interesting word.

Shane: Yeah. I just didn't expect some of the things

that went on. Like…their worship, you know, the singing was so heartfelt! You saw men and women with their hands raised and tears running down their cheeks. It was an experience. There were so many people and there was a peaceful feeling. Nothing like I imagined.

D.J.: Wow, Shane! Sounds different than what we've dealt with…huh?

Shane: You know! Sean was totally messed up!

D.J.: Dang! That must have been something to see! What did he do?!

Shane: Check this out…Sean got saved. No…no…I mean born-again! He was crying from the altar all the way home! It kind of freaked me out at first, but Carol said he was cool. She said it happened to her.

D.J.: Sean got saved?! Hold the press this is big news! Do you think this is real?

Shane: Most definitely. You got to know, my brotha doesn't play with God. He's done a lot of things, but he doesn't play with the Big Guy!

D.J.: I guess you're right there. I met a new honey last night, Shane. He is fine and…

Shane: Oh girl…I'd love to hear the details, but I got to meet Maverick, so I don't have a lot of time. Give me the collapsed version!

D.J.: Okay! His name is Jeffrey and he's single, available with money to spend. I'll tell you more about him when I have the time. Maverick...huh? It kind of surprised me to see him at that crazy fellowship!

Shane: You know! We have been kicking it pretty tough ever since. Girl, he's deep. Deeper than what I expected.

D.J.: I thought he seemed different. He kind of reminds me of a preacher or something. Shane is going to marry a preacher! Hahaha!

Shane: Whatever D.J.! I don't think I'm cut out to be a preacher's wife! It sounds too crazy! I haven't quite lived a "holy" life! More like a party till I drop, with an occasional booty call kind of life! Can't say I'm proud about my life at all, girl. I could see myself cussing church folks out, though. Yeah, I'm not the one.

D.J.: Shane! We all have done our dirt, but people change...don't you think? You have. You ain't as busy as you used to be. Now that I think of it, you haven't been busy since Tom and Leo. And that's been months.

Shane: Yeah, I guess. Tom's too goofy. Leo keeps bugging me for booty calls. I'm so done with both of them. I really can't stand Tom, though. He better get a clue...because I ain't the one!

D.J.: Tom's a jerk! I don't know Shane, if Leo's still calling you after all this time, something might be there. Or you got him whipped! Hahaha!

Shane: Girl! Hahaha! Whatever D.J., he blew it big time and I really was digging him for a long time. Well, time has gotten away from me. I better get going to meet Maverick! Thanks, girl! I'll talk to you later.

D.J.: All right, Shane. Be careful, girl, this stuff is pretty potent. It doesn't take much.

Shane: Okay…let me get myself together. Uh oh, D.J. the room is spinning!

D.J.: Whoa are you okay? See I told you to…

Shane: Hahaha! D.J., I'm just kidding! For real though, you know it takes a whole lot to slow me down. I'm sorry, but your expression! Hahaha! Girl, I'll call you later! Ciao!

D.J.: Okay, you keep playing! This stuff creeps up on you. You know what Shane, you got issues. Girl, bye!

She cracks me up! Well, I'm on my way to see my baby! Yeah! Yeah! Yeah! He's my baby! I'll just roll up here and park. Let's see, I am really high! Wow, I really need to be cool. D.J. was not playing! Okay, okay, okay! Let me find a place to park, lay back a minute and catch my composure! Who's the chick in the hooch wear? She looks a hot mess! Some ho looking for a sucker. Man, why did he want me to meet him here? There are a few girls around here prostituting…oh, there he is.

Okay…who is this chick up in my man's face? Dang! I'll kick her tail up and down the street! Oh, he's talking to her?! He's looking around all guilty. And he's giving her a business card!? What the hell?! For real?!

Forget this…I've seen enough. I'm out! What? He has the nerve to come over here? You've GOT to be

kidding me.

Maverick: Hey, baby, thanks for meeting me here.

Shane: What's up Maverick? Who was that girl you were talking to?

Maverick: Uh well she's someone I met a long time ago.

Shane: Listen, I'm not sure why you had me meet you here and I'm not cool watching you give your number to a prostitute.

Maverick: Oh Shane, it's not like that…

Shane: Nope. I can't do this Maverick. I'm not the one.

Maverick: Wait a minute!

Shane: You're just like the rest. Let's not do this. I'm out. Step away from my car.

Maverick: But Shane…aw come on.

I've had enough of this bull. I can't do it, I don't want to and I'm not going to. Catch up with me in the next chapter. Sigh!

Chapter 13
Deal Breaker

Sorry I left you hanging...whoa, I'm tore up from the floor up! I've been like this for days, every night after work, until I fall asleep. That old Maverick keeps calling here. I don't want to hear anything he has to say! NOTHING! I knew he was too good to be true...jerk! What? I should give him a chance to explain? Explain WHAT? I got eyes! Never! So what if he's the finest brotha I've seen in many a day's! So what I feel electricity when he's near me! So what I can't stop thinking about him. So what his parents are probably the coolest folks I ever met. If he ain't right with me, it don't mean a thing! Like they say if you don't expect nothing good...that's just what you'll get. Or uhm...if you don't expect nothing good...you won't be disappointed. WHATEVER! Stupid saying.

KNOCK! KNOCK! KNOCK!

Dang! This man just doesn't get it! What does "I don't want to talk to you ever again mean?" Jesus, help the man, would Ya! Give him a clue! I'm so done with playas – so done! I should tell Sean. He'll kick his butt for me.

KNOCK! KNOCK! KNOCK!

Maverick: Shane, baby, I know you're in there. What did I do wrong?! Please don't let this go like this without an explanation. Shane! Shane?!

Go away playa! Good he's leaving. Now, the plan for this evening is to hang out with the Sistas and put this mess behind me. No more Maverick, hello someone else...whoever you are! Maybe Leo is in town.

Okay, I'm off to The Club, come on. Hmm well, it looks like the coast is clear, shall we cruise!? Let me throw in a little ole school. I need to chill out completely. Brothas! I just don't get it! Is there anyone out there who isn't hooked to someone else or isn't just a plain old nasty playa?! It would be great for once in my life to meet a man who would just be focused and in love with me. No distractions. No secrets.

I hope I didn't give this man my whole heart. I sure was trying to be cool. Maybe I'm over reacting. I should act as if I could care less what he does or who he sees. Who am I kidding? Either way, he won't get the pleasure of knowing I care. I hate it that I care! I hate it that I fell for him. I hate me for letting my guard down again to another loser! Don't you hate it when you do that?! Huh?! Don't act like you don't know what I'm talking about! I can't have any liars hanging with me! Hah!

Ahh good, my girls are waiting outside for me! Let's go see what's up!

Essence: Hey Shane, what's up!

D.J.: I'm sorry...you are? You look so familiar.

Lynn: What up!

Shane: Ladies, Shane is back! Have I missed anything?

Essence: Yeah, Maverick is looking for you!

Shane: Oh him. Well, no need to worry all is well in my neck of the woods!

Essence: He said you're pretty pissed with him!

Shane: Anything else?

Dang, he's just running off with the mouth! Mom used to call it diarrhea mouth.

Essence: Yeah, he told me to give you this letter.

Shane: What? How did he know to give it to you?

Essence: Well, he told me you won't give him an inch and he figured we'd see you before he did. He's around here somewhere. I guess you don't have to be a rocket scientist...we were out here waiting for you!

Shane: Let me see it.

Essence: Here girlfriend. Listen, let's go inside and get some drinks. The first round is on me!

Shane: Cool. I need one!

Essence: Shane, you are lit already. What is really going on with you? What did old boy do? Speak of the devil...geez!

D.J.: Hi, Maverick!

Maverick: Hello, D.J....ladies.

Lynn: Hi.

Essence: Hello.

D.J.: Shane, we'll get a booth, what do you want to drink?

Maverick: Hold that thought, she'll get back to you on that.

D.J.: Shane, are you cool with that?

Shane: No. Whatever. He doesn't run me. I'll be there to get my drink! You know what I like.

Maverick: Shane, I'm sorry for what you saw the other day. I wish you would have told me why it upset you so much, instead of hearing it through other people. It wasn't the way you thought...

Shane: Uh...what?! Boy, bye! I'm going back in.

Maverick: No, it's not enough to leave it this way. I need you to know what that was all about.

Shane: I don't want to know. A picture is worth a thousand words. Main words...you're not who I thought you were and I don't care. You guys are all alike. I know that girls reputation! That tells me a whole lot about you! She was all up in your face. Maybe that explains why you haven't tried to kiss ME!

Well, there you go Shane. You just put it out there! I didn't mean to say that out loud...geez!

Maverick: Shane, that's not fair. When I met her five years ago, she wasn't like that. We never got close. She just happened to be at the park, when I pulled up. I couldn't believe my eyes when I saw her. She was a mess. We grew up in church. Her parents moved uptown, they ended up getting a divorce and she lived with her Dad. I said hello to her, next thing I know she was trying to sale herself to me. She's in bad shape. These are the type of people my family helps...remember?

Shane: Mmhm...That's nice. Save it for the soaps. I see you made sure she had your number. Whatever Maverick! Let me go. I have a drink waiting for me! I don't want to hear this, it's just making me angrier.

Maverick: That's nice? That's all you can say? My parents pour their hearts into these people – you seen it! All you can say is save it for the soaps!? Wow, Shane.

Shane: Would you like me to play the violin while you cry? Boo hoo! Let me go...

Maverick: You've been hanging with me all this time and you still don't get me. You're pretty self-absorbed, Shane. I can tell you that! Vain Shane Vanity.

Shane: Excuse me? You talking trash...for real!? Don't talk to me like that, Maverick! You don't know me!

Maverick: Look, I've tried to explain myself. Thank you for your time. Your friends are waiting for you. And by the way...the card I gave her was for suicide prevention. Unfortunately, it didn't stop her. See you around Shane.

Shane: Uhm…Maverick?

Maverick: You got my number.

Shane: Uh...nope. **Nope. No, no, no...I'm not biting. No!**

Maverick: It's on you now.

Walk away and keep walking. Now let me get to my drink! What sounds good to drown my sorrows tonight? She killed herself!? Is he trying to put me on some guilt trip or is this mess true? Oh man… Nope! No! I'm not going there tonight. I can't!

Essence: Hey girl, that brotha has it bad for you, don't he?

Shane: Whatever! **I think my foolish butt just blew it!**

Essence: Whatever? Oh is the flame going out? Is he up for grabs now?

Shane: No, he's not! Why would you say something so stupid Essence? Don't any of ya'll go there or you'll feel the wrath of Shane! Dig?!

Essence: Sorry Shane…it was a lame joke.

Lynn: Shane, she was just kidding! Ain't nobody trying to get their behind beat by you. You love sick puppy!

D.J.: Yeah, you ain't pulling my weave out in handfuls!

Shane: And you know that! Hahaha!

Essence: Shane, look, Maverick is sitting over there watching your every move. Read the letter.

Shane: Oh yeah, let's see what else he has to say. But I'm reading it in the ladies room. He's not going to get the pleasure of seeing my reaction. Come on Essence.

Essence: Shane, are you okay? I've seen you hurt, but not like this. You're really digging ole dude, huh? Maybe you should have stayed home, we would have come to you and hung out. Shane? What's it say?

Just finish me off...I wasn't expecting this.

DEAR SHANE,

   I REALLY HOPE THAT WE CAN GET THROUGH THIS MISUNDERSTANDING. I'M NOT RUNNING SOME KIND OF GAME ON YOU. I CARE DEEPLY FOR YOU.

   SHANE, I SEE US TOGETHER, SERIOUSLY. I SEE US WITH A FUTURE AND KIDS. WOW, I REALLY WROTE THAT DOWN! I AM STARTING TO FALL IN LOVE WITH YOU! THERE I SAID IT. IT'S EASIER TO WRITE IT THAN IT IS TO SAY IT. WHEN I LOOK INTO THOSE BEAUTIFUL BROWN EYES, I MELT. I'M DOING GOOD TO HOLD MYSELF TOGETHER WHEN I'M WITH YOU. I HAVE SO MUCH MORE TO SAY TO YOU, BUT I NEED TO KNOW IF YOU'RE GOING TO GIVE ME ANOTHER CHANCE. PLEASE RECONSIDER.

                        LOVE, MAV

Essence: Shane. Shane? Here's some tissue. Girl, what did he write?

Shane: I wasn't expecting this. Listen, I need to get some fresh air.

Essence: Okay, I'll walk out with you.

Shane: No, Essence, I'll roll my window down on the way home. I'll be okay…really.

Essence: Home? Oh come on, Shane! Since when could a guy send you running home crying? You can't be serious! I'm starting not to like him, Shane.

Shane: Yeah…well. My make-up is all messed up now. Essence, this just hurts so much. You know me better than anyone on this Earth. I just can't fake it tonight. I'm gonna go home.

Essence: Aww. I sure have been missing you. I have so much to talk to you about.

Shane: I'm sorry. Call me and we'll get together. I do want to catch up, I really do. I just need some air right now.

Essence: Do we need to go kick this guy's tail or what?!

Shane: No. Essence, leave your bat in the trunk for now. I just need to think. Listen, I promised ya'll a party tonight. Here are three J's. I'm out for the night, call me when you get home…if you want! Ciao, ladies!

Essence: Bye Shane. I'll call you later.

D.J.: Goodness, that brotha is busting up our group! He's starting to get on my dang nerves!

Lynn: Yeah, but you know it happens to the best of us! I've never seen Shane like this though.

87

Essence: It's cool. It's all good. Shane has a good head on her shoulders. And I got a good strong bat in my trunk!

D.J.: Look, Maverick followed her out.

Essence: I'll be back! Excuse me, Maverick!

Maverick: Yeah?

Essence: Maverick, give Shane some breathing room. If you really care for her, let her talk to you on her terms not yours. She will talk to you when she's ready.

Maverick: I hear you.

Essence: Do you? You're watching her every move. Let her think everything through. She ain't no fool and she's just tired of getting hurt. If she wants to be with you, you'll have a good thing. If not, all the pressure in the world won't get her heart.

Maverick: I just want her to understand that I'm not playing games.

Essence: Sure…we've all heard that one. She's my girl…so you just watch your step…if you hurt her again, you'll be walking with a limp…and I'm the one for the job, my brotha!

Maverick: Essence, are you done? Please move so I can leave. I'm out.

Essence: Mmhm, out of your dang mind! Wow, he's running to his car to follow her. I'm calling her to let her know. Creep!

Chapter 14
Religion or Relationship?

I can't believe this. I guess I can, but what am I supposed to do with this information now? What am I supposed to say, Maverick, I'm really sorry for being so judgmental and cold? Oh, and I love you too? Do I love him? I guess I must feel something for me to be so bent out of shape! I am tripping on this one! Jesus, help me! I need some air so I can clear my head. Why did I get so high?

Okay, I'm home. Let me hurry up and get in the house. I hate being chased. Wait a minute, I forgot my purse in the car. What?! Geez, does his car have flying capabilities? I'm getting creeped out.

Shane: Hello? Yeah he's here Essence. I'll be okay – talk to you later. Maverick, why are you here?

Maverick: Shane, are you okay?

Shane: Of course I am…I'm just getting my purse! Why did you follow me home? I'm a big girl, I can take care of myself.

Maverick: You seemed really upset and ran out of the club, I just wanted to make sure you got home okay. You're pretty high tonight.

Shane: I didn't run out, I walked. Poor me, I'm a real basket case! Are you happy with that?! Listen Maverick, it's been a rough week, I need to clear my mind and relax. Something I wanted to do at The Club. Why are you here?

Maverick: I really want to make things right. Can I come in for a minute? I promise I won't stay long.

Shane: You don't give up do you?

Maverick: Not on people I care about.

Shane: Grrr! Okay, you can come in, but not for long. You can talk. I don't have anything to say.

What the heck did I say yes for?! Goofy.

Maverick: Can I stay long enough to make us some coffee? I could really use a cup.

Shane: I guess. I'll be right back.

Why couldn't I just say no? This fool is really tripping! Doesn't he know all I need to do is pick up the phone and all my problems are taken care of?! I know Essence talked to him, because she called me. That girl is crazy sometimes! I'm glad she's my friend and not an enemy.

Coffee can't mend a broken heart, but it can help you stay awake while you drive away from here. I need to change into some sweats and we can sit on the balcony...maybe that will bring me down a bit.

Shane: Mhm, coffee smells good.

Maverick: Yeah, don't you look cute in those sweats?

Would you like to sit on the balcony?

Shane: Sure, that's fine. **Now he can read my mind?**

Maverick: Shane, baby, I'm so sorry.

Shane: What you did hurt me. Are you clear about that? If what you said was true about that girl, I am real sorry too. I'm really not heartless and it came out like I was. What was that all about?

Maverick: She gave up, Shane. She overdosed later that night. Sometimes you can see it on them. I could see it on her and tried to reach out. Sometimes people can be in such a dark place, they can't be reached. But we still have to keep trying. We can't give up on them.

I know that dark place, but I've never wanted to end my life there. I don't know...is this something I want to be involved in?

Shane: Uhm...wow. Yeah, I understand what you're saying. My Mom used to have some real dark days. It was tough sometimes.

Okay, we've hit that awkward silence. He better not be judging me. I feel pretty selfish in this moment and don't know what to say. Hopefully he'll come up with something else to say. Any time now. Awkward!

Maverick: I guess the reason I've been so persistent is that I've seen a good many people give up and a lot hold on until God pulled them out. I really don't know. I can't say I could have done things differently, whether

91

you were there or not. I really did try. But my pride isn't so big that I can't ask for forgiveness anyway. Every word in my letter to you is from my heart. I can see us together for a long time. If you'll have me.

Shane: Maverick, slow down. Listen, how do you know that I'm the one you want to be with like that? What is your heart saying or are you sure it's not lust? What do I do for you?

Lust? Yeah right, he won't even kiss me. Geez!

Maverick: If it were lust, I'd have been pursuing that. I haven't kissed you yet for an important reason, Shane. This doesn't mean that I don't want to grab you up and lay one on you. But my feelings of respect and honor for you are great, girl! I know how I feel because of my respect for you! And I know how I feel when I'm with you...and when I'm not with you. Besides, I don't want to take advantage of you under the influence of...the hype. So what if everyone is claiming to be doing it. I'm not everybody. I want my thing to last a lifetime.

Shane: Maverick, you are very different from what I've encountered in men. I'm trying to size you up, but I'm not sure who to compare you with. Wait...what? Under the influence? You've got to be kidding me!

Maverick: Shane, it's time to be honest with you.

Shane: I thought that's what you were doing.

Maverick: I have, and there is so much more I'd like to share with you. Is your head clearing yet?

Shane: Yeah, enough. I have a question for you. You

say you don't want to take advantage of me while I'm under the influence...of the hype. Hmm. What do you think about me getting high? You don't do it, do you?

Maverick: No, I don't do it. To be honest with you...I think you're way too beautiful to be doing it...but...instead of ragging you about it, I pray about it. I have been praying for you, Shane. I'm sure you'll be cool in this area in time.

Shane: You've been praying for me? For real?!

Too beautiful? So now he thinks I have an ugly problem. Wow. Poor little old me needs prayer...hmm.

Maverick: Yes, I have. I'm not saying it to get a pat on my back or to offend you. This is something that I do.

Sean did say this man could pray...now this is a buzz kill for sure! I really can't say I'm impressed. I think he just threw a little shade my way. Hmm.

Shane: I've been getting high for a long time Maverick. I can't think of anything better to do, especially when times get tough. When times are good, I use it to celebrate. No problem! You make me feel like it makes me ugly or something!

Maverick: Slow down Shane, that's not what I'm saying!

Shane: Am I your next charity case? I'd love to hear this one, okay...keep talking.

93

Maverick: Shane, come over here to me, let's cuddle. It's getting chilly.

Shane: Nah, I'm good.

Maverick: Listen, I've been going to The Club for the purpose of seeing you and hoping to talk with you. I've wanted to get to know you and hopefully kick it with you. I don't drink and if you've noticed I haven't been on the dance floor that much. I do enjoy dancing with you. My goal was to get to you.

Shane: You're spilling all your secrets tonight, huh!?

I hope I can handle this. He really sounds like a stalker.

Maverick: Yeah, a few of them I guess. I told my Mom about you. I told her something very personal and I don't want you to laugh at what I'm about to say. I'm very serious about this. I told her during times that I've been praying. God has been telling me that you are someone very special in my life.

That's why I took you to the B&B so she could meet you. She told me to go for it. She's a praying woman and I wasn't sure what to do. So I just hung around where you hung out, until God moved on your heart.

Shane: Hmm, well, something happened.

I couldn't honestly say it was God with the way my thoughts were getting all lusty and stuff. Yet another awkward moment.

Maverick: Don't play with me Shane!

94

Shane: I'm not playing with you! Really, Maverick, how does God talk to you? I mean, how do you know?

Maverick: You know, you're the first person to ever ask me that! Everyone is different! For me, I start out with worship music…music that tunes me into His goodness and mercy. It tunes me into how Great He is. Then I get quiet inside. I open up the Bible and read a while.

Shane: Quiet inside? What do you mean?

Maverick: I stop thinking about everything else and get real quiet, focused and wait. After a while, I hear Him speak to me...it comes as a thought to me. But the thought is different than what I would think...that's the best way I can explain it. It becomes a...conversation. Like I said, everyone is different!

Shane: Oh. Is it scary?

Maverick: Oh no, not at all! Actually, it's the sweetest encounter I have every day! He is awesome Shane. In His presence, He removes all doubt and fear, and I know I can do what He wants me to do!

Shane: Maverick, this sounds so incredible! God always seemed so far away...so distant to me. I've always felt like my prayers got lost in the clouds and never reached Him. I get high, I get lost in the feeling of it. It feels good for a time, then I start to feel lonely and sad again.

Maverick: Shane, I'll be honest with you. Getting high opens you up to the spirit realm.

Shane: Meaning? What do you mean?

Am I in the mood for creepy? Nope.

Maverick: This might be going deeper than you're comfortable with. Listen, getting high is the devil's counterfeit to the presence of God...that's it in a nutshell!

Shane: Really? I never heard that before.

Oh boy, creepy. Will I get any sleep tonight? It's hard to sleep with my eyes open in complete terror! Geez!

Maverick: Yeah. In His Presence is fullness of joy! What I'm saying is you feel this incredible peace and joy! You feel on top of the world...with no hangover. Even when you're going through hard times.

Shane: Hmm, sounds like something I would much rather have. You had me going there.

Maverick: Some One.

Shane: Yeah okay. Some One. Okay, enough uncomfortable talk.

Maverick: Well, Shane, I don't want to over stay my welcome. I better be stepping on home, let's get back in. I want to make sure you're secure and all.

Shane: Okay! Maverick, I really thank you for sharing with me tonight. You've given me some good things to think about, to dream about, and to even pray about. I have one more question for you Maverick! How do I pray...to get my prayers heard and answered?

Maverick: When you pray always close with "In the Name of Jesus, amen". He's like the phone number to get the call through to God. I'll teach you more about it. It's getting late. Again, I'm sorry for the confusion.

Shane: Me too. Okay, thank you. Be careful.

Maverick: I will.

I am so happy that Maverick and I have worked things out and very irritated because it cut into my time with my sistas! Anyway! He is incredible! Physically, I want to be close to him, but he has shown me total respect and has kept things in a good place. If he tried I'd probably fall right out! I've given my love to the wrong ones...obviously. All I got was a feeling of regret and shame. Well, I didn't get their last name! But this thing with Mav seems so different, and I really want to do things right!

A conversation with God...how incredible is that?! I know there is something going on, but I have to be sure before I think in those terms. Right now Ms. Diva Shane is doing good to get up every morning and face the day. Maverick makes it easier...but it's hard to get excited about a new love, when I can't get closure from previous broken relationships...especially with my Dad.

Lord, I'm sure you heard what Maverick said to me. I hurt inside and I'm tired of being a pothead. Especially if it's opening me up to creepy stuff. I don't know what to do about my life. Is it possible that You told him I'm special? Can my life change? I want so bad to be loved without the fear of abandonment. I don't want anyone else to leave me, God! You did an awesome thing for Carol, and she's been through hell! You've done something for my brother Sean...is there room in Your heart for me? Please Jesus, save me for real! Uhm...in Jesus Name, Amen.

Well, sweet dreams! See ya when I see ya! That would be in the next chapter. Hah! Turn the page!

Chapter 15
Maverick's Prayer

RING! RING!

Rico: Hello!

Maverick: Rico, man, do you have minute?

Rico: Yeah man, what's up?

Maverick: Listen, remember the girl I was sitting with at the gig?

Rico: Yeah...what about her?

Maverick: Well, she's the one.

Rico: Oh, I see...she's the one you acted like wasn't there...right?

Maverick: Anyway! Listen, I actually took her down to meet the fam at the B&B!

Rico: What? You're that serious?! Dang! What did she think?

Maverick: She's cool with it. I know she's special because she didn't refuse to get out of the car when we got there! Hahaha! But her eyes were as big as quarters!

Rico: Yeah...Hahaha! That's cool!

Maverick: Man, I'm calling to ask you to keep us in prayer.

Rico: I can do that! Yeah…she's real pretty. Question for you…is she saved?

Maverick: Uhm…she's kind of…well, she's asking questions.

Rico: I'll tell you Dawg…that's a dangerous set up, you know that…right!?

Maverick: Well, I've been praying about this man, I know it's not the "ideal" set-up to start…but I know that she's someone special in my life.

Rico: I hear you. My concern is this. You always say you want to marry a virgin, a woman who is saved and on fire for the Lord. I've seen this girl around, man. I wouldn't call her fast or loose, but I know she gets high and fools around a bit. Where do you really think this is going?

Maverick: I see God working things out. Her brother came to the B&B a while ago. He just got born-again. She's asking questions about prayer and about how she's hungry for the real deal.

Rico: Okay…that sounds promising. Not to mention she has a beautiful set of eyes.

Maverick: Yeah, and she's so beautiful inside. I knew her when she was real young…she went to our church camp way back when. I have a good feeling about this.

Rico: Well, Mav, I'm on my knees…just making sure

you hold tight to your standards. Limit your time alone with her.

Maverick: Man, she's not fast! I can handle myself…

Rico: Yeah? Get real man. She's not what you call slow either. Until she's all the way in…hold up, I take that back. You know it can get real hard…holy or not. Just be cool. You don't want to get caught in this thing with unnecessary soul ties.

Maverick: Yeah, you're right…I sure don't want to do that. She may not be a virgin, but I know that God can make all things new. Does that sound crazy?!

Rico: Man, its cool. I wasn't a virgin when we got married, but the love of my Holy Ghost-filled, fire-baptized woman of God is on point! People make mistakes, you just can't hold it against them. We're in this relationship, and it's working out great! Huh? Oh…okay! She heard what I said…I got to go and uh…handle some business my man! Score!

Maverick: Yeah, whatever! Keep praying for me!

Rico: You got it! Keep me posted, man! I'm out!

Maverick: I will, man...out!

CLICK

Maverick: *Lord, I'm not one to throw caution to the wind. I believe Your word that the steps of a righteous man are ordered of the Lord. I don't want to move outside of Your will. I want to walk uprightly and stay close to You.*

Father God, clear Shane's mind and take away the desire for the counterfeit of Your presence. Replace that void with Your love. Help her to see herself as You see her and the world around her. Touch her heart so that she will soon fall in love with You and want to serve You with all her heart. I know You can do all things and I thank You for Your love, faithfulness and brand new mercies every day. In Jesus Name – Amen!

Chapter 16
Miracles by Almighty

Wow, we are so busy today! And if my boss walks over here one more time to see if I finished typing his proposal I think I'll scream! He just handed it to me 15 minutes ago AND these phones are ringing off the hook! I wish these people would stay in their seats! Jesus, take me now...NO I take that back, I can't leave my boo Maverick here to miss me! Ooh Maverick! I wonder what he's doing right now!

RING! RING!

Shane: Blue Lights Unlimited this is Shane, how can I help you?

Mom: Shane, baby?!

Shane: Mom?! Is everything okay?

Mom: Shane, baby….there has been a crazy accident! Sean is in the emergency room!

Shane: What!? What happened?!

Mom: They were driving and these things came off a truck in front of them and they got pinned in and….

Shane: Mom, slow down...listen, which hospital are you at?

Mom: The one downtown! Med Cross Hospital! Shane, please hurry, I don't know what to do!

Shane: I'm on my way!

My boss looked at me cross-eyed when I told him I had to leave! He can be so goofy at times! Once I explained, he had the decency to let me go. He told me to call him when things calm down. Okay...let me make sure I have all my stuff...I'll try to catch Maverick on the way!

RING! RING!

Maverick: Hi Sweet thing!

Shane: Maverick! Meet me at Med Cross Hospital in the emergency room! I'm on my way! I should be there in about 10 more minutes!

Maverick: Okay! What's wrong?

Shane: Sean's there, Mom sounded like she was in shock and couldn't explain it to me. I'll see you there!

Maverick: Okay! Bye!

CLICK

Maverick: Dad, Shane needs me at Med Cross Hospital....will you be okay? Sean's in the emergency room!

Mr. Grace: Oh Lord! Yeah, go on, I'll call Rico to come in early. We have enough on staff for now! Go on and call me later! We'll be praying.

Maverick: Okay!

MED CROSS HOSPITAL EMERGENCY ROOM

Shane: Uh excuse me, I'm here to see my brother Sean Vanity.

Nurse: Just a minute...yes, Sean Vanity has just been moved from the critical care unit to a private room. Go through those doors and on your left you'll find an elevator, he's on the 5th floor room 522.

Shane: Do you know if my Mom is there? I don't see her!

Nurse: One of our assistants walked her up, she was very upset. She's with him now, he's trying to settle her down before she goes in to see your brother.

Shane: Oh my Jesus! What happened?

Nurse: I'm sorry I don't know the details. It says he's in stable condition now though.

Shane: Okay...through the doors…. elevator on left...5th floor...522. Wow.

Nurse: Yes Ma'am, are you going to be okay?

Maverick: Shane?!

Shane: Uh…I am now, thank you. Oh Maverick…

Maverick: What's going on?

Shane: I'm not sure, come on! Let's go up to see him.

Just when you think life is flowing, something

happens! Jesus, please make everything all right! I really don't know what I would do if something were to happen to Sean. We are so close, and he's really all I have. My Mom is there but she remarried and really lives another life outside of me and Sean. We're not really a part of her life like we were as children. Oh God, Mom said "they". Who else was she talking about?!

Chapter 17
Hidden Under His Wings

Maverick: Shane, come back to Earth....baby girl, everything will be okay.

Shane: Yeah, I hope so. Mom! Are you okay, where is Sean?

Mom: They took him to run some more tests.

Shane: What happened?

Mom: I don't know Shane. Sean was about to tell me when they came and got him. Carol is here, but I haven't had a chance to see her.

Shane: Where is she?

Mom: She's down the hall in room 538.

Shane: Maverick, can you stay here with my Mom, I want to go see Carol...I don't know if she has any family here for her.

Maverick: Okay...

Mom: Maverick come on and sit down with me.

Oh God, I hope Carol is okay. What on earth happened?! This is straight from some crazy soap opera!

Knock! Knock!

Shane: Excuse me, Carol?

Nurse Bell: Honey, hold on, I'll be done in one minute.

Shane: Oh, I'm sorry.

Nurse Bell: No problem, I'm just making Ms. Carol more comfortable...there you are. Okay, Honey, come on in. I'll check on you in a while, Ms. Carol.

Shane: Thank you. Carol? How are you doing?

Carol: Hey, girl! Isn't Jesus good?

Shane: Huh? Uh yeah, you and Sean are alive! Carol, what happened?

Carol: We were on the freeway going to Hot Soul & Rockets for lunch. We got behind this big old semi carrying them big metal pipes they put underground or something. Next thing we know, one started rolling off the back and coming toward us. When Sean dodged it, we ended up hitting a divider full force. Girl, I think I wet my pants...it was crazy. Don't tell anyone I said that. Hah...ouch!

Shane: Ooh take it easy. My God!

Carol: Yes Shane, my God had everything to do with it. When we looked around, another one of the giant pipes crashed down right were we had just moved from. Shane, I'm talking about a matter of seconds. We could have, and I believe should have, been killed! I'm talking CRUSHED! But you know...God isn't through with us! He's not through with us! Thank you Jesus!

Shane: Wow, wow, wow! This is giving me goose bumps! My God, this is straight wild! So why are they keeping you here? Did you get hurt?

Carol: I banged up my knee, bruised my ribs and hit my head. So they're keeping me for observation. I heard Sean broke his arm and was knocked unconscious...how is he doing? They said he came to. Have you seen him yet?

Shane: Oh my Jesus! No, he wasn't in his room when we got here, they had taken him out for tests. I really need to see my brother! **This is crazy! Oh no!**

Nurse Bell: Excuse me ladies. How are you holding up Carol?

Carol: I'm fine. Where is Sean? His Sis really needs to see him.

Nurse Bell: That's fine. Are you okay Shane?

Shane: I will be, I just want to see my brother.

Nurse Bell: Your brother Sean is back in his room and wants to see you.

Shane: Okay, thank you.

Nurse Bell: Ms. Carol, you have another visitor.

Carol: No one knows I'm here...who is it?

Carol's Mom: Me, baby. I came as soon as I heard about the wreck. Are you going to be okay Carol?
Carol: Mama? Mama is that really you?! Oh Mama,

Jesus saved me! He saved me!

Shane: Excuse me, hi, uh...I'll talk to you later, Carol. Love you.

Let me get to this brotha of mine! I've got to dry these tears! Wow, Carol hasn't seen her Mom in ages! Thank God she came...I pray that You help them find the love they lost, God. Please do that for them! In Jesus' name, amen!

Sean: Yeah, it was something else...but you see I'm alive....

Shane: Hi Big Brotha!

Sean: Lil' Sis! Ow I'm really sore, you're gonna have to save those hugs for later.

Shane: Oh, I'm sorry! **Real smart Shane, duh!**

Sean: Ow, ow, ow! I gotcha! Hahaha!

Shane: Okay now, I get the message, you will always be a clown till the day you die! Which won't be any time soon!

Sean: Well Sis, I was pretty close today!

Shane: Yeah, I spoke to Carol.

Sean: You did!? How is she doing?

Shane: She has a banged up knee, bruised ribs and she hit her head. Even with all of that, she is praising God like crazy. She had me crying...it was wild! When I

110

was leaving her room, her Mom came in.

Sean: Wait...what?! We were just talking about how she wanted to work on getting a relationship back with her Mom! That's cool, Shane.

Maverick: Sean, I'm glad you're all right! You had your Mom and little sister pretty shaken up.

Shane: I'm okay....Mom was the one that was worrying me!

Mom: You kids! When they said Sean was unconscious, that's when I freaked out! I thought he was in some kind of coma or something. You know those quacks don't always tell you what the...

Dr. Obadiah: Hello family, I'm Dr. Obadiah and I wanted to talk to you about Sean.

Mom: Uh...okay.

Dr. Obadiah: Well, your Sean is an amazing man! He was knocked unconscious and we ran some tests. It seems that there was no damage done to his skull or brain. As a matter of fact, we're not sure why you were unconscious when you came in. There are no bruises...as you see we even shaved his head....nothing was found.

As we discussed Sean's condition, it was pointed out that if Sean would have been conscious at the point of contact with the divider, he would have tried to avoid it and rolled under the cement pipe that they had just escaped. It's quite amazing actually. Jesus, You're becoming more and more real to me...

Sean: Well Doc, I needed the haircut, thanks. Hahaha Whoa...God is good!

Shane: Amen!

Mom: Lord Jesus!

Maverick: Yes, thank You Lord Jesus!

Dr. Obadiah: We'd like to keep Sean another day for observation. If all looks good, he should be able to go home tomorrow. Sean, do you live with anyone?

Sean: No.

Mom: Don't worry about that, baby. We'll bring you home until you're good as new.

Sean: Thanks...oh, boy.

Shane: Hah! I'll stop by and check you out Sean...I'll even bring Carol by.

Sean: Better yet, take me to see Carol...uh...after all she's pretty banged up you know....uh it's easier for me to walk than for her.

Dr. Obadiah: Not so fast Sean, I'll have one of the nurses take you to see her in a wheel chair for right now.

Mom: Yeah...that's good. Well, I need to get home and get things prepared...we'll be back later Sean, okay! Give me love.
Sean: Okay Mom, love you! Tell step-Daddy I said hi!

Mom: I love you too, baby! I sure will.

Shane: Mom. I'll see you later!

Maverick: Would you like me to walk you to your car?

Mom: Maverick, that would be nice...Shane you have a really nice boyfriend...

Shane: Uh...yeah, I do. **He is fine, yes indeed!**

Maverick: Shane, I'll be right back.

Shane: Okay! So brotha dear...God kept you alive for a reason. I don't want to overwork you today, but we will have time to talk when I rescue you from Mom's house!

Sean: Yeah! Shane, can you call Carol's room for me.

Shane: Sure!

RING! RING!

Carol: Hello?

Shane: Hi Carol, Sean wants to talk to you.

Carol: Oh yes! Hi Sean!

Sean: Hi Carol....baby, how do you feel? I miss you....
Shane: I'll talk to you later Sean....hugs. Bye.

Well, I'll step out in the hall and wait for Maverick. Sean is amazing to me, this man must truly have a call on his life. I've never seen anyone survive so many things. God, what am I here for? What do you have for me to do? I need a J! This is usually the time I have my evening puff! I got to find a way to stop this weed craze!

Chapter 18

Shame to my Game

I'll hang with Maverick for a little while, than I have to ditch him to get high. I'd love a drink too. Dang, what is the matter with me? Why can't I just stop this mess? Do I need help with this? Hmm I see Lynn has tried to call me, I better give her a call.

RING! RING!

Lynn: Hello?

Shane: Hey, girl!

Lynn: Shane, I've been trying to call you! It's been on the news about your brother! Is he okay?

Shane: Yeah Lynn, he's fine...him and Carol.

Lynn: Carol? Carol the crack head...his old girlfriend?

Shane: Carol is his old girlfriend, but she's not a crack head anymore! Carol is a new woman... Sean's got a new girlfriend!

Lynn: I don't know Shane...if she's not, what happened? Once you get into that mess, you're stuck for life.

Shane: Not if you have Jesus. Lynn, look...everyone is fine, please let everyone know. I got to go! Bye!

Lynn: Shane? I didn't mean any harm. Bye.

I'm ready to straight cuss Lynn out! What an awful conversation to have at this time. Dang that was irritating! I just wanted to get with her to smoke! But I ain't about to deal with that crazy talk! Dang! Dang! Dang! I need to know that if it's real for Carol and Sean, it can be real for me. I don't want to be a pothead the rest of my life! I want my life to matter too. They seem so happy, even with all of this pain and agony going on. How can anyone be happy laid up in a hospital bed broken? How can somebody not be high but have peace and contentment? I want that, and I don't want to smoke or drink to get it. This stuff doesn't help anymore...if it ever helped at all.

Maverick: Shane? Are you alright? You look heated!

Shane: Hey, are you ready to go? I am.

Maverick: What's wrong?

Shane: Nothing...I'm just hungry and stressed. Sean is on the phone with Carol and they both need to rest. Let's go...I told him I'd call him back later on.

Maverick: Okay, baby girl, that's fine. What are you in the mood for?

Shane: Anything...

Maverick: Okay...I'm parked near you. Follow me, I have a nice spot in mind!

Shane: Uh...okay! I'll call my boss on the way, so give me a minute!

Good! Now I can hit this real quick! God, I don't know if You're okay with me doing this! I ain't too proud of it myself. But until You help me stop...well...could You help me stop one day? And when You do it...be gentle! Oh, isn't this nice...Chinese Chopsticks Buffet! I love this place! Maverick is the bomb! Hey! Let me spray some perfume and get out of my car first! Oh shoot, he's coming this way! Caught again, geez!

Shane: Maverick, go ahead on in, I'm right behind you!

Maverick: Okay, hurry up.

Shane: Okay!

Yeah sweet baby, let me air out a bit. Squirt a little more perfume on... I know he's not stupid, but I don't have to give him contact either! I got the munchies! I think I'll try the chopsticks this time! There he is sitting near the window! Listen, I'll check you out in the next Chapter...I won't have much to say for a while...I've got to get my grub on! Ciao for now*!*

Chapter 19
Rollercoaster Ride to Reality

This man has been pretty incredible! I don't know what I've done to deserve him, but I am straight cool with it! We talk, but I still haven't gotten inside his head just yet. We haven't kissed...I'm going to attempt to change that tonight...after all I need to thank him for his kindness and being by my side. Good Lord he looks so good tonight. The way he sits there soaked with confidence. Why me? Why not me? Am I that bad of a person? No...There are worse! But...there are better! What does he see in me that keeps him hanging around?

Maverick: Shane, what are you thinking about?

Shane: Huh? I'm just thinking about my brotha...thank you for coming.

Like I'm going to really tell you what I was really thinking.
AFTER THE GRUB FEST

Maverick: You crack me up, Shane. I haven't laughed like this in a while. So, would you like anything else or are you ready to go?

Shane: I guess I'm ready to go. I've tried everything they have out. I just need a toothpick. Hah!

You can serve me up those luscious lips, my sweet baby!

Maverick: Come on, you look pretty tired. Let's get you home.

Shane: Yeah...it's been a real eventful day!

No more days like these God...thank You very much!

Maverick: Yeah...well, I'll tell you what. These kinds of days make you think seriously about life after death. If something more serious would have happened, could you say that you would have hope?

Shane: Meaning if Sean or Carol would have died?

Maverick: Not necessarily die. That's a horrible thought. But serious injuries...would you have a sense of peace, or would it shatter you?

Shane: Let me think about this on the way home. I'll meet you there later.

Maverick: That's cool. I need to stop by the B&B and see how things are going, and then I'll be on my way.

Shane: I have to swing by my job and then I'll be home. I'll see you about 8:30. Don't take too long, I might be sleep.

Maverick: Better not, girl!

This man keeps me on my toes! My hope? Life after death? What? Hmm. Sean and Carol were just praising God and they're lying in hospital beds! Who's the common denominator? Jesus Christ. I guess He's their hope...I don't know where Maverick is trying to go with this one. One thing I do

119

know...I'm going to feel those luscious lips on mine tonight I need to go in and brush my teeth and get this breath smelling a whole lot better! Chinese food can stank up some lips! Matter of fact, I hope he sticks a toothbrush in his mouth too! Hah!

RING! RING!

Shane: Hello?

Mom: Shane?

Shane: Hi Mom! Is everything okay?

Mom: Uh...yes. Shane...I love you baby!

Shane: I love you too! How's Sean doing?

Mom: He's resting comfortably. The doctors are going to do more tests on him in the morning. They seem a bit puzzled as to why he blacked out. Then they say it actually saved his life. It's all confusing don't you think?

Shane: Well, I think God has something for him to do, and if that's what it took to save his life, that's what it took. Mom, you do know Sean got born-again right?!

Mom: He got saved as a little boy, of course I know that.

Shane: No, Mom, I mean really saved...as an adult. It's called born-again!

Mom: What's the difference, once you do it, it's done.

Shane: I used to think that...I'm not so sure now. At least for myself, I need more than what I got as a child...a whole lot has happened since then. It sounds like someone's outside my door. Hold on Mommy!

KNOCK! KNOCK!

Shane: Who is it?

Maverick: Shane, it's me.

Shane: Oh, okay...come in. Mom, Maverick is here, can we talk more, later?

Mom: Yeah, I'm pretty tired. I'm going to try and lie down and rest my nerves. Baby, call the hospital in about an hour and see how Sean and Carol are doing...call me if something is wrong...let me sleep if everything is all right. I'll touch base with you when I get up...okay. The doctor gave me some stuff to help me rest.

Shane: Yes Ma'am I will do that! Love you. Bye.

Mom: Love you too, baby. Bye-bye.

Shane: Hi, I'm glad you're here, is everything okay at the B&B?

Maverick: Yeah. How's your brother doing?

Shane: Resting comfortably last I heard. I'll be calling the hospital in about an hour to check on him.

Maverick: So Shane, what do you think about all of this?

Shane: Well, Maverick…it's a lot right now. I need to chill from the drama for a minute and calm down.

Maverick: Yeah, come sit beside me and let me hold you for a while.

Shane: Uh huh.

I am relieved and very happy! Very, very happy! Oh yeah! Oh yeah! I hope he can't hear me shouting in my mind! Thank You Jesus, thank You! Give me those lips! Give me those lips! Give me an L…give me a I…give me a P…give me a…S! Hah! Don't judge me.

Maverick: How's that?

Shane: Fine, thank you.

Now this is wonderfully great! It smells like he brushed his teeth too! It's going to be a nice evening! I just want a kiss - I can hold out for the rest - just a little kiss or two or three!

Maverick: Shane, what radio station is this we're listening too?

Shane: Kiss and Tell 99.7. It's nice huh?

Maverick: Well, everything is pretty provocative. Do you listen to this all the time?

Shane: Uh…well, not all the time. Why?

Maverick: It's just that…holding you close like this, and hearing this kind of music makes me….well,…let's say, it's a good combination for a married couple.

Shane: A married couple? What? Maverick, what's wrong? I'm not trying to seduce you. **Wow, awkward!**

Maverick: Shane, listen, I respect you with my whole heart and I really care about every step we take in this relationship. I'm very attracted to you...God knows the whole story! But, I am holding out for marriage. And it's getting hard right now for me to stay.

Dang, he looks frightened! Holding out? Oh no...he's a virgin?

Shane: So, you've never been with a woman in that way?

Maverick: Uh...no. I came close, and it made it very hard on the relationship. I don't want that to happen with us. Can I ask you a question?

Shane: Nope. Don't ask me anything. And I think it would be better if we stick to public meetings. I don't want you to come by here anymore Maverick. I don't need you holding me, I'll be just fine.

Maverick: Shane, I didn't mean any harm!

Shane: Damage is done! You need to stick to those little fake church girls. The ones that haven't been touched and are perfect little blossoms, if you can find one! That's not my story and I sure as hell don't want to contaminate your holy self! Please get out of here! Right now!

Maverick: Whoa! Shane!

123

Shane: GET OUT NOW!

Maverick: Uh...okay, okay Shane. Here we go again.

SLAM!

What?! So what I tried! It didn't work and I'm irritated! There is enough shame in my game, I don't need to be rejected on this issue too! All of this for a lousy kiss? It was just a kiss! Geez! I wasn't pulling on his clothes or mine...dang it! It's always too good! IT'S ALWAYS TOO GOOD TO BE TRUE! God, I didn't know how important it was to save myself! I just didn't know! I never thought I'd meet a "Maverick" in my life! And it's not like I was a big ho either! Now I feel filthy because I didn't know and now it's too late. God, this hurts so much! I can feel my heart breaking off in pieces! And he looked all scared and stuff...talk about feeling like something freaky! My feelings are broke down to the ground!

You better catch me in the next Chapter. I'll be crying myself to sleep tonight! Don't worry, I'll make it through the night. He better be glad I stopped seeing Leo or I'd have called him over here. I guess that wouldn't help anything. Geez! Oh yeah, I better call Sean's nurse before I let the tears flow. Sigh If anything is wrong...you'll find out with the rest of us! Good night.

Chapter 20
Secrets That Sabotage

KNOCK! KNOCK! KNOCK! KNOCK!

Rico: HOLD ON! HOLD ON! THIS BETTER BE GOOD! WHO IS IT?!

Maverick: It's me Rico!

Rico: Man, you see this bat? What's wrong with you? Get in here!

Maverick: Rico, Man, I blew it with Shane! I blew it. I've never seen here so hurt in my life! She had tears, man....she was so hurt!

Rico: Whoa. Slow down! What happened?

Maverick: I just blew it with Shane.

Rico: How?

Maverick: Her brother was in this crazy accident earlier today. I met her at the emergency room, he's okay and all. We got something to eat and talked for a long time. I met her at her place later and she had music going...the Kiss and Tell station. I asked her to sit down and let me hold her for a while, only I didn't realize what kind of music was on at first and the words to the songs and her perfume started freaking me out! Man, I wanted her so bad!

Rico: Sigh…So, what happened Mav?

Maverick: I panicked and started talking about my virginity and...

Rico: You more or less slapped her in the face with it...right?

Maverick: Yeah...I didn't mean to come off like that. She looked so hurt. Man, she was really hurt and embarrassed.

Rico: It's like this Mav, if she loves you and that's her way of showing affection. But if she didn't learn the why's and the when's, she unintentionally blew it. That doesn't make her a bad person, just misinformed. It doesn't take away who she is as the woman you love...at least it shouldn't.

Man, if a woman feels love coming from her man and she really loves him, her past falls away. Even when there are children involved. I should know. People are people, and we all make mistakes. We're not supposed to base what we've done, on who we are today. Because who we are today can be a million miles away from whom we used to be. Live and learn...and move on.

Maverick: Yeah...man she threw me out! Rico, I don't think I can fix this one.

Rico: Go talk to God about this one. He has your answers. It sounds like Shane was in a very vulnerable frame of mind. She needed you close, and felt rejected. Maverick, man, I told you to be careful. I'm sure it will be all right. Pray tonight, get some sleep, talk to your Mama, not about this though, and call me tomorrow.

Maverick: All right Rico, thanks man! Later.

Rico: Later. Next time call…this bat had your name all over it tonight!

Maverick: Whatever Dawg! Bye! *Lord, I surely didn't mean to hurt Shane! Forgive me for what I really wanted to do. I know it's important to stay pure for my wife and that's what I wanted my wife to do for me, but does that mean she doesn't love me? My thoughts haven't been pure…my fantasies…my dreams about different women…even more about Shane. I'm not perfect. I want to be with her so bad…I really want to do this right, just to prove to myself it can be done! How can I preach to others about something I can't do myself…Lord, help me! Tomorrow's got to be a better day!*

A NEW DAY

Mrs. Grace: Maverick, Maverick! Hello?!

Maverick: I'm up here working on the roof. I'll be down in a minute.

Mrs. Grace: Okay, baby, please be careful!

Maverick: Uh huh!

Mrs. Grace: So Freda Lee, how long has it been? You're all grown up now! Maverick will be so excited to see you!

Freda Lee: It has been a while! You look great Mrs. Grace!

Mrs. Grace: A compliment? Mm-hmm! What brings

127

you around here Freda Lee?

Freda Lee: Well, I'm in college right now and I'm working on a term paper about social economics. I thought this might be a good place to start. I hoped it would be okay with you to…

Mrs. Grace: Social what?

Freda Lee: Social economics…I'm comparing…

Maverick: Mama did you…

Mrs. Grace: Maverick you remember Freda Lee?

Maverick: Yeah…hello. It's been a while.

Freda Lee: Hi Maverick…

Mrs. Grace: Well, you two talk amongst yourselves, I've got plenty to do. Freda Lee, make sure you stop by and explain to me about what you want to do, before I start doing anything. Explain it to Mav too, so I have back up…

Freda Lee: Yes Ma'am, I promise.

Mrs. Grace: Maverick, if you're done with this ladder, put it up before folks start getting crazy ideas!

Maverick: Okay!

Freda Lee: Well, well, well! Maverick don't you look fine.

Maverick: Yeah right…dirty and sweaty!

Freda Lee: Anyway...uhm it's good to see you again. Maybe we can grab a bite to eat or something later today.

Maverick: No...But thanks.

Freda Lee: No? What do you mean no?

Maverick: I'm not interested.

Freda Lee: Okay, who is it this time Maverick? Who do you think you're in love with this time?

Maverick: Freda Lee what you and I had a long time ago ended a long time ago. You messed up and I moved on. I'm not interested in anything you have to offer.

Freda Lee: Maverick, you never gave me the chance to explain my side!

Maverick: What is there to explain? You claimed you were saving yourself for marriage. Then I catch you under Jackson giggling in the back seat of his car. And you know, ya'll didn't notice me for a while before I walked away! You DON'T have anything I want anymore. You lied to me! You never loved me, you were just using me!

Freda Lee: He forced me! Let me explain!

Maverick: You liar! It didn't sound or look like that to me! Look, I don't know why you came around here. But you need to stay clear of me, dig?!

Freda Lee: Whatever! Just tell Mrs. Grace I'll call her

for the information!

Just to think I wanted to marry that Freda Lee. She said she understood why it was important to save herself, but she didn't. And she was always so self-justified for what she did, no remorse, just a load of lies. And here is Shane...her heart has been broken, I know that for a fact! And I panic and make things worse! Oh God, please don't let me lose Shane. She's who I want...I can't sleep at night...I can't keep my thoughts on anything else.

Mrs. Grace: Maverick, what on earth was going on out here I thought you and Freda Lee were getting ready to throw some blows!?

Maverick: Yeah….well. Freda Lee ain't all she appears to be, Mom.

Mrs. Grace: Boy you just now got the news flash? You have been around here for hours looking like you lost your best friend. What is going on with you? How's Shane been?

Maverick: Mama, I hurt Shane's feelings so bad the other night, I don't think I'll ever be able to work things out.

Mrs. Grace: Aw, you know I hate getting in other folks business, baby! So I'm gonna go and…

Maverick: Mama, I need your help with this one. Even Rico said you had answers. I've just been waiting for the right time to talk to you.

Mrs. Grace: Rico? Lord, help me! Okay, just this

130

once. Tell me what happened.

Maverick: The evening when Shane's brother had his accident, we were at her place. She had some cozy music going and we were sitting down and I was holding her. She seemed pretty shook up about the day. I got nervous and started backing off and saying that I'm holding off for marriage.

Mrs. Grace: Oh Maverick, did she grope you or something? She doesn't seem to be that kind of girl!

Maverick: No! She sure did smell good though! I panicked and came across very uptight. She said she wasn't trying to seduce me and when I looked at her, she had tears running down her cheeks. She looked humiliated. I didn't know what to say. She made me leave and told me never to come back again.

Mrs. Grace: Baby, wow, I know how she must have felt. Let me explain her side, maybe this will help you find the words.

Shane strikes me as a young woman who has been looking for answers to deep questions in the wrong places for a while. She has a lot of love to offer, but it will have to be someone who can accept her as she is today and can see who she will someday be. Like your Daddy was and is with me. Maverick, it took a while for your Dad to earn my trust, respect, and love, because I was so messed up. And I believe Shane truly loves you and I know you love her, but is your love for her based on her past or your past? She seems to be searching for God and she sees the God in you. Let the God in you lead her to Jesus Christ! Cool it with the virginity thang, baby! It's great and I want you to hold

on to it because it's important! Just know true love
isn't based on if you're a virgin or not, it's much deeper
than that. We all make mistakes.

Mav, does she make your stomach leap when you see
her? Does she send electricity through you when you
get kind of close? Do you call her sometimes just to
hear her voice in secret? Cause if you say yes to all of
these questions, baby, there is a whole lot of hope
beyond the scope! Hah!

Maverick: Yes to all of the above…so how do I do
this?

Mrs. Grace: Tell her that you love her and her past is
behind both of you. That all you see in her eyes is your
future. Tell her she sends electricity through you and
that you haven't been able to sleep for days! Tell her,
son, that you are really sorry.

Maverick: Mmm that's very romantic.

Mrs. Grace: That's the same line your Dad used on
me to bring me around. And most importantly, he
made good on those words. Can you make good on
those words to Shane? Do you think you can handle a
kiss? Aw probably not! But it would at least let her
know she's desirable…without jumping her bones.
And give her flowers. Some nice ones.

Maverick: Mama, I love Shane more than life! Can
you call her? She keeps hanging up on me.

Mrs. Grace: Nope. Keep trying. If it's meant to be, it
will work out. What did Freda Lee want?

Maverick: She said she would call you later. Mama, one huge lesson I've learned about women. Virginity or the lack there of doesn't make the woman, it's her character, her love for God, and her dedication to Him. That's what makes a virtuous woman.

Mrs. Grace: I'm giving you an A, baby! If you haven't learned anything else, that's the one thing I want you to know about women. Why, look at me. It takes God to truly make a good woman or a good man. Trials make you strong, and better able to hold on! Boy, I'll be praying Shane comes through for you.

Another thing…forgive Freda Lee and move on from that hurt. Accept that girl for who she is. If she wasn't faithful, that was her. Not saying she can't change, but if she's still lying, don't spend another moment being mad. That doesn't reflect on you…you did right. But let that past hurt go, because it's affecting what you have now. Shane didn't know you before, don't make her pay for the mistrusts of your past. She's got enough to deal with. And loosen up…not too much though! But if you can kiss her and walk away without lowering your standards…try it. If not, don't go there. She'll respect you, especially if she loves you and understands how important it is to you. One thing you'll have a hard time with is convincing her she's worthy of your love…especially knowing you've been "waiting" for that special one. Time is passing you by…don't wait too long to talk to her, Mav.

Maverick: Thanks Mom, come and give me a hug. Shane reminds me a lot of you. So full of life and she keeps it real.

Chapter 21
We Are Not Our Mistakes

Essence: So Shane, when do you plan on leaving?

Shane: Well, I have a flight out tomorrow. I'll be gone for a few days to interview and find an apartment.

Essence: Girl, this is so sudden! What does Maverick have to say about all of this?

Shane: He's fine with it! Listen, I need to finish packing.

Essence: Don't forget be there at 8:30 p.m. And don't be late! Buzz-a-plenty!

Shane: Uh…Okay, okay! Bye!

Please…enough with the weed already! I'm getting tired of it! Where did I put those other boxes?

KNOCK! KNOCK! KNOCK!

Shane: Who is it?

Sean: It's me, Sean!

Shane: Come on in the doors unlocked, I'll be right back. I'm getting some more boxes from the basement.

Sean: Okay sis! Have a seat Maverick, I'll handle this.

Shane: Okay, so Sean how are you doing? What... What is he doing here?

Sean: Now Sis…

Shane: Didn't I tell you I didn't want you here anymore!?

Sean: Now Shane…hold up! You are getting ready to move away and you both need to get things right before you go!

Shane: I think everything was very clear the last time we seen each other. I'm not good enough for him!

Sean: It seems to me, there has been a lot of soul searching going on with this man. You need to…

Shane: NO! I don't want to cry anymore.

Maverick: I didn't come here to make you cry…please let me say what I need to say to you. Please Shane…please.

Sean: I'm not leaving until you do, because he brought me here, Sis. Get to it so I can do my thing.

Shane: You both are really irritating me! Say what you need and then go.

Sean: I'll be sitting right out there on the patio! Take your time Mav! Let's see what you got to drink. I hope you got some of that delicious lemonade…

Maverick: First let me say that I never ever meant to make you feel, in any way, inadequate. I was the one in the wrong. It was me saying all the wrong things. Shane, the taste of my boot was awful!

135

Shane: What? Yeah right, you put both of them in and choked!

Maverick: You're right! I did. And from the bottom of my heart I'm sorry and I ask for you to someday forgive me. But, I need to explain myself to you. I didn't say the things I said in judgment of you. Shane, I've seen a lot and it helped me make the decision I made to wait. That's where I'm at. Seeing people dying from AID's and prostitutes will do that to a person. But, that doesn't take away from who you are to me. Or even who they are. God loves us all.

Shane: Wow, so now I'm a potential AID's victim? What is wrong with you!?

Maverick: No, no…that's not where I'm coming from. Shane, let me start over…geez I rehearsed this moment in my head and I still blew it. What I'm trying to say is…

Shane: Maverick, I'm not a virgin, but I'm not a T.H.O.T either! I made a decision a while back to wait until the right one came along, at least I did at first. I made mistakes and it hurts me to say it. I thought I was in love…more than once. Each time it just got easier and I thought that's what was expected. You come in my life and all of a sudden I feel inadequate. I mean, there was a time when I had standards like you, but it seemed unrealistic in my world. I didn't mind the encouragement and the deep talks we had, because it made me tap into the real Shane. But you stepped on an area that is shameful and very sensitive to me, because it can't be changed. I can stop smoking weed, but this…it's already done.

Maverick: When I first laid eyes on you, we were kids at camp. I didn't really know you then. So your past was before I got know you. I fell in love with the now Shane, not the yesterday Shane. I love you and our past is behind both of us. All I see in your eyes is our future. I sincerely mean what I'm saying to you.

Shane: What about YOUR past. It seems to me you're making me pay for the sins of your past friends or something. Your standards are out of my reach, Maverick. I've got to go out of town to handle some things tomorrow. I'll get everything in order, when I get back. If all goes well, I'll be moving permanently. So I really need ya'll to go now.

Maverick: I see you're packing, but leaving for good? Shane, how can I change your mind?

Shane: I'm sorry. Your words touched me, but you need a girl who better matches what you are willing to accept. It's too late for me to be that girl for you. It hurts like hell, if the truth be known, but I don't know how to get around it.

Maverick: No Shane, it's not over between me and you! It's not over. I don't want anybody else. Please don't leave me.

Shane: Maverick, I don't have anywhere to go now, even if I wanted to stay!

Maverick: I have room at my place!

Shane: Oh no way! I don't live with any man!

Maverick: I can stay at the B&B, that's where I'm at

most of the time anyway!

Shane: I don't know Maverick. If I don't go, I won't have a job. This is a promotional transfer. They have already posted my position.

Maverick: Shane, I'll take care of you. I want too!

Shane: No, no, no! **Your place?** I thought you lived at the B & B. **I'm done with this conversation.** What time is it?

Maverick: It's 7:45.

Shane: My friends are having a party for me at The Club tonight, I have to be there by 8:30 and they don't want me to be late!

Maverick: Well, can I meet you there?

Shane: I don't want you to come. If you do, that's up to you. You can't change my mind, so if that's what your plans are for tonight…you're wasting your time.

Maverick: Sean, I can take you home now.

Sean: Sure Man, come on. Shane, I heard about your party, but I'm staying clear of that crowd…you know why!

Shane: Sean, I'll deal with you later!

Sean: I'm sure you will Lil' Sis! Don't hate me, I was just trying to help. You madder than I thought. Bye.

Men! Just when I think I've got things figured out, here comes another fork in the road. I have to say, Mav is putting a whole lot of effort in. Can't get mad about that, right? Well, I better get ready for tonight. I got this dress just for the occasion. I can't wait to wear it! It just might make Maverick want to drink! Hah! Well, I'm not going to talk about how I'm feeling right now. I have plenty to deal with, like guilt and a whole lot of doubt. Anyway, I just want to move on and stay strong. Don't worry about me, I'll be fine. I'm glad Essence changed her mind and decided to pick me up tonight. I really don't feel like driving. She can catch me up on her love life. I'll catch you at the Club.

Chapter 22
Punked By the Best

Essence: So…life goes on. There they are.

Shane: Ladies!

Lynn: Long time no see!

Shane: Hey, girl! You look great!

Lynn: Thanks! You too!

D.J.: There you are…ready to party?!

Shane: Always!

D.J.: Come on, let's hit this joint. We need to catch up!

Shane: Uhm…love to catch up, but I'm not smoking tonight… Don't judge me.

Essence: Uh oh! There is Maverick, he's coming our way.

Lynn: He seems pretty serious tonight, ya know. Aw, he brought flowers!

Maverick: Hi Ladies, can I steal this beautiful woman for a while?

Lynn: Who me, Maverick? Shane won't like it? Hahaha!

Shane: Whatever! **Flowers?! Ooh!**

Maverick: Hello again. These are for you. May I have this dance?

Essence: Well, so much for the party! Hmm, something is up. Did you hear Shane? She said she wasn't smoking tonight? She didn't even want to do it on the way here either. It didn't stop me, though. Hah!

Lynn: Yeah...what is really going on?! That isn't the Shane I know. He must be havingsome crazy effect on our girl. And she's leaving us too? I'm done.

Essence: Yeah...she's living her life. Go Shane! I hope he talks her into staying, though. I don't know what I'd do without her.

D.J.: How much did Maverick pay you to get her here?

Essence: He paid for dinner AND drinks for all of us at the River, Jazz & Jammin' Rib Club, he even sent some money to go to the waiter! Girls, I don't know what he does for a living, but he makes a good piece of change!

Maverick: Shane, can I have this slow jam?

Shane: I guess...for old times' sake.

Why are they waving and blowing kisses? Okay, where are my girls going? Out the dang door?! Are you freaking kidding me right now?! I thought this was a party for me?! No they didn't! Sigh...I have just been punked! I'm gonna smack that Essence!

Maverick: Maybe for you, but I want to start some

new stuff. Mmm you smell so good, and you look fantastic in that dress.

Shane: Thank you.

So all of this is all about THIS! Why is everyone on his side? What about me? Wow, he's never held me so close before! I don't want him to prove his manhood to me before we...or uh...he gets married. I want this man so bad my teeth chatter! I want to be his wife! For him to wait and fall in love with me...to give his love to me, it makes my knees buckle. Shane, girl, stand strong...if you can! Jesus help me for real!

Maverick: Shane, I want to give my love to you, no one else. I want to make love to you on our wedding night. I believe with all my heart, you will one day be my bride. The thought of you leaving is making me crazy, because I can't see my life without you. Baby, don't you know we can work things out?

Shane: Maverick, calm down before you blow it tonight. It's getting late and I have to get up early.

Maverick: I'm sorry, Shane. I just need to know that we can work things out.

Shane: Maverick, I'll call you before I leave.

Maverick: Can I come in tonight?

Shane: No, you seem intent to prove your manhood tonight. Don't do it. You're trying to step out of who you are to keep me, but don't you know, what you have done is honorable to me. Don't change, Mav. I'm very curious as to what made you flip?

Maverick: It's not that I wasn't attracted to you. I just panicked because I haven't felt that much passion for anyone in my life. I haven't kissed you because I would push the envelope with you, and I know it. That night I wanted to kiss you a thousand times and lead you into your bedroom.

Shane: Hold that down…stay clear of that! I need to hit the bathroom, I'll be right back.

Thank God the slow jam is over. I need to hit the bathroom, a joint, and the road! Is it me or is it hot up in here? Man is he pouring it on heavy! What do you think about all of this? It's jacked up how we can guard something so important and lose our reason why. It's a set up! Don't most girls start out wanting to be a virgin on their wedding night? I know I did. But you fall for a guy and think he's the one and you want to give him your "special" love. Then come to find out that's all he wanted or he just loses interest. That's the one thing of value we have, so when it's gone…it's gone. What do I have left to give this man? Oh boy, I think I seen ole Tom in here. I've got to get out of here before he makes a scene.

Shane: Since you must be my ride home, let's blow this joint and go somewhere else. I can't believe my girls punked me and you're in a talking mood.

Maverick: Uh, okay. Is everything all right?

Shane: Sure it is. The party left, so there's no need to stay…right? I'm disappointed, so let's leave.

We got out the door before Tom could catch up!

THAT was close! Geez! Mav won't stop talking. I'm getting a little tickled. I have to hand it to him, he's putting in a great effort. A bit too late though...

Maverick: I want you to be my wife, Shane. I want you to have my babies...I love talking with you and doing things together. During this time we've been apart, I felt so empty and lonely. I couldn't sleep or stay focused. Didn't you?

Shane: Yeah, but I felt rejected more than anything. I don't want to be with someone who isn't happy with who I am, in all my jacked up self. I don't want you to walk away from me disappointed and wishing I were the things you always wanted and coming up short. That's not fair to me, Maverick.

Maverick: Shane, I really realize now that I hurt you, and I'm really sorry. I think I'm desperate to make you stay. I'll do anything you want.

Shane: It seems your flesh wants me, but what does your soul really want? Don't get them confused and don't confuse me! You've wanted a virgin. It's kind of crazy when I think about it though. Because you can miss the greatest love of your life because of a technicality. I'm human, Mav. If I believed that a man like you would have been in my future, you better believe I would have waited! I've just seen so much heartache, I didn't think anyone out here cared!

Maverick: Shane, I've done a lot of thinking and growing up. When I wasn't seeing anyone, I had this fantasy of what I wanted my wife to be like. But I left out something on my list...her humanity. And I realize how unrealistic it is to make a list without taking the time to get to know someone. I admit it was...it was...

Shane: A set up! It was a set up Maverick! How many people are sitting around waiting to meet Mister or Miss Perfect and they come into their lives, but they never ever notice them, because they don't add up to everything on their list. And they live a lonely imperfect life because they can't get past their list or themselves.

Maverick: I hear you. I also believe that God hears our prayers too. And He gives us the desires of our hearts. And even though I had a list of what I thought I wanted...God knew what I needed. When I saw you, something happened in my heart and I knew...I just knew you were the one...a long time ago.

Shane: But you also have a certain standard. I'm out here getting high...I've lost my virginity, Maverick... it's gone. Where do I fit in your world?

Maverick: Shane, you fit in my heart. And you do fit in my world. My world deals with unconditional love, Shane. We minister to those that are hurting. We don't sit around and judge the people coming in, we just love on them. My God! What a fool I've been to put my convictions on someone else without offering grace. It's one thing to hold a standard for myself, but it's another to push others away because of something they didn't learn or understand! I see my Mom and Dad, their love. A perfect example of God's grace. (*I've been going about this all wrong.*)

Shane, you do fit in my world and you have the qualities I want in my woman. You have an uncanny way of looking at something in a different way. And

145

you move me to look deeper…into myself or whatever situation we may be observing. You have a great sense of discernment, Shane.

Shane: Maverick…

Maverick: You give me a sense of worth that I never felt before and it feels so good being with you. You make me feel like I count. You make me laugh and those beautiful brown eyes melt me, Shane. You look inside my soul. How can I throw all that away, when it's all I've been looking for?

Shane: Hmm…I do all of that? Why couldn't you have relaxed that night and talked like this? Now I have made decisions…

Yeah…I made these decisions without counting the cost or even thinking beyond my pain.

Maverick: You know I want you to do what you feel is right for you. If it includes me, which I pray that it does, I will be here with open arms. If not, I will be broken-hearted. I want to spend the rest of my life with you Shane. I can't say that any other way…I wish I had time to prove it to you! Well, here we are.

That was the longest ride I've ever had. Thank God he brought me straight home. I've got so much on my mind, there is NO WAY he's getting in tonight.

Shane: Well, thanks for bringing me home. I'll be back Monday afternoon. And I'll call you every chance I get while I'm gone…okay?

Maverick: Why are you going?

146

Shane: I need distance and time to think.

Maverick: You can't think here?

Shane: I don't want to think here, I need to get away from here and see something new.

Maverick: Well, call me on my cell phone. If you don't call me, I'll call you!

Shane: I don't doubt it for a minute! Good night.

Maverick: I love you Shane Vanity…good night!

A little wave and watch him pull out of the parking lot. Finally, Lord, I don't have a clue of what I need to be doing with Maverick, or myself. That man was straight persistent! Lord help him! He cooled my jets, though…I'm not putting myself out there anymore!

If you were me what would you do? I want so much to be with him, but if I'm not what he wants down in his heart, it's just a set up for failure. I've been hurt enough. What does a real relationship consist of? Why do fools fall in love? Why? Why? Why?

Home sweet home, at least for a little while longer. Now I feel pretty goofy. Why did I decide to move so hastily? Was my decision based on living my life on a grander scale, or am I running away? It doesn't seem as exciting to leave as it does to stay! I'm ready to…

RING! RING! RING!

Shane: Hello Maverick.

Maverick: How did you know it was me?

Shane: Well…you're kidding right?

Maverick: Anyway…do you need a ride to the airport tomorrow?

Shane: Yes, as a matter of fact. My previous plans fell through so I could use one, but it's pretty early!

Maverick: I'm your man…I mean I'm the man for the job!

Shane: Uh…okay. I have to catch a 6:30 flight, so I need to be there by 5:30 in the morning.

Maverick: Okay, I'll be there at 5:15 since you live so close.

Shane: Sounds good. Maverick, thank you.

Maverick: Anything for you Shane. Good night.

Shane: Good night.

It seems like I just might have the upper hand now. Kind of like a power trip. But I don't want to feel like this, I want to feel safe in his love. It's almost like he's begging me to be with him. Is this what happens to folks anxious to be loved? Or scared of loss? Is that how I am? Now that I look back at my bad decisions…wow…I thank You Lord for getting me out of the messes I made. Now if You could just show me how to accept good love. Is it possible for You to love me through him?

Well, Mav and I will talk in the morning before I go. I want to settle some things with him, to take him off of this edge. I do love him and I'll confess my heart. I don't want him wondering about my love. That's the last thing anyone should ever wonder about...if their love is being reciprocated. He spilled his heart tonight...wow!

Oh, I'm so tired! Well, I'll see you in the next chapter. It's getting good...don't you think!? Ciao for now!

Lord, please show me what to do. In Jesus' Name...Amen.

Chapter 23
Travel Destination: ME

BUZZ! BUZZ! BUZZ!

Now what was I getting up early to fly across the friendly skies for? Oh yeah...to find me! Lord, help me find me...or find You! Things seem so cloudy! I've got to clear my mind! I'm kind of proud of myself for last night...I didn't smoke any weed and I didn't give in to Maverick even though I could have!

(Yawn!) To find me would be the ultimate adventure! Or better yet, God! I would ask Him, "Why am I here and what am I supposed to be doing with my life?" Is it about a big party or is there an actual purpose to life? Man, life used to be so simple when someone else was making the decisions for me...why do we have to grow up!? And love...what is love exactly!? Is it about great sex, romance, and good conversation or is there more to love? One thing I know...Maverick is in my life for a reason.

RING! RING! RING!

Shane: Hello Maverick.

Maverick: Oh Shane...I guess it would be me this early! Good Morning my little dove, are you up and at 'em?

Shane: Yes I am...good morning.

Maverick: How about I pick you up at 5 so we can

talk a little before you go?

Shane: Sounds good! What time is it...4:30? I just stepped out of the shower, I packed last night...I'll be ready at 5!

Maverick: Sounds good! See you at five, baby!

Shane: Okay.

CLICK!

It feels good to hear his voice. It makes me feel guilty. Am I stealing something that belongs to another girl, because she had sense enough to wait for marriage? Do I deserve to be with a man who waited all of his life for me, but I didn't wait for him? Am I excused or justified for just not understanding the importance of my virginity?

Geez! There is so much shame in this area if the truth be told! I never wanted other men walking around "knowing" what it's like to be with me, only the man that truly loved me...my husband! For some crazy reason I didn't wait until the deal was done. It didn't happen! Or was I afraid it would never happen?! Dang this hurts! I let myself down. It's not Mav's fault...it's mine. So now what? I guess I need to know how to forgive myself. Well, let me finish getting my make-up on and double check everything.

HONK!

I know he's not blowing the horn for me to come out! What's he doing?

Shane: Maverick, it's too early to be blowing the horn...shh! What's the deal?

Maverick: I'm sorry, I hit it trying to reach for my keys... they fell down under the seat!

Shane: Mmhm! My bags are right at the door. Did you find the keys?

Maverick: The keys? Yes. Come on, let's get you in the car. I'll lock up for you. Are you all in? Okay, let me grab your bags, lock the door and get your bags in the trunk. Are you sure you have everything Babe?

Shane: Okay. Uh, yes I'm pretty sure. If there's anything I missed, I can buy it there.

What is going on with him? He sure is acting chivalrous just a little more than usual! Hmm... What's really going on?

Maverick: Okay, let's get going. So Shane, what hotel are you going to be staying at? Will it be nice?

Shane: It's not the top of the line, but it's something I could afford.

Maverick: The reason why I asked is that I reserved you a room at a five star hotel for the whole weekend! Its downtown and I had the other hotel refund your money back to the credit card on file.

Shane: What!? Why did you do that Maverick!?

Maverick: Well, I felt responsible for this trip. If things would have been working better with us, you

152

wouldn't be leaving, so I figured if you needed to go, at least have something to remember me by!

Shane: What's with the grin?! Maverick...what am I going to do with you? If I didn't appreciate it so much, I'd be mad! Any other surprises?

Maverick: Who me? A limo will be picking you up.

Shane: Whatever! Hahaha!

Maverick: Oh no, baby...I'm serious.

Okay, we're here! Can you believe Maverick!? I really have to see this to believe it.

Maverick: Okay, let's get your plane ticket and get you on your way. Shane, did I tell you that I loved you today?

Shane: Not that I remember.

Maverick: Shane, I love you.

Shane: Maverick, I...uh...I...I love you too.

Why was that so hard to say? Oh boy, my stuff is out there now!

Maverick: Do you mean it or are you just trying to make me feel good because you're leaving my sad behind here?!

Shane: Yes, I do love you Maverick! That's why I'm so messed up about how you've saved yourself for that special someone! I just don't feel like I deserve it, because I didn't wait! And why I didn't wait was because I thought I found that special one, and he turned out to be a dog! He got his kicks by going with virgins! After that, I was so broken hearted it didn't matter anymore. And I just kept on blowing it.

Maverick: Shane, you can stop explaining. I'm not a confessional. And baby, don't think my wait isn't worth it! When we do get together, because I plan on marrying you, it will be right because we're right. I've made mistakes along the way too, but it doesn't define who I am, just something I did in ignorance!

Shane: Yeah...what did you do?

Maverick: We'll have time to talk about it another day. I promise! Just remember what I said. I did some soul searching and I'm speaking to you from my heart, we deserve each other, Shane, we really do.

Shane: Uh...I guess my flight is ready! Maverick, I really appreciate what you've said, it's made me feel a whole lot better! I love you baby, and I can't wait to come back!

Maverick: Me too! I love you Shane. Call me when you get there, I want to hear about your room!

Shane: Okay.

Finally, a kiss! Not a deep one, but one that I still feel the tingle on my lips! Oh! This man is yummy. Sigh...I want this man for life! Oh Lord, help a sista out!

Well, I'll catch you when I get to the hotel! Four star

hotel, that is! That should take us to the next chapter. Toodleloo!

MAVERICK: *Mmm! Her lips are always as soft as I imagined. I want Shane so bad, but my love wants to respect her! I don't know why a man would jump a woman's bones...I mean I know why, but waiting shows value! Once you know what's right, you want to show respect...you should anyway. I think about how Shane went through that crap...I could kick this man's tail! He violated my sweet baby! When it's our time, I will be sweet and tender. I'll be gentle and loving! And she will be addicted to Maverick! Oh yeah, I haven't done it yet, but I've thought long and hard on how I'll do it! Big plans...oh yeah, baby girl!*

Shane, my love, I've got major plans for you! Now, I need to take care of some stuff before I catch my flight. I want things to be right for this evening! She is going to be so surprised to see me! Haha! I can't wait! I'll travel a thousand miles to kiss those soft lips again!

Chapter 24
Am I Dreaming

What an amazing limo ride! Wow! This hotel is absolutely beautiful! Oh my Jesus, You treat me so good! Wow! This is much too beautiful to enjoy alone! I wish Maverick was here! This is wonderful!

RING! RING! RING!

Ooh, let me twirl and kick my leg to answer the phone! Hah!

Shane: Hello?

Maverick: Hi, baby. Are you in your room yet?

Shane: Maverick! You are...I can't believe...what am I gonna do with you!? Ooh! Look at the beautiful flowers...WHAT!? You...Maverick...you are so sweet, thank you...they are absolutely beautiful!

Maverick: You are very welcome my love! I've got to go now, I'll call you later. Just relax and enjoy yourself...okay!

Shane: Oh...Maverick I miss you already. It's so beautiful here! I wish you were here...I really do! The view is breathtaking!

Maverick: Aww! I miss you too, baby! I'll call you later.

Shane: Well...I guess if you have to go... okay, bye.

Maverick: Bye.

Hmmm...Where on Earth did he get this kind of money? Business must be real good! This is an expensive room...very expensive. As much as we talk, I haven't really asked him how much he makes. Or is that tacky?! I know that his parents run the B&B and it's totally run down! He could be putting his money into that, instead of me. Look at this place!

Great Shane! Now you can't even enjoy yourself. Well, let me check out the bathroom. Ooh isn't this nice...real nice! A girl could really get used to this kind of living...for real!

RING! RING!

Shane: Hello?

Mr. Cisco: Hello Shane?

Shane: Yes! Hello Mr. Cisco!

Mr. Cisco: Hello Shane! My secretary told me you changed hotels and it's good to know you made it in. How was your flight?

Shane: My flight went well. You truly have a beautiful city!

Mr. Cisco: Yeah, it is pretty nice here. Listen, Shane, I wanted to call you myself to explain to you that I have been called out of town for an emergency meeting with our CEO. There are more changes in our Executive Structure and all Executives have been called to meet.

This means that our meeting will have to be postponed.

Shane: Oh, I see. Are we still meeting while I'm in town?

Mr. Cisco: Oh, uh...I don't think my schedule will work for this week. Once the meetings are wrapped up, I can take a better look at my schedule. This could take a couple more weeks before I can meet with you. I found out about this meeting while you were in the air. I'm really sorry for the inconvenience, Shane.

Shane: Uh, okay... *So what about my paycheck?*

Mr. Cisco: So Shane, listen...I have taken care of all of your spending expenses for this weekend! I want you to take in the sights, dinner, tours, and night life, whatever your heart desires! You can even go on a shopping spree if you'd like!

Shane: Are you serious?!

Mr. Cisco: Of course! One of our couriers will be coming to your room any minute. She will be giving you one of our loadable credit cards with a $3,000 credit limit and a $5,000 check. The card is good anywhere in town! And the check is to cover your month expenses at home.

Shane: Oh how wonderful! Will I have to pay it back...if anything were to change?

Mr. Cisco: Oh no Shane. Even if you don't come on board, this is our way of keeping our doors open. I sent a letter explaining the details. I don't want to burn any bridges. You come highly recommended and I want to meet with you in the future. Like I said, it's going to take a couple of weeks before I can get back to you. Consider this a short, all-expense paid vacation.

Shane: Are you kidding?! Mr. Cisco, I appreciate all you have done. I look forward to meeting with you in the near future!

KNOCK! KNOCK!

Excuse me, Mr. Cisco, there is someone at my door could you hold on a second?

Mr. Cisco: Sure, it should be our courier.

Shane: Who is it?

Courier: Delivery for Ms. Shane Vanity from Mr. Cisco…

Shane: Oh yes! Hi! Thank you very much! Mr. Cisco, I do have the envelope with everything you mentioned.

Mr. Cisco: Great! Again, enjoy our beautiful city and I hope you meet a friend while you're here! Good-bye Shane!

Shane: Thanks, good bye!

GOD IS GOOD! OH YEAH! OH YEAH! Oh man! I don't want to go out on the town by myself! I better call my baby! Let me dial him up…gosh I hope he can talk! He better talk to me.

Maverick: Hello?

159

Shane: Maverick, I have got some awesome news...listen, baby...

Maverick: Shane, hold on real quick.

Shane: Uh...okay.

Maverick: Shane, are you in your room?

Shane: Huh? Yeah, that's what I wanted to tell you...I really wish you were here because...

Maverick: What, baby?

Okay is it me or is he having a hard time listening to me?!

KNOCK! KNOCK! KNOCK!

Shane: Well...wait a minute, someone is at my door. Mav, I'll call you right back. Who is it?

Delivery for Miss Shane Vanity!

Delivery? Wow, all I can see are flowers. Let me open my door and take a peek.

Shane: Wow, thank you! They're beautiful! Come in and sit them over there! Huh? Leo?! What are you doing here?!

Leo: Hi Shane! Happy to see me?

Shane: Uhm, well, of course I am. How did you know I was in town? **Oh boy, this could go very wrong if I'm**

160

not careful. My heart whispers Maverick, but my body screams Leo! It must be his cologne. His cologne won't leave me alone!

Leo: Well, you know that I own flower shops in a few cities. I happened to be working on the books when this order came through with your name on it. Since it was a pretty expensive arrangement, I thought I'd hand deliver it to see if it were you and what was going on with you.

Shane: Wow. Okay. Well, thank you for hand-delivering them to me. Uhm. I'm doing well.

Leo: Will you be in town for a while?

Shane: Uhm, yes I will for the week…on business.

Leo: Great! How about we take in the town this evening? I can show you a good time.

I KNOW you can my man. Jesus, please help a sista out!

Shane: Uhm, ya know Leo, I won't be able to. The flowers are beautiful and look there's a little envelope. Leo, where's the card?

Leo: Oh yeah. It's right here. Who's Maverick?

Shane: Maverick is my man. That's who I'm seeing now.

Leo: Oh really? Okay. I tell you what. If he falls through and it doesn't work, let's pick up where we left off. You've never given me a real chance to be your man. You were always on the move.

Shane: Me on the move? Really?! Where we left off? Where was that exactly? Transient romance just doesn't work for me. You barely called. You show up out of the blue here and there. I fall or I fell into your arms every time you popped up, only to not see you for however long, until the next time. A phone call here and there isn't good enough. So, sorry, I don't want to pick up where we left off, Leo. It sucked! You need to know that we're over and I've moved on. I'm no longer a stand-by for you.

Leo: Aw Shane! Come on, it wasn't that bad was it? What does this Maverick have that I don't have?

Shane: Time and everything else I need to make me feel special.

Leo: Flowers? I always brought you flowers. Time wasn't the issue until you decided you didn't want to wait on me. Yet here we are. Can he handle the rest like I can?

Shane: Don't worry about what he can handle. It's time for you to step, Leo. Thanks for the delivery.

Leo: Yeah, I didn't think so. Okay, Shane. I'll check you out later. Bye, beautiful.

I can't believe I'm shaking. That was harder than I expected. He's that guy. You know that ONE who knows what makes you weak. I know he's not any good for me, but he's the one I got to get out of my system! Lord, please don't let him show up again! Please!

Chapter 25
He Doesn't Need To Know, Right?

Ring! Ring!

Shane: Hello?

Maverick: Hi, baby! Everything okay? Why didn't you call back?

Shane: I'm sorry. I'm all yours now. Let me tell you about my flight, limo ride and…oh, wait a minute! First I want to thank you for the beautiful flowers! I really love them!

Maverick: You can.

Shane: You can what?

KNOCK! KNOCK! KNOCK!

Shane: Let me call you back. Who is it? Oh my GOSH!

Maverick: You can thank me right now!

Shane: MAVERICK!? Oh my! Oh my… Hi, baby!

Listen, you might want to step out of the room for this grand hello! Mmm! This kiss should be real good! Aww man, another peck! Not bad though! He lingered. Hah!

Maverick: Oh baby, it's so good to see you! I've missed those lips!

Shane: Aww…me too! Okay…let's cool it!

If you've missed my lips so much, make them happy to see you, man. Aww, my baby needs to learn how to kiss me. I'm the one to give him the lessons. His pucker's way too tight.

Maverick: Shane, I came here just to kiss those luscious lips…don't deprive me.

Shane: Maverick! No. I want you to be a man of your word, don't compromise with something so special… please don't. It's important to know there are men in this world who value love. Once you get started it's hard to stop…so stop!

Maverick: But baby…oh…okay. I'm sorry, wow Shane, I'm sorry.

Shane: Are you okay? You're funny! Hahaha…

With his sad puppy dog eyes and uptight lips. Wow!

Maverick: Yeah…you've made me fall deeper in love now. You value something I have valued for a long time. It's more than that, you value our love.

Shane: Yeah…yes I guess I do. You're special and you make me feel special too. Let's not blow it because it "seems" right! Let's wait until it is "right"!

Maverick: You have my heart and my word…so what's the big news?! Who was that guy walking down from your room? *Hmm, I've seen him before.*

Oh no, no, no, I'm not about to wreck this moment.

164

Since he doesn't know you're watching, you can't tell him neither! Have faith in a sista, okay! I got this under control...I think. Don't judge me.

Shane: Uhm, he delivered those beautiful flowers you sent me. So here's my good news...Mr. Cisco, the man I was supposed to meet with called to postpone our meeting!

Maverick: And that's why you're happy? What does that mean?

Shane: It means that he gave me a nice check for my home expenses and a credit card to use for my stay here this weekend! He said I can shop, go to dinner, and take tours! Whatever I want to do!

Maverick: Wow, baby, that's great! And guess who will be here to be your tour guide?

Shane: You?!

Maverick: You're wish is my command!

Shane: Oh Maverick! Will you be here the whole week?

Maverick: Unless there's an emergency to pull me away, I'm here! Have you eaten yet?

Shane: No, not yet! I'm in Heaven! I need to freshen up a bit!

Maverick: Okay, I'm a few floors down. Dress casually we'll get something to eat and see the sights!

Shane: Okay! Give me about 20 minutes!

Maverick: Sounds good, that'll give me time to put a little something together! Ciao, baby!

Shane: Ciao!

Okay...pinch me I must be dreaming! That one song comes to mind...am I dreaming, or am I just imagining you're here in Shane's World! God, I'm calling on You big time! I've been seeing Maverick for several months now...we're just now starting to kiss. Truth is, Leo hit a nerve and my flesh is all fired up! I don't want to use anyone, but this is a battle with my heart and flesh! We're in a very romantic place. Anything can happen, but I don't want it to! Please help me honor our love...In Jesus name, Amen! For real!

This time will be good for us. I'll see Maverick without all the interruptions and ask the questions I need to ask. Hopefully Leo doesn't pop up. I'm going to freshen up and call one of my girls real quick! This is just too crazy and cool!

RING! RING!

Shane: Hello?

Leo: So that's your new man, huh?

Shane: Leo? Why do you keep bothering me?

Leo: I'm not bothering you. I'm just making sure you're good, Shane. You should at least give me a chance. We haven't sat and talked in a while.

Shane: Yeah, I know. It's going to be even longer if at all. I've got to go. Please keep your distance while I'm here. I didn't come here for you. I came here to get my mind clear...

Leo: Oh, so things aren't as wonderful as you're pretending?

Shane: I didn't say that. What I meant was...never mind! I don't need to explain myself to you. Sigh. Bye, Leo.

Leo: Later, Shane.

I have a feeling Leo is going to be a problem. Will wonders ever cease? When I wanted his attention, he was always on the move. Anyway, I need to get ready for my amazing date! I love Maverick, not Leo. As long as Leo stays at a distance, I think I'll be okay. I just pray that Mav doesn't have to leave early. That could be another problem. Stay focused, Shane! Geez! Time to have some fun! I'll see you in the next chapter! Ciao for now!

Chapter 26
One Knee for One Answer

Wow, so far this day has been incredible! Maverick really knows how to have a great time in a strange land! Sitting here on the dock of the bay, just watching the waves and the birds flying overhead... this is so soothing. Makes me want to sing. Hold up! I actually feel good without weed! I haven't even thought about getting high today! I wonder if his prayers are working. The only way I'll know if I'm free is when I get home.

Maverick: Shane, what's on your mind?

Shane: You know Maverick, I haven't even thought about getting high today!

Maverick: Oh yeah? Cool!

Shane: Yeah! I'm glad you showed up. I'm really having a good time with you.

Maverick: Me too, Shane.

Shane: Maverick, I'm curious...with the fancy hotel, limo rides, and beautiful flowers, what do you do for a living? I know you help your parents and all, but...

Maverick: As much as we talk I've never told you?! Oh...well, I have an internet business trading stocks. It keeps a good amount of cash in my pocket and I'm not chained to a desk. So in my spare time, I help my parents through the day. My biggest contribution to the

B&B is maintenance. My dream is to totally restore that building. As a matter of fact, that dream is starting to become a reality. Business is booming and that's how I was able to be here with you. Let's just say, I could live anywhere in this world if I so desired. It's all legit, Shane, you're in good hands.

Wow, that's cool. This isn't an interview...or is it? Hah!

Shane: Impressive. Baby, it's cool that you help your parents too! I have some great ideas for the building, if you ever need interior design! Like decorating the rooms with amazing art, stucco, colors and textures. I have a beautiful designer wallpaper in mind that would look gorgeous in the hallways. Beautiful window treatments and trim, and the colors have to be right with the lighting....

Maverick: Shane....

Shane: Fresh new carpet. Maverick, what are you doing?

Uh oh, why is he on his knee? Can't do this today, bro.

Maverick: Shane, you are the most beautiful woman I have ever known! You're gorgeous inside and out, and you're mesmerizing in conversation, your heart is compassionate and I just can't imagine living my life without you.

Shane: Aw, that's so sweet of you to say that, Maverick. But why are you kneeling? Come on up and sit beside me, okay.

Please get up. Please don't go any further. Please!

Maverick: Shane, will you marry me?

Shane: Wait!? WHAT?!

Maverick: Shh! Shane, baby...I didn't stutter! Will you marry me?

Shane: Are you kidding me?! Uhm, Maverick before I can answer you I need to know some things. This is going to take some time for me to figure out. Please get up, we need to talk. I need you to share straight from your heart and answer honestly.

Maverick: Okay Shane...I'll answer all your questions.

Shane: I don't want you to tell me what you think I want to hear. Do you understand? Even if it's something that might hurt me. Trust me enough to make the final decision with the answers you give me. Let me decide if they are the right answers or not. Okay?

Maverick: Talk to me Shane, ask me anything. If I can't be real with you now, what's the use of going any further? I don't want to live a lie.

Shane: Okay Maverick. You say that it doesn't bother you that I've been in other relationships in the past? The way things are going in this world I just want you to know I'm straight, so that you know. Are you really a REAL virgin, no games?! Not technical or on the down low to get your kicks? I don't want any pop up surprises. You know what I mean?

170

Maverick: Oh! Wow...for real!? That blows my mind. I'm not one bit interested in men. I'm straight as an arrow. Oh, Shane, that hurt, baby! Is it that hard to believe that I could hold out for a good woman's love? No hanky-panky. Do you know what kind of women and men I've grown up seeing? There are a lot of folks that are lost and unsure of who they are or who they want. I've seen a lot, Shane. I'm solid about what and who I want.

Shane: I had to ask! Then tell me, what do I do for you? What do I do that lights your fire? What is it about me that stands out from all the rest?

Maverick: Years ago when I saw you at Whispering Winds Church Camp, I remember one day going over and sitting near you. I had an extra grape pop hoping you might take it because you were so sad. I finally got the courage to offer it to you and that was the first time I seen you smile. When you looked up at me, your eyes pierced my soul. Knowing that you noticed me...that your beautiful brown eyes were gazing into mine...it just shook me. You probably don't even remember me. But that day, I prayed that I could someday make you happy again.

Shane: Hold up! I remember that! My Dad used to always buy me grape pop. And I asked God if He loved me, could He show me some kind of way, just to let me know everything would be all right...then this chubby kid with braces came up cheesing and offered me a grape pop. That wasn't you, was it?!

Aww, I want to fall out laughing right now! Private note: Ladies, don't count out the guys you think aren't your type – they will surprise you! I'm in shock

right now! Wow!

Maverick: That was chubby me…braces, glasses, tight little fro, and all! And I believed in love at first sight. It seemed like I fell in love with you then. As I got older I thought about you sometimes, but I started to think it was just puppy love or a big crush. But I always remembered your name and your eyes.

When your brother came to the B&B, he talked a lot about his family. He mentioned your name a few times. I couldn't believe it, but I wanted to see how you turned out.

Now this is really blowing my mind! Can you believe this?!

Maverick: I happened to go out with a friend to pick up some pizza…that's when I saw you after all those years. You turned out so beautiful, I couldn't stop looking at you. You noticed me staring at you and fluttered those beautiful eyes and smiled. I about fell over. That's when the eye tag began. I wondered if you remembered me or was just flirting with a handsome stranger.

Shane: Oh wow! You are for real aren't you?!

Maverick: Oh yeah! I hoped you would have remembered me, but my appearance had changed quite a bit. I lost the weight, the glasses, and the braces. Haha!

Shane: Yeah, you changed a whole lot, I didn't know that was you. Thank you for being so sweet to me. It gave me a little hope in such a sad time in my life. So,

I know you've had other relationships. Are you still affected by any of them? There's no way I would believe you never dated anyone seriously in all of this time.

Maverick: There was one relationship that was kind of serious. She turned out to be a faker. She was just using me for what she could get. I caught her with another guy and I ended it.

Shane: Where did you meet her?

Maverick: I hate to even say it. But I met her at a church conference. She played me on all my "requirements" and made me think they were important to her too. I'd much rather deal with someone who is honest about who they are or what they've done, than a pretender. She pretended she loved me, but her actions proved differently.

Shane: Sounds like she took you for a ride. I'm sorry to hear that. I guess we've all been used in some way. No matter where you meet them or who they are, it still hurts. Come on, let's take a walk on the beach.

I love that we're talking and getting things out in the open. I had a feeling he had been in love before. Well you can go talk amongst yourselves while we continue with our date. But before you go...

Let's take this moment to give God some praise! You believe this? I'm totally shocked! I wasn't expecting this at all! Are you happy for me? I sure hope so! I know when you first tuned in I seemed to be a pretty smoked out case! Partying was my life, I lost my

virginity for all the wrong reasons, and I came from a jacked up family life! Well, I don't believe in living happily ever after! But I do feel like I'm on the right track to a better life….better than I was! As long as Leo don't show up. Don't judge!

Time to Reflect and Pray

Okay, this is a time to pray and seek the Lord for answers. This is a decision that affects the rest of my book shelf life. I don't want to get married with the attitude that if it doesn't work, we can get a divorce. I'm a child of divorce and it's painful. Just being a child of two parents that decided they didn't want to go on any further together made it hard for me to figure things out. I couldn't imagine what it must have felt like as an adult making those decisions, because I was a child.

Mom was crushed...all life left her eyes for years. I don't think my Dad had a clue of the damage he left.

Lord, I know I got saved as a little girl, and I have done some crazy stuff since then. I'm still working on giving you everything...but can you help me to love without fear. I don't want to be abandoned again. I always hear that You will never leave me or let me down...so if that's true, I need You to give me the answer to his question. Should I marry him? Did You bring him to me? Lord, do You want me to marry him?

Give me a sign...anything...something to let me know You are answering my questions. I'm so scared. I'm so scared, Lord! You know my heart has been broken over and over again. Is there something wrong with me that makes men break my heart? Did I do something to cause this kind of pain?

Maverick is a good man! I don't want to miss it. I want to be in love...good love...God's love. I want Your love this time. If he walked into my life all those years ago with a grape pop...now with love...bring my Dad back into my life to help us heal the loss of our family. That will be my yes. If Daddy never comes back, I'll never say yes.

This is between You and me, Lord. I'm not going to say anything about this request...I need to see You come through for me. I want to know that You want this for me too. And if this can happen, I'll see to it that I'll give my life to you...completely. Pinky promise? Can you answer this crazy prayer for me, Lord? In Jesus Name...Amen.

You can't blame a sista for trying.

Chapter 27
Back Home at the B&B

Mrs. Grace: Well, baby, how did it go?

Maverick: Uhm…she didn't say no. She needs time. Since I had to come home a couple days earlier than I planned, I hope she spent those few days to seriously think about what she has with me.

Mrs. Grace: Well, you wait on the Lord and see what He's got to say about it all. Better to have a woman who wants to be with you than one who's trying to play games to trap you.

Maverick: You're right Mom…yeah. How's everything going?

Mrs. Grace: Okay. We had this man come in…he looked about my age. He didn't strike me as a man that has been down on his luck a long time. He just seemed like all hope is gone. Your Dad found him sitting in the park staring into space. He struck up a conversation with him and found out he didn't have anywhere to go. So he brought him here.

Maverick: Hmm…I wonder what his story is. I'll check in on him.

Mrs. Grace: Uhm…oh yeah! Carol and Sean called me today. They said they want to come and help out. What do you think about that?!

Maverick: I know Shane said they loved them some Mrs. Grace…I'm not surprised. It would be nice to see

Shane come down here too. She…oh never mind.

Shane: She…what?

Maverick: Oh! Hey lady!

Mrs. Grace: Hahaha! Shane, you got him!

Shane: Hello beautiful people! I'm rested and refreshed, so I thought I'd come down here to see what I can do to help ya'll out. Is it okay?

Maverick: I just said I wished you'd come down here and help out.

Shane: Yeah? I just felt like it's time to go a little deeper in this…love thing.

Mrs. Grace: Good girl! That's a good thing, baby! When you're ready, come my way, I have a project for you!

Shane: Yes Ma'am!

Maverick: Wow, girl…it's so good to see you!

Shane: Yeah…you too. It's good to be back in our neck of the woods.

Maverick: Yeah. It's good to know they were able to let you continue your lease since things changed. Are you really cool with that? Are you going to go back out there and interview?

Shane: The way things are going right now…I don't think so. I'm happy to be home. I'm not looking to run away anymore. Mr. Cisco called me. I was appointed to a new team in the company here. It pays more and I won't have to work as many hours. So I can come by more often. Now I just have to unpack.

Maverick: Congratulations…that's good to hear! I'll come by and help you put things back together.

Shane: Thank you…that would be real nice…everything is everywhere. But right now, I want to go and see what your Mom needs me to do.

Maverick: She's in her office…up the stairs to the left.

Shane: Thank you, baby…I'll talk to you later.

Maverick: Mmhm*! Now she knows she is fine all over the place! Lord have mercy!*

Lola: M-m-m! Sounds to me like Mavy is in love!

Maverick: What?! Lola…I'm more than in love.

Lola: Yeah, it seems to me you in lust too. I could help you with that!

Maverick: Lola, you need to get your life together. I ain't looking for anything THAT free. A woman's love must be earned to make it worth having. A good man is willing to work hard for the prize of a good woman.

Lola: Who said anything about free or love for that matter?!?

Maverick: You mean to tell me you'd settle for anything less than love? Or…

Lola: Mavy…can't nobody love me. I'm worthless. The only thing I have left is good sex. For a little bank I can rock your world.

Maverick: Never that. It's only as good as the love.

Lola: Spoken like a true virgin! Aww, hahaha!

Maverick: No! Spoken like a real man. Sex don't make a man…anyone can do it! A real man knows how to treat his lady. A true man respects his lady and is faithful to her. A true man will tell the truth, even when it hurts. A true man prays for those that need Jesus…I pray for you Lola.

Lola: Well…ouch Mavy! You keep praying, hear! And while you're at it, pray me in a "real man"! I can't say I ever had one of those!

Maverick: I'll do that just for you Lola. And I'll pray that Lola loves Lola first…that's where it will all start for you.

Lola: Yeah, well… Well what's the first step to that?

Carol: Honesty. You got to come clean with yourself, like I did. I'll take it from here Maverick.

Maverick: Okay…Carol…great timing. I'll leave you ladies to talk. *Ahh! Shane is standing against the wall, I don't think she seen me see her. I hope that crazy conversation didn't bother her. Hmm I'll let her see Carol at work and see what happens. Get her Holy Ghost!*

Lola: Carol? Is that really you?! Oh my God! You all

cleaned up!? How can this be?!

Carol: Yeah, baby girl! It's me! Delivered and in love with Jesus!

Lola: Jesus huh? Mrs. Grace can't stop talking to me about this Jesus! But He's forgotten all about me Carol! He left me in a pile of crap and never came back for me.

Carol: Oh no, baby girl. He didn't put you there. Satan thinks he's somewhat of a puzzle master, but he's missing pieces. He tried to set you up to fail by rejections and heartache. God has big plans for you. He promised He'd never leave us nor forsake us. We can try and walk away from Him, but He'll never leave us…He's our first love!

Lola: Then why am I so jacked up?! I hate my life! I'm tired of living like this Carol!

Carol: Haven't you heard? Satan is the enemy of your soul? He wants you to feel this way.

Lola: Enemy? What did I ever do to him?

Carol: It's not what you've done to him. It's just the fact that he hates humans. We were created in God's image and likeness. He hates us for simply being alive. We remind him of God and his upcoming date with Hell and the lake of fire. But if we don't know these things, he tricks us into thinking we have no value. He lies to us by whispering negative thoughts in our minds. Tormenting lies!

Lola: What kind of lies?

Carol: How nobody wants you and nobody loves you. That's crap. Girl, God made you to be loved. God is love. God loves you! Do you think He would make you unlovely, unlovable, or unloving? He's not capable of doing that! We're too precious to Him. That's why He sent His Son, Jesus, to the Earth as a man…to walk through this life and understand what we go through each day. Then He became the perfect sin sacrifice and died just for you and me!

Lola: So He's dead? What's good about that?! What can a dead man do for anyone?

Carol: Listen Lola, Jesus is not dead anymore! He rose from the dead! He got up out of that grave to snatch the keys of death and hell from the devil and now He's in control! Jesus is alive forever more!

Lola: Wow Carol. I need control…control of my life.

Carol: Girl, to have your life…you must lose it to Him.

Lola: Now what the heck does that mean!?

Carol: It means that you have to give Him you…let go of all the things that you think define you. It's like you hand Him your life, in exchange for all that He actually created you to be. He knows what He wanted us to be from our beginning. Somewhere things got twisted in our lives. Life happened and some of it was real painful. Our innocence got stolen and we lost our way. You know what I mean? We got lost in this big crazy world of filth and sin before we knew it.

Lola: Yeah Carol, I don't know how my life got so

crazy. Wow uhm…I want to do this. So you're saying that I can trade in the way I am for what He made me to be? If I can be free like you – I'm all in. Can you show me how?

Carol: Baby girl, I thought you'd never ask! Come on in the chapel and we'll go to the altar and handle it right now.

Wow, that's the most amazing thing I've ever heard. I want to follow them in the Chapel and fall on my knees too! I can't stop myself, I have to go too. It's time to give all of me to Him! Whether I see my Dad again or not – it doesn't matter. I know I want Jesus for sure.

Shane: Carol…uh…wait for me. I want to do this too.

Carol: Come on Shane, there's plenty of room!

It's time to get things right in my relationship with God - all the way!

Maverick: Yes! Thank You Lord! Bless You Jesus!

Sean: Who's in the Chapel Mav?

Maverick: Shh! Just look inside!

Sean: Oh yes! That's all right! Yes, baby girl…finally!

Maverick: Man this is gonna be a great day! I need to make my rounds, I'll talk to you later Sean.

Sean: Okay.

Chapter 28
Coming Clean

Maverick: Hello Sir. The dining room will be open for dinner in about 15 minutes. We'd love for you to join us.

Sam: Oh, I don't feel much like eating.

Maverick: No? Well, can I at least interest you in a cup of coffee or some soup?

Sam: You have anything else good to drink?

Maverick: Sure, we have a bar downstairs.

Sam: A BAR?! No booze! What is this place? Do you think I'm a drunk or something? I meant soda pop, juice or tea, son! I don't drink. I never did. I thought ya'll helped people…that ain't helping nobody!

Maverick: Uhm, well it's a juice bar. That's about as good a drink you'll get here. Mom has these amazing fruit smoothies to help get you back on your feet. Would you like to try one?

Sam: What? Uhm…yeah. Aw man, you got me good, that's for sure! Hahah! I was thinking, Lord get me out of here! What's your name?

Maverick: Maverick. My parents own this place. What's your name?

Sam: It's Sam. Listen Maverick, I do want to eat, but my body is hurting so bad, that I just can't do any more walking. Can you bring me something to eat?

Maverick: I can only do that if you'll let me sit with you.

Sam: That's fine…you make me laugh.

Maverick: I'll be right back!

Sam: Hey! Don't forget my amazing smoothie! Hahaha!

Maverick: I'll even bring you a straw!

Sam: Hahaha, you do that!

BACK AT HOME

Wow! What an incredible ride! I feel so…so clean inside. I haven't cried this hard since my Daddy walked away. I think I cried out that pain and everything else that ever hurt me. I'm born-again, I'm actually saved! Who would have thought that it would have happened to me at the B&B! Of all the places in the world! A place, at one time, I thought I was too good to drive past, let alone step foot inside. I have been so wrong and so blind to the reality of God's grace. When you're not a part of the work, you don't have a clue of what's going on in this world. God can and will meet you anywhere, all we have to do is ask.

I've got to call my girls! They are too lost! They're hurting and they just need Jesus. That's all they need or should I say He's all they need. Hmm! How will I do this thang! I haven't talked to them as often as I used too. I hope they don't shut me down.

RING! RING!

Shane: Hello?

Leo: Hey girl, where have you been? I've been trying to get a hold of you for a while now!

Shane: Uh…I've been around. Why? What's up?

Leo: Shane, I know things haven't been right with us. Can we sit down and talk?

Shane: I don't think…

Leo: Shane, you can't just turn me off like this. I know you're seeing dude. I've seen ya'll together and I thought I didn't care at first, but…

Shane: But!? The other girl you were messing around with turned out to be crazy…right?!

Leo: No, no, no! That's not what was going on. Who told you I was messing around?!

Shane: It doesn't matter, Leo. You only gave me booty calls. You never really invested any quality time in me. I was your late night bump and grind.

Leo: Can you honestly say that you gave me the chance? You were always out with your girls getting high. You kept me at arm's length. The only thing that brought us together was the sex. Don't you think I liked you?

Shane: If you liked me so much, you would have taken me out more, instead of meeting up with me later. And the truth about it is…I felt dirty when you would leave me in the middle of the night, that's when I knew we had nothing real. What kind of mess was that?!

Leo: Shane…I'm sorry.

Shane: Yeah…right. That's all you can say. You never gave me a real explanation. Really Leo, I don't want to talk about this anymore. I got to go…

Leo: No, Shane. It's best we talk this out.

Shane: Why?

Leo: Because it's important. Shane, you are important to me. Listen, I'm going to be honest with you. I never meant to hurt you. I never meant for you to feel used. The problem didn't lie with you, it was me. When we met, I was going through a really bad divorce.

Wow! Now ain't that some real crap?!

Shane: I was right…you were married!

Leo: No! Like I said, when we met I was going through a long dragged out divorce, and I didn't get close to you until the night it was final.

Shane: Oh really. Why didn't you tell me this? Were you having a private celebration?! Bye, Leo!

Leo: I didn't know how, Shane! I wanted to be with you, but I was scared as hell to go there with you. And I didn't want you to be caught in the confusion of it all.

She was pretty wild at the end. I didn't know what to expect, so I kept things discreet with you. It was a long time ago, Shane.

Shane: Leo, leaving me in the middle of the night? Not taking me out to nice places or just hanging out in the daytime made things worse for me. It tore me up to feel that way. If you were going through a divorce, I guess you still cared for her, since you would leave in the middle of the night. Man, you're a real piece of...piece of...work!

Wow! I guess my heart has been renewed. I can't even cuss him out like I want to! Grr!

Leo: Not true. Shane, I know you're seeing dude. I'm going to ask you straight out...is this really serious?

Shane: Yes it is. This phone call just helped me realize how special I am to him. He's a good man. I can't say that about you.

Leo: I don't want to give you up like that.

Shane: You can't give up someone you never had. You left me hanging way too many times. How can you think that you can walk back into my life like this?

Leo: The thing is...I never willingly walked out. You pushed me away!

Someone was looking out for me and helping me get out of this Leo mess! Grandma? Jesus? Thank you!

Shane: Leo, I got nothing for you. I'm happy with the man I'm with. I just can't risk my heart with you anymore, it hurts too much. Months have gone by, this conversation is way too late.

Leo: It's not too late to me. I just wanted to get things out. It's cool if you want this dude. When it gets old, I'll be right here. And you know the loving is good, right? I'm never going to stop trying, Shane.

That's what's so sad, it was. It really was. I can't lie.

Shane: Sigh…take care, Leo. I appreciate you coming clean with me. The mystery has been solved. I need to go now.

Leo: Well, I guess I owed you that much. Shane, I don't want it to be over, but…I can understand why you're moving on. He better treat you a heck of a lot better than I did. If he doesn't…he'll be a great big fool like me. I know if I ever had another chance with you…I'd do it right. I'm really sorry. Okay beautiful, I'm out.

Yeah…right!

Shane: Good-bye, Leo.

CLICK!

Yes, you are out…out of the picture. Dang you Leo! Going through a divorce!? I was rebound booty all that time? What kind of crap is that!? I am so angry right now! Why? Why am I so upset with him? It doesn't matter, he deserves my anger! I deserve so much better than this! He didn't deserve the time I gave him! Dawg! He didn't have sense enough to

wait! And she's crazy too!? He also jeopardized my life...to hear him tell it! Oh Lord, this hurts me. He used me, no matter what he said...he used me to get over his wife. And in the process he bruised me. Used and bruised...oh, Jesus, heal my heart...heal my heart from this mess. I'm ready to move on. There's nothing left behind me. Aw man, I need to cry for a while. If Maverick calls, I'm not picking up...he can't hear my voice. He knows when I'm upset. I've got to get myself together. I'd get a joint, but that's not the solution anymore. The pain will still be there. I think a good cry will do me right.

Hey, if you care, could you send up a prayer for anyone you know that's hurting like this, please. Sometimes it's about grieving the loss of the relationship, even though we know it wasn't what was best for us. I'll check you out later. Thanks.

Chapter 29
Blast from the Past

KNOCK! KNOCK!

Oh, shoot! I'm not ready just yet! I know this is Maverick! Let me get my robe on and hurry up!

Shane: Who is it?

Maverick: It's me, baby!

Shane: Okay, Maverick, I'm going to open the door, just wait a minute before you come in, I'm not dressed yet.

Maverick: Okay…hurry up, it's cold out here!

Shane: Okay!

Maverick: Man, the hawk is out! It's mighty cold out yonder!

Shane: Oh no. Well, I need to switch it up. I was going to wear something else. Choices, choices! What's a girl to do?

Maverick: Haha Why aren't you ready yet? Up late?

Shane: Kind of. I got a late phone call and I just…

Maverick: A late phone call from whom?

Shane: Well it wasn't you, because you didn't call.

Maverick: Yeah, you know it was pretty busy yesterday. It was a long day and I couldn't get a break in to call you. You were on my mind the whole day. When I got home and settled in, I planned to call you, but I fell asleep. I'm sorry about that. So tell me about this late night phone call.

Shane: Uhm, I know we talked about my past a little, but I never gave you any details. There's a guy I used to see...we never officially said it was over. I mean...it's been over for me, he just needed to hear the words.

Maverick: Mmhm...go on.

Shane: Basically, he told me some things that I didn't know that kept the relationship so jacked up. And I made it clear that it was over nonetheless and I was happy with the man I'm with now. That's you, Maverick.

Maverick: What made him call you now or have ya'll been talking all along? What's this dude's name? Do I know him?

Shane: I haven't spoken to him in over six or seven months, about the time I met you. I guess he's been leaving messages. I just never called him back.

Maverick: So, how should I be taking all of this in? What am I supposed to do or not do? What's his name, Shane?

Shane: His name is...Tom. Maverick, that chapter is closed in my life. I'm not looking back. I have no desire to reopen it either. You're not supposed to worry…okay.

Maverick: Yeah? Prove it! Marry me, Shane!

Shane: Oh Maverick! I…I…

Maverick: What's up? Why can't I get you to commit on this level? Maybe you're still hung up on this Tom guy. That's it isn't it? Was he the one at the hotel?

I knew that was still lingering in there somewhere. Leo's the chokehold. Now he's NOT the one I'm going to talk about right now. Don't judge me.

Shane: Nope. Very wrong answer. It's not that I don't want to commit. I want to be sure I'm giving you what you really need. And that I'm getting what I really need too. So much has happened and…

Maverick: So much has happened and will happen, baby. You have to fit us in the equation some time. I'm not thrilled that this Tom is calling you, Shane. I'm not cool with it at all. Don't throw me a curve ball. I need to know that you love me, Shane. I'm not about playing games! Don't…

Shane: I'm not playing games with you. I just got born-again. I'm not sure what's going on with me now! Things seem so different. I look back at how bad I blew it and… Listen, if we're going anywhere, we need to leave. I'm ready – let's go. I don't want to talk about this anymore…please.

Maverick: Okay, that's fine. Let's talk about something much more important than our love. Let's celebrate your First Love, Jesus Christ. I didn't mean to overlook something so beautiful. I can imagine your world has turned right side up. I'm so proud of you, baby! I'll give you time to sort this other situation out. I'll back off.

Shane: Back off!? Why would you do that? Are you kidding me?! I need you more now than ever. I want to study the Bible with you Maverick! I want to know more about our Savior! That uhm…Tom situation is far behind me.

Maverick: Hmm, we'll see. Okay, the first thing is to get you some tools that will help you out. Do you have a Bible?

Shane: I have the one my Grandma left me.

Maverick: Okay, is it one you can write in?

Shane: Write in the Bible?! Oh no, not my Grandma's Bible! Never!

Maverick: Shane, if you bought a book and you liked certain things in it, don't you write in it or highlight it to make it stand out?

Shane: Well…yeah, I guess. But not my Grandma's Bible, Maverick. Anyway, she highlighted and wrote all over it. I just don't want to mess it up. I love reading her notes. It helps me see through her eyes.

I miss her so much.

Maverick: I'm sure it's special to you. So, we'll get you a new one that you can write in. Now…church. Have you decided what church you want to attend?

Shane: Well, I like where Sean and Carol go. I mean…it has done wonders for them. I'd like to go back there again. I know you and Rico go to my Mom's church sometimes. I'm not going there. No way.

Maverick: Actually Shane, we also visit the church Sean and Carol go to. Next time you want to go, I can take you, if you'd like. In the meantime, Rico and I are starting a church service at the B&B on Saturdays. It's part of our new outreach department.

Shane: Oh…really?

Maverick: Yeah…but I don't want to move you away from where you feel God's leading you to go. The most important thing is to get in His Word and get strong in your faith. It will be a minute before we get this up and running. It will give you time to decide if you want to be by my side as a pastor's…

Shane: Maverick! Are you kidding me? Don't finish that sentence! Hold that thought! I refuse to be overwhelmed again with you. Listen, I'm happy for you and Rico! I believe ya'll will do a wonderful job! Let me do one thing at a time. I'll support you in whatever way I can…just without the pressure! Who says that I'll stay saved?

Maverick: Shane, whom the Son sets free, is free indeed. Stop freaking out and take a deep breath!

Shane: But still…I know me.

Now ain't that some crazy mess to say? Really, Shane? Really, girl? I've got some work to do.

Maverick: Shane…don't believe the lie! You are saved through and through. I see it in your eyes. Just don't worry about me and Rico. Do your thang, girl! Get rooted and see what God is doing in your life. He's about to blow your ever loving mind!

Shane: I will do that Maverick. I'm not worrying anymore about anything. God is in control of my life and I'm willing to go wherever He leads me.

Maverick: Oh! Spoken like a true woman of God! Haha! I love you Shane! I hope you'll attend church with me sometime.

Shane: Yeah, I'd love it! Well, let's get going…

Maverick: Yes ma'am! You know after you left, I helped out with a new client last night.

Shane: Oh yeah? What happened?

Maverick: He's a nice guy. An older gentlemen. He has a good sense of humor. We talked about how he ended up at the B&B. He said his woman left him for another man. She locked him out the house, emptied his bank account, and left him, right after he lost his job.

Shane: That's too bad.

Maverick: Yeah, he was sitting on a park bench when my Pop's found him. It's pretty sad.

Shane: Aww…that's too bad. What's his name?

Maverick: Uh…I think it's Sam.

Shane: Hmm…Sam? Sam what?

Maverick: I don't usually ask last names. Sometimes people don't like to give out too many details. I figured he just gave me any old name.

Shane: Well, what does he look like? Well, let me ask you this. Does he have a mole right under his right eye shaped like a heart?

Maverick: Uhm, how did you know that…you've already seen him, huh? That's some kind of birthmark.

Oh my God…oh my God!

Shane: You're kidding right? Does he really Maverick? Uhm, can you tell me more about this man, please?

Maverick: Shane, what's wrong.

Shane: Just tell me more about this man…okay!

Maverick: Well, he wasn't feeling too good. He said his body ached and didn't want to eat anything. So I sat with him a while. I told him I could bring his food up, if I could sit with him. We joked about him having something good to drink. I told him we had a bar and freaked him out. He cracked up and said he didn't drink. I offered him a juice smoothie, because Mom swears by them. He was fine with that. I went to get his food and the smoothie and brought it to him.

That's too many details. Geez!

Shane: How did he look? Is he tall or short? Is he

thin? Can you describe him to me?

Maverick: I can take you on my rounds to meet him, if you'd like Shane.

Shane: Uhm…I'm just wondering. I'm not that curious. I don't want to bother you with taking me on your rounds.

Maybe I'm imagining this. I'm sure there are plenty of men with heart shaped markings on their face. It could be one of those tattoos. I guess I wasn't clear when I asked. I don't want to make a big deal about this.

Maverick: You know that wouldn't be a problem, baby. I already mentioned you. I'm sure he'd like to meet you. I need to make sure we order some more grape pop. We're getting low. Sean loves it. He drinks a couple every time he volunteers.

Shane: Grape pop? Why would you mention that?

Maverick: Oh, because Sam asked if we had any. I told him we needed to order some more. I guess he likes grape pop too.

I'm speechless. This is all a crazy coincidence! There's no way!

Chapter 30
Back Home and Alone

Oh no, no, no. This is crazy…why do I have this crazy sinking feeling in the pit of my stomach that Sam is… I don't want to go there! I'm not ready for this! Not this way! Not like this! Not at the B&B!

Maverick: Shane is something wrong? You look frightened.

Shane: Has Sean seen him? How long has he been there?

Maverick: He came the night before last. Sean helped in the kitchen and fixed a plate to take to him later that evening. I guess Sam ate in his room again. Sean didn't say anything to me…anyway.

Shane: Maverick! I think I might know this Sam! If Sean is around him, make sure you're there.

Maverick: Are you sure? Sean? Why?

Shane: Did you mention my name?

Maverick: Yeah, just your first name. We were talking about relationships. When I started talking about you…hold up! When I started talking about you, he got real quiet and had this sad expression on his face. He told me he was getting tired and wanted to lie back down. I didn't think anything of it, except…

Shane: Except what?

Maverick: Except he put his face in his hands when I started toward the door. When I turned to say good-bye, he didn't look up, he just mumbled good-bye. I left.

Shane: Maverick! Sam might be my Dad! What's wrong with him? How did he end up here? How long is he going to stay?

Maverick: Let's go by and see. Let's play it down, and I'll introduce you. Then you'll know for sure.

Shane: Uhm, uh, no. Nope, I don't want to, I'm scared, baby!

Maverick: I'll be with you Shane. What could scare you?

Oh God, is this for real? I remember what I prayed for! Oh, I'm so scared! Lord, be with me, be real close to me today!

Shane: Okay...let's see if it's him. I could be wrong. I got a little crazy there for a minute. I'm sorry about that!

Maverick: I understand completely, Shane. Don't worry about it. If it is him, you're not going to beat him up or anything, are you?

Shane: No, God took that anger away from me. As a matter of fact, I prayed that I'd see him, to work through the past hurt so I could move on and make a decision about us.

Maverick: You're a praying wonder aren't you!?

200

Shane: Yeah! Just like you, my man of God!

Maverick: We just stepped into another level in our relationship…can you feel it?

Shane: Yeah, I feel it.

I just don't think I'm feeling seeing my Daddy like this though.

Mrs. Grace: Good I'm glad ya'll are here! We can't seem to find Sam anywhere. The last time I looked in on him, Sean was sitting in with him. He seemed upset, but he said he was alright.

Maverick: Uh oh.

Shane: Oh God! How long ago was this? Have you seen Sean?

Mrs. Grace: Sean is in the kitchen prepping for breakfast. He still seemed a bit off. Shane, maybe you can find out what's going on with your brother.

Shane: Yes Ma'am, I'll check in with him.

Mrs. Grace: Maverick, help me find Sam. His health is really bad, he needs medical attention.

Maverick: What's wrong with him?

Mrs. Grace: Oh shoot! I know where he is. I was so busy talking with my girls that I waved your Daddy on. Sam was with him. I think he took him to the clinic. Yeah, I'm pretty sure that's where they were on their way too. Oh well, false alarm. But I still want to know what's going on with Sean and Sam.

Maverick: Mom...there's a good chance that Sam is Sean and Shane's Dad.

Mrs. Grace: What!? Are you kidding me?

Maverick: No kidding. And from what it sounds like, Sean found him.

Mrs. Grace: Oh I hate to pry, but this is something I think we need to keep in prayer. I see God's hand in this thing. From how we found Sam, to his very own children serving in a place he may have never thought they would find him. Yeah, God is in this thing!

Maverick: Yes He is. Wow, this is really blowing my mind. I'll go check on Shane to see if everything is okay. I might need to step in so Sean can talk to her.

Mrs. Grace: Yeah, that's a good idea. Keep me informed. I'll stay in prayer today.

Maverick: Okay.

MEANWHILE IN THE KITCHEN

Shane: Good morning Sean.

Sean: Shane! My girl! Wow, my little sister is born-again! I can't get over it! I bet you slept good...real good. I know I did after all that crying!

Shane: Yeah! I'm born-again. Sean, it feels so good!

Sean: Yeah, it's something!

Shane: So...you spoke with Sam?

Sean: Huh?! Yeah, I spoke with...Daddy.

Shane: Talk to me...how are you feeling? What's going on with him?

Maverick: Hey Sean, go on I'll finish setting up for you. My Dad took Sam to the clinic Shane.

Sean: Okay, I cut up the onions. I just need about 20 potatoes peeled. I'm about to hurt the fried potatoes and onions. Throw down on some scrambled eggs and sausage and I got the pots of coffee brewing!

Maverick: Haha! Sean you are the man! It's good to see you here smiling and helping out. Thanks man!

Sean: No, thank you, Maverick. Thank you! Come on Shane, let's talk. You want some coffee?

Shane: No, I'm good. Sean, now I know without a doubt that you are truly saved, especially with Daddy around. You didn't beat him up did you? Why did he go to the clinic? How did he end up here?

Sean: No! I just realized that God has to get a hold of him. There is nothing that I could say or do that's going to make him feel worse than he already feels. It was a shock when I saw him. It shook me up! Shane...he asked me to forgive him. I did. He asked about you. I told you you got saved yesterday. He started crying and I started crying. Mrs. Grace walked in on us. We tried to play it off. We were getting pretty ugly. You know that kind of cry that gets your face all wrinkled, and your nose starts getting red and stretching wide enough for two trucks to drive through?! It was a bad scene, Shane! Snot running and stuff...

Shane: Wow really?! You are straight crazy Sean! That sounds so ugly! T.M.I! Hahaha!

Sean: Yeah, it was.

Shane: Wow, you forgave him. How did he end up on the street!?

Sean: The lady he left with, Ms. Rosie, met some other guy at another church and ran off with him.

Shane: Her poisonous thorn has yet pricked another! You can't do what he did to us and think it won't come back to haunt you. You know?!

Sean: Yeah I guess so. He really tore our family up. Or should I say, the devil used him to hurt us. But through all of that pain, guess where we stand today?!

Shane: Where?

Sean: In the arms of a loving God, Shane. We can trust that He will never leave us or forsake us. We can't even be plucked out of His hand, Shane! We'll be alright. And I have a feeling, Daddy will too.

Shane: This is a lot to take in. I don't know if I can see him just yet. I think I need some time.

Sean: Yeah, I just happened to see him in the hallway on my way in. My mouth hit the floor. It was all on my face. I guess I always dreamed of what I would say to him if I ever seen him. But I was a drunk then. So my plan had changed drastically! I didn't want to punch him and cuss him out anymore. I felt sorry for him. He looks so broke down and sickly. I could have acted like I was gonna punch him, but he might have had a heart attack and crumbled in a pile.

Shane: Wow, yeah I don't think I can handle this right now. I'm going to get Maverick to take me out of here. I'm not ready to deal with this yet.

Sean: Do you want me to tell him anything for you?

Shane: No….no…nothing, right now.

Sean: Okay. Hey Maverick!

Maverick: Yeah?

Sean: Hey man, take my little sister away from here for me. She needs some air.

Maverick: Shane, you ready to go? I thought you wanted to stay.

Shane: Yeah, please. I don't want to stay.

Maverick: Okay, let's go.

Sean: I'll check on you later little sis! Everything will be all right! I promise you!

Looks like our lives are about to change in a major way.

Chapter 31
Why Do We Have To Love

I can't figure out for the life of me what to say to my Dad. I feel like that little girl he walked out on. How do I look him in the eye and say...what?! What would I even have to say to him? I'm confused! I want to hate him and yet I want to run into his arms and be his little girl again. This is so hard. What would you do? After being abandoned this long and when he does show up he's all sick and stuff. Part of me says, "That's what you get for hurting us!" and another part of me just feels so sorry for him.

Maverick: Shane, baby, are you okay? Do you want to take some time and talk?

Shane: I don't even know what to think, Maverick. My Dad is a broken man. I want to smack him for the pain he put us through when he left us. Then at the same time I want to cry and run into his arms. Dang! Why did he come back this way? Why couldn't he come back into our lives because he wanted to!? Why did it have to be this way?

Maverick: I don't know, baby. All I know is that God is working some things out in your family and your hearts. Does that make sense?

Shane: I...I guess so. I've waited for this day for so long. And now I'm scared to face the day...to face him.

Maverick: Scared to face your love for him?

Shane: Yeah…yeah…love. When he walked out, I figured all of what I had learned about love was a lie. I couldn't make heads or tails of it after a while. Maverick, I think I want to smoke a joint…I think.

Maverick: Well Shane, it's your choice. I just have one question for you.

Shane: What's that?

Maverick: After you finish, will this situation be resolved? Will it make any difference with what's going on?

Shane: Resolved? No I guess not. Maverick, I just want to be somewhere…anywhere else, just to get away from these feelings.

Maverick: Don't throw all of what you've accomplished away over this. I'll hold you as long as you need me too. You can cry on my shoulder until I have to grab a towel. Shane, baby, I'm here for you. I'm here to help you through this…to pray you through this. I love you.

Sounds good my love, but I want to be numb right now. I don't want to feel anything. I know. I know.

Shane: Love. What is love, Maverick? Why do we have to love?

Maverick: Because that's what Jesus did. He loved us. Shane, think about it. He loved us enough to lay his life down, raise Himself up and conquer death and hell. Can you imagine who He was thinking about?

Shane: I...I don't really know.

Maverick: Shane, He was thinking about you and I...even Sam. The human race! His love for us said, "Loving is okay"! That's why He came. He wanted to make sure that we would someday experience real love. Shane...He is real love! Isn't that what you felt when you got born-again?!

Shane: Yes, it is. It was very real in that moment. And even now as you're talking about it, I feel that love warming me up. Keep talking Maverick, this is really helping me.

Maverick: Jesus' love can put any hang-up to shame any day of the week. Be it any kind of addiction or malfunction, because it brings life.

Shane: Maverick, I can honestly say that His love out classes all of these things. It's kind of funny to hear you say something like that when you haven't done these things.

Maverick: There are things I can't tell you now. But there will be a day when I will share more private details about my life, if you ever decide to marry me.

Shane: That's smooth, baby! You think you're slick! I'll tell you what, if you want to marry me, you better be preparing your biography...because I ain't marrying you first. You need to tell me those little details long before I give you any answer.

Maverick: Haha! No I didn't put that in there to be slick. I'm just saying being a virgin doesn't make me foreign to sexual desires...I just haven't acted on them.

Or any other desires…like drugs, alcohol and all that's out there.

Shane: Okay, okay! I get it. Okay, Jesus' love is the ultimate love. And He wants us to love one another. A few days ago, that would have been hard to accept. But now, feeling His love makes things different. I need a little time to think of the words to say to my Dad. I want to talk to him. He went to the clinic…what for?

Maverick: I don't know, but I'll call my Dad to find out once we get to your place.

Shane: Okay. Another obstacle to deal with is my Mom. I think I better talk to him before I even mention it to her. She'll just bring up the painful past and make it harder to handle. I can't say I'd blame her if she did.

Maverick: Yeah.

Shane: I don't know what it's like to be abandoned after 12 years of marriage, being left to raise two children alone. When I start thinking about what we went through, I want to vindicate my Mom, Maverick! I want to fight for her honor!

Maverick: I sure can understand that, Shane.

Shane: Pray for me Maverick! I need you to pray for me right here and now!

Maverick: Okay Shane…let's pray.

It's so incredible to have a man who is willing to stand beside me through all kinds of crap. I've lived a crappy life. I haven't made the best decisions in so

many situations in my life. Yet God sent a man of God into my life. He's not Jesus - no way, but he's a good man. Maverick is a man with purpose and direction. What do you think? Things have changed a whole lot since you stepped into my world. I still think it's too good to be true, but then it would be nice to have restoration.

Restoration...now that sounds do-able. I guess I'll hold off on that joint. Prayer is the better choice.

Chapter 32

Virtuous Woman Class

Well, Carol talked me into coming to a woman's Bible study and I'm a little shaky. There's so much going on and I didn't think I had the time for this, but Carol felt I did. And of course Sean was right behind her egging her on. So, here I am. Let's see what this is all about, shall we.

Sister Grace: Ladies, welcome to our Virtuous Woman class. We are so happy to see so many ladies in attendance this evening. If you haven't had the opportunity to sign in, please do so now. Once you do, please take a paper beside the sign-in sheet and a pencil.

Shane: Carol I'm a little nervous...

Carol: Baby girl, all is well. I really wanted you to come to this meeting. It has helped me out so much! My whole life has been opposite of the way God has really wanted me to live. The topic tonight is going to be good!

Shane: What's it on?

Carol: It's called "What You Don't Know Can Contaminate Your Soul".

Shane: Oh my Jesus, stay close!

Carol: Amen!

Sister Grace: Great! Is everyone settled now? Good,

good, now let's begin with prayer. *"Father God, we thank You for bringing us together for Your Word. Lord, anoint each of Your daughters with Your eyes that they see themselves as You see them. Anoint our ears, so we can hear You clearly. Bless each of us with Your Presence this evening. Your Word says when two or three are gathered together, there You are in the midst of us and we do welcome You this evening. May Your word bring strength to a weary soul and enlighten us, in Jesus' Name...amen."*

Amen! Wow, I'm so excited! Sit in with me and let's learn something together.

Sister Grace: For those of you who are new to our class, my name is Sister Grace. Thank you all for coming. Ladies, as you may have heard, our class today is called "What You Don't Know Can Contaminate Your Soul". What we're going to address this evening is sex. I will open and then turn the class over to Sister Mercy to bring the teaching to a close.

Isn't it interesting how God can address those certain issues in my life when I have the questions just waiting to be answered!

Sister Grace: We'll first address Fornication. Fornication is any sexual activity outside of marriage. If it's outside of the realm of marriage, it is considered sin. In God's Word, marriage is defined as a union between a man and a woman. This is found in Genesis Chapter 1. We were made in the image and likeness of God. We are made of three parts: Body, Soul, and Spirit.

If you've brought your Bibles, please feel free to follow

along with me. I'll be reading from Genesis Chapter one, verses 27 and 28. *"So God created man in His own image, in the image of God created He him; male and female created He them. And God blessed them, and God said unto them, be fruitful, and multiply, and replenish the earth, and subdue it: and have dominion over the fish of the sea, and over the fowl of the air, and over every living thing that moves upon the earth".* Now let's go down to verse 31 *"And God saw everything that He had made, and, behold, it was very good. And the evening and the morning were the sixth day."*

Let's note a couple things here. God started with a man and a woman. The first thing he did was bless them and commanded them to be fruitful, multiply, and replenish the earth and subdue it. This is the first glimpse of a direction of the union between a man and a woman with God's blessing. It was actually the first wedding in the glory of God. And through that blessed union, we get to make babies! God is so awesome He made being fruitful with great benefits. Can I get an amen, wives?! Ahh, finally a few giggles and smiles!

Sister Grace: So let's think about the world today. Right now the biggest temptation is sexual sin. All sorts of things are going on. Is it possible to believe in a lie? Yes it is AND it's extremely dangerous. When Adam and Eve ate from the Tree of the Knowledge of Good and Evil, they turned everything upside down, and the human race has been on a rapid decline ever since. Even with the great flood in Noah's day, it didn't wash the sin away. That's why Jesus had to step in. Glory to God!

In the New Testament it talks about having a reprobate

mind. Let's turn to Romans Chapter One. Reprobate means being morally corrupt. Living in this condition when you die, means hell is your destination. There are many people walking this Earth indulging in reprobation and don't even realize it. Unaware that they are deeply loved and God wants to heal their hearts and give them a higher purpose than what they're living. And they are doing crazy things by demonic influence. They may rationalize these things on a whole different level, but never understanding why they do them.

The greatest deception Satan uses is "everyone is doing it" and thinking if we "accept" sin because it's something the world is doing somehow should make us believe it's right or okay with God. If that were the case, Jesus died in vain. Right? Well, He didn't. A life that's not surrendered to God is an unsettled one. Filled with chaos, anxiety, and rage. Seeking any kind of love and comfort in the world and never finding it is heartbreaking. God knew this and had an escape plan to perfect love, healing, and peace. The One to open that escape hatch was His Son, Jesus Christ.

Man, that's pretty wild! A reprobate mind? Thank You Jesus for calling my name!

Sister Grace: So when Jesus died on the cross and rose from the dead, He opened the door for reconciliation with our Heavenly Father. That means that He reconnected our relationship with God, which gives us the opportunity to make things right with Him. Isn't that great news? Yes indeed! Okay ladies, at this time, I'm going to let Sister Mercy take over from here. Sister Mercy.

Sister Mercy: Thanks Sister Grace! I'd like to interject a little. When we think about the original purpose of man, to be fruitful and replenish the earth, you have to know that Satan stepped in to destroy Gods plan. Doesn't that make sense? Yet, we only look at the moment of pleasure, not the future beyond our death, in our decision making. But you know, Satan looks at the long term consequence. After all...look where we are today...a society out of control. There are many people who don't want to hear the name of Jesus and don't want anyone to tell them what's wrong and what's right. They think they're rejecting us, but they're rejecting the mercy of God. It's because of His love for us that He gave us laws to preserve the human race, not to destroy us. And the biggest obstacles in sharing the Gospel of Jesus Christ is convincing the world that Jesus loves us and we have an enemy of our souls. Earth is not the final destination!

Proverbs 27:26 says "Faithful are the wounds of a friend, but the kisses of an enemy are deceitful". In other words, we can share God's truth and it may be hurtful to receive, but if it's done with love, it can actually cause healing. I repeat, it's supposed to be done with love. But there are those who "say" they love you and are all in your face and lure you into compromise. Next thing you know you're in a big mess trying to figure out what happened. The enemy will whisper that unrepented sin is "okay" knowing it will give you an evil end. So it's important to be careful and prayerful. Ask God to show you who's a faithful friend and who's in your face trying to draw you away from Him. Okay?

We're so glad you all came today! We pray that this lesson will help you in your daily decision making. We pray you think twice before you let your desires over take you. Amen? Our teaching tonight is based on First Corinthians Chapter 6:18-20. So make sure you take some time to read it and marinate on it. Sex is a beautiful gift and is so blessed when we're in God's will. When it's done within His marriage covenant, all shame and guilt have no place. It's really amazing. Some of us have past experiences and know the difference.

The title of our next week's teaching is "Know Your Audience". Did you realize God is watching over you all the time? He doesn't sleep! Oh wow, we have a few ladies in shock. Haha, its okay! He gives us a chance to get things right with Him. He loves us. You'll have to come to our next class to learn more. Being a born-again believer in Jesus Christ is a lifestyle, it's not a title, ladies.
God can give you the strength to focus your desires in the right place if you ask Him to. He gives us wisdom to stay out of situations that will snare us. We must be ever-present in our daily lives. Amen?! Amen!

Sister Grace: Thank you Sister Mercy. Ladies, let's close in prayer and dismiss. If you have any questions come see us after class. God bless you all.

Man, I've been blind for a long time! This is the first time I've understood the purpose for sex, the reasons we need to keep it in check and why we really need to know the Word of God. My girls would trip knowing what we've been doing wrong all this time! I'm going to study tonight and talk to Maverick. Wow, this is what he's learned and has stuck to all this time. Then I'm going to ease into this

conversation with my girls...wrong thinking can have you bust hell wide open! Then you'll be sitting in hell wondering why you're there! Ain't going to happen on my watch! I got to share this info! Hey...you should do the same! Me and Carol are going to hang around for a minute. I've got some questions to ask these amazing teachers, so I'll see you in the next chapter! Don't worry, I'll catch you up.

Chapter 33
Making Sense of Chaos

Well I'm on the phone with my Boo and I've been waiting on you! What took you so long? Yes I've got jokes because I'm happy! I'm gonna try to stay as upbeat as I can! I'm telling Maverick all about the Bible study and what I learned! I just read him the scripture, 1st Corinthians Chapter 6:18-20 and I quote! *"Flee fornication. Every sin that a man doeth is without the body; but he that committeth fornication sinneth against his own body. What? Knoweth ye not that your body is the temple of the Holy Ghost which is in you, which ye have of God, and ye are not your own? For ye are bought with a price: therefore glorify God in your body, and in your spirit, which are God's".* **I read it and he broke it down even more! I love him. My cheeks hurt from smiling so much! Hah!**

Maverick: Wow Shane, this is really some good information! It feels good to know that you have a better understanding of where I'm coming from. It's not easy at all, but it's important!

Shane: Yeah! I'm just so shocked of what I've gone through. It really makes sense now. God gave us His laws to protect us physically, emotionally and spiritually...wow. It feels so good being saved and getting fed by His word. I see what you mean when you said it's a lifestyle. It really is! It's not so hard when you understand the why, you know what I mean?

Maverick: Yeah, it's cool. Uh, Shane...listen, your Dad asked about you today.

Shane: Huh? Yeah, well…uhm, how's he doing?

Maverick: He's in the hospital in critical condition.

Shane: Wait…what?! Why?

Maverick: He's in pretty bad shape. We just found out that he lived out of his car until the police towed it. He'd just been walking around wandering the streets for weeks. When my Dad met him, his feet were swollen and he could barely walk, that's why…

Shane: That's why you were taking his food to him?

Maverick: Yeah…so they are saying that infection has gotten into his blood stream or something like that. He just needs a lot of attention right now.

Shane: Oh Lord…Maverick! We need to get him the best doctors we can! I need to see if I can get him on my insurance…and I need to make some phone calls to…

Maverick: Baby! Baby girl….slow down! He's in the best of hands. I made some calls to a few doctor friends of mine, to get him the best care. They are flying in tonight, they may already be here to take a look at him, and if they need to have him flown out…all expenses are taken care of. I think it's a good idea to add him to your insurance. But I'll take care of all the deductibles for you.

This makes me cry. This man is the real deal. I'm not ready to say good-bye to my Dad. I haven't even said hello again.

Shane: Maverick…how can I thank you? How can my brother and I thank you and your parents for all that you've done for our family? It's more than I could have ever prayed for.

Maverick: It's just how things worked out…all God needed to hear was your moan. He knows your heart.

Shane: Maverick?

Maverick: Yeah, baby?

Shane: I want to see him now.

Maverick: Sounds good, do you want to see him tonight or do you want to wait to see him in the morning…it's pretty late.

Shane: Will he be okay till morning?

Maverick: Let me make a phone call and I'll call you back to let you know.

Shane: He's really in bad shape, huh?

Maverick: Yeah, but they are doing everything they can. Last time I checked, they said they were giving him medication to get the infection under control.

Shane: Okay…call me right back!

Maverick: Okay…bye.

Shane: Bye.

Lord, you know I need to get things straight with my Dad! Please give him more years. We need time, Lord! Time to heal and find a new place of love! Father God, please listen to me. I love my Daddy and I've missed him all these years! I believe you brought him back to us, so please let me have that time. Lord, I want him to be able to walk me down the aisle to the arms of my groom, Maverick. Please, Father God, let him see my babies and...

RING! RING!

Shane: Maverick?!

Maverick: Yeah...well, he's doing pretty good. They said he's resting comfortably. The doctors I told you about are here and have taken a look at him. They said they will be able to help him. They may need to fly him out toward the end of his treatment...but we'll deal with that when we get there. So we can wait to see him in the morning. He's going to have a bunch of tests, so I'm sure you being there will help his frame of mind.

Shane: Okay...okay! What time do we need to get there?

Maverick: Tests start at 8:30 a.m. So we need to be there about 7.

Shane: Cool! Thank you, baby! I love you Maverick!

Maverick: Shane, I love you too...I'll always love you! Get some study time in if you can focus. Most important, make sure you get some sleep. Okay? God has it all under control.

Shane: Yeah…I believe that. (Yawn!) Oh excuse me…I'll talk to you in the morning. I'll be ready. Good night.

Maverick: Sounds good…I'll see you then. Good night sweetheart.

Well, this has been a rollercoaster ride, hasn't it? So, I'll tell you what I'm starting to understand. I have found out that although I've made some mistakes in my life, God still loves me. I'm not a virgin because I made some crazy lusty choices that ended in heartache and all the guilt and shame I've gone through over these years. The pain of losing my Daddy to another woman and living without a heart of forgiveness drove me to try to numb the pain with over partying and promiscuity. Wow, it's been a while since I've had a joint! Wanted too, but worked through it and didn't! I'm so proud of me!

Fancy that! Hahaha! That's cracking me up! All this time I thought I needed it to get by, but I'm finding out that as long as I'm working on me and focusing on Jesus…His love pushes away all the desires for anything else. Don't get me wrong…I loved smoking weed, because it took me away from my thoughts for a while. Only buzz kill with that is my problems were still there when I came down and I was fuzzy all the time. But it's time to start dealing with the pain and putting it in its proper place…FAR BEHIND ME! I want a better life…the kind of life I've always dreamed of. What seemed like a faraway dream is now something within my grasp.

A good man, a second chance with my Daddy, my brother happy, healthy, whole and in love! I think the biggest deal of all is actually being born-again and finally feeling saved. I have the real deal this time! That's the best feeling of all. Anything else I can handle, now that I've got Jesus in my heart! Next stop...Mom.

Reader, yeah you! I'm praying for you. I pray that you know Jesus and allow Him to heal your life. Well, I tell you what...I hope my journey has helped you see your life a little more clearly. Maybe it makes some sense of the chaos.

Don't go away though, it's sure not over yet. But I just wanted to share my heart with you before I fall asleep. I'll see you in the next chapter. Ciao for now!

Chapter 34

A Set Back Is Just a Set Up

RING! RING!

Shane: Whoa…what time is it? Uh, hello?

Mom: SHANE?! WHY DIDN'T YOU TELL ME YOUR DAD IS IN TOWN?! What the hell is wrong with ya'll?!

Shane: Uh, Mom, slow down!

Mom: Slow down!? Are you kidding me!? Baby, I know we don't talk often, but this somehow seemed to slip your mind the last time we did! What are all the secrets about?!

Shane: Mom, how do you know Daddy's in town?!

Mom: ARE YOU SAYING YOU DIDN'T KNOW? BECAUSE IF YOU ARE, I KNOW YOU'RE LYING TO ME! DON'T DO IT!

Shane: Mom, please calm down. It's just a question. Who told you about this?

Mom: A couple ladies at church are nurses…are you kidding me?! They told me your brother and Carol stopped in to see him too. And YOUR brother won't return any of my phone calls! I'm totally pissed at you two!

Shane: Uhm…Mom, I know this is very unexpected, but why are you so upset?

Mom: Oh Shane! Why wouldn't I be?! There was a time when he was my world. Don't you understand anything?! This man walked out on me and I had to...

Shane: But Mom, that happened a long time ago and uhm...you've remarried since then. I didn't think it mattered. I mean, I wasn't trying to see him, but now that he's pretty sick...

Mom: How dare you talk back to me! Whatever! How could you both betray me? The least you could have done is give me a heads up! I had to hear from someone OUTSIDE of my kids! This is a HUGE deal to me!

Shane: Mom, I knew you would want to know, but at the right time. Aren't nurses supposed to keep this stuff private? I didn't mean to upset you. **I sure didn't think you would respond this way, though.**

Mom: Oh Shane! I'm mad because ya'll didn't tell me! I got to go! Tell me this one thing! What's wrong with him? Probably ain't nothing really wrong with him anyway! He's nothing but drama!

Shane: Mom, I'm going to see him this morning.

Mom: What!? Why?!

Shane: He's having some extensive testing done. He's been in really bad shape. He has a lot of infection in his feet and it's moved into his bloodstream. That's all I know.

Mom: Serves him right! He used those old stanky rusty feet to walk out on us! On all four of us! Don't you ever forget that! Do you hear me Shane? You and your brother should never forget what he did to us!

Shane: How can I forget? I was there Mom. But, in order for me to begin living my life, I have to forgive him and you do to!

Mom: That'll be the day! Anyway, I moved on with my life. He doesn't deserve my forgiveness!

Shane: Mom, think about what Jesus did for us...

Mom: Jesus?! Don't you get all holy with me, Shane! I don't want to hear it! Bye!

CLICK!

Wow! I wasn't expecting that response! Lord, help my Mom to get through this time. Help us all. Also, help her to forgive my Dad so that she can live in peace, in Jesus' Name, Amen. Four? Hmm, not sure I heard her right.

RING! RING!

Oh brother, who could this be! What time is it?! Oh shoot, I better get ready! This must be Maverick.

Shane: Hello?

Maverick: Are you ready?

Shane: I will be by the time you get here.

Maverick: Hmm. You sound kind of flustered...have

you changed your mind, baby?

Shane: No, I still want to see him. My Mom just called and she just flipped out on me! Someone told her my Dad was in the hospital. Maverick...she is so upset!

Maverick: Wow, baby, I'm sorry to hear it. I'm on my way. We'll be late if we don't stay on schedule.

Shane: Okay, I'll see you in a few. Bye.

Maverick: I love you baby, see you later.

CLICK!

Do me a favor, go on over to the hospital and wait for me there. Listen in on my Dad's room. I'll catch up with you in a while. Geez I'm so confused. It's not going to be easy to juggle both of my parents to find a happy medium. Now would be a good time to smoke a joint, a drink or something. I'm trippin'...should I really do this? I really don't have the time, dang it! I'll cover it up real good so Maverick can't tell. Oh Lord, forgive me...just this once. Uh! I better hurry up! What? Does this bother you? Sorry! I'm not perfect and neither are you. I'll see you in a few! Aww man! I don't have anything. Oh, I have wine! Just as well. You still here reading? Go on, I'll catch up with you in a few.

AT THE HOSPITAL

Doc Z: Okay Sam I'm going to get you started with your medications to get you nice and mellow for the tests this morning. How did you sleep?

Sam: Sleep? With all these nurses coming in every 15 minutes to see how I was doing…I couldn't close my eyes good!

Doc Z: Did they disturb you? They're only supposed to check your vitals by monitor…let me know who the nurse is and I'll take care of that for you.

Sam: You better not Doc, unless you're getting her phone number for me! Haha! You know you got some sugar dumplings in here! Haha!

Doc Z: Did they drug you already?! Haha!

Sam: Yeah Doc! With the love drug!

Doc Z: Well, let's get one of my gorgeous nurses to set up your medicine right now and I'll be back in after she's done.

Sam: Yeah, okay Doc. I…I was kind of hoping my kids would stop in before I go in.

Doc Z: Well, I hear you have a visitor on the way.

Sam: Really! Who is it?

Doc Z: You'll see…right now I need you to relax.

Chapter 35
On The Ride In

I think Maverick is the bomb...but he knows I'm a little buzzed right now. Now I wish I didn't do it, but I felt like I really needed it at the time. Dang...how can I be so shaky after all I've been going through lately? I've been saved and working on my life...now I take a nose dive off the wagon and fell under a wheel. He must really think I'm a basket case. I need to throw all these crutches away! I'll do it soon as I get home so I don't have anything to fall back on. I should have done it a long time ago. Goofy!

Maverick: So Shane, have you thought about what you're going to say?

Shane: About what?

Maverick: Uhm…to your Dad.

Shane: Oh, I guess I'll figure it out when I see him. It wouldn't be cool to cuss him out just before he goes in to be tested…wouldn't that be a crazy trip! Hah!

Maverick: Yeah…it would make it rough.

Shane: Yup. I just have to see him. I can tell you this is really hard for me, especially after my Mom's crazy phone call!

Maverick: Do you see where she's coming from?

Shane: Yeah, I can dig…it's just that it really upset

me, Maverick! It was crazy! She's usually in pretty good control of her anger, but she really lost it and she hung up on me and stuff. She told me she didn't need me to be acting all holy because I told her about the forgiveness of Jesus Christ and how we should forgive… Mav, she shut me down.

Maverick: Wow, baby, that's cool.

Shane: What's cool?

Maverick: The Gospel of Jesus Christ under high pressure.

Shane: Whatever…now I'm sitting here buzzed feeling stupid. I drank some wine before you came, to calm my nerves. I over did it, sorry.

Maverick: Now that's a step in the right direction.

Shane: What?! Did you hear what I just said to you? I drank wine, Maverick! Buzzed! And what's so jacked about it is I don't want to be. It's crazy how you can do something and can't change the effect of it, so you got to ride it out. I'll have to wait to come down. I want this visit to be short…I want to be clear in my head when I really talk to him…okay.

Maverick: Yeah, baby. I love you Shane and I'm proud of you.

Shane: I don't know how, do I really deserve you to be proud of me right now? You're a fake, Mav! Trying to fake me out.

Maverick: Shane, what kind of question is that? It's

not that you have to deserve my love…it's just that we're a perfect fit. I knew that from the moment I laid eyes on you.

That is just nonsense to me! What a buzz kill! Geez!

Shane: Yeah, okay Maverick. I'm not in any condition to deal with that comment right now.

Maverick: Deal with it? Girl, I'll wait till you come down. We really need to talk about love.

Shane: Yup…love. I'm confused about love. It seems to me that it's more than just a feeling otherwise more people would still be together today.

Maverick: It's a matter of choice, Shane. Okay, we're here. Are you ready? Maybe walking might help you.

Shane: Oh…like I said, I want to have a short visit right now.

Maverick: I'll make sure.

Shane: Thanks.

Maverick: Going up!

Shane: Oh gosh…this feels crazy.

My stupid decision to drink on an empty stomach was about the stupidest thing I've done in a long time. Geez!

Maverick: I've got you…get it together before the doctors stop you.

Shane: Okay…I'm cool, I'm cool…really. I'm sobering up real good knowing I'm going to see my Daddy for the first time since he left.

Maverick: Excuse me, where is Sam Vanity's room.

Nurse: Oh, he's down three doors to the right. He's had medicine to calm him down, so he might be a little woozy, but he's alert.

Good, we'll both be a little woozy. Hah.

Maverick: Well, that makes two of you…

Shane: Whatever Maverick. **I feel even more stupid now. Sigh.**

KNOCK! KNOCK!

Sam: Come in.

Maverick: Hi Mr. Sam I am! How are you sir? I brought someone to see you.

Sam: Hi Mav…who'd you bring? Oh Lord! My baby girl. My Shane! It's really you.

Shane: Hi Daddy.

I don't want to get too close to him right now. I don't even want to touch him. Because if this is a dream and I wake up, I'll be even more devastated.

Sam: Before I say another word I got to tell you I'm so very sorry, Shane. There is no excuse for what I did! I was a big idiot! I was a fool, Shane, a dang fool.

232

Shane: Yeah, I agree, but right now we can wait to discuss this.

Maverick: Shane…

Shane: I mean…you need to be calm for the testing. I accept your apology…let's just wait to talk.

Sam: Okay, baby girl. I can wait. Why did you come?

Shane: Because I'm concerned about how you're doing. After all, you are my father.

And I wanted to see you with my own eyes. He looks worn out. I hate the devil.

Maverick: Uh, okay…well Sam. Shane's under a lot of pressure. This is a lot to take in.

Sam: Oh Shane…

Okay, visiting him before he goes in for tests wasn't a good idea. He's crying, now. This is not good.

Doc Z: Okay Sam…oh hello.

Maverick: Hi Z, this is my lady Shane…Sam's daughter.

Doc Z: Hello, nice to meet you. I've heard good things about you.

Shane: Hi. I guess we better leave so my father can get those tests done. I'll come back by later today. You relax and pass those tests and we'll see you later. Okay?

Sam: Okay…thank you for coming by. You too Maverick…thanks man.

Maverick: Yes sir.

Sam: Thank you…she's beautiful.

Maverick: Yes she is! We'll see you later.

Doc Z: Okay, it's time to get started

Okay…I need a good cry. He looked so sick…Oh God…he looked so bad. I just couldn't bring myself to touch him or anything. I didn't realize how deep these hurt feelings are. And he looked so broken. What would I do if he died? Knowing he left us, but thinking he might still be alive was one thing. I kind of had hope that maybe someday we'd work things out. Seeing him in the flesh has brought back all kinds of feelings. I didn't think I was this mad. Knowing that he's been wandering the streets here in town sick really bothers me too. He was that shame to reach out to any of us. Or was he scared? Whatever it was, none of it's good.

Maverick: Shane, come here, baby. I know it was hard to see him like this, but Z said he's going to get better.

Shane: Yeah, I really hope so. I don't know why I'm still so mad at him though. I thought I'd feel differently. Maybe it was the call from Mom.

Maverick: Let's get out of here before he sees you crying.

I'm so tired. Drinking my wine didn't help me at all. I'm tired of this goofy mess. That's it! I'm finished with getting buzzed for real. Nothing has changed. It just had me unsteady during my first visit with my Dad. And if he were to die, this last buzzed visit would be all I have to remember. Decision is made, now I need to apologize for my lack of soberness and figure out a few things with my Boo.

Shane: Maverick, I'm getting a clear head now. Listen, first I want to apologize for handling this whole thing with my Dad in a childish way. I'm real embarrassed about it. Don't say anything, let's just move on. Back to what we talked about earlier...I don't understand love. You said it was a choice.

Maverick: Uhm...okay. Yeah, baby, man was given free choice.

Shane: Yeah, I know. And that means you can choose today to be in love and tomorrow you can choose not to be, right?! Because that's what seemed to happen to my family.

Maverick: I guess it depends on the person. Personally, if you are truly in love with someone, you just don't stop like that. I mean, I don't. I'm in it for the long haul...but that's how I am with everything I do.

Shane: Well, if you could write that down, sign it in your blood and get it notarized, I just might consider it...

Maverick: Shane, this is the deal with me. I love you. I'm here whether you want me or not. What I felt when

I first saw you doesn't come anywhere close to what I feel now. You have my heart. If you decide to reject my love, you've pushed away one of the best things in your life.

Will you ever figure it out? I hope so. Don't think so hard about it, just experience my love. I'm not cut out of the same stock as your Dad. To leave my woman and my children is unthinkable. Frankly, I don't understand that type of thinking. My scenario would be leaving me with the kids and her running off. Maybe I'm a fool, but it's about dedication, loyalty, and faithfulness. Anything less is unacceptable. Can you hear me, Shane? Does this make sense to you?

Shane: Yeah...I hear you saying that abandonment is just not your style. I really believe you...I do. And I don't want to lose a good thing because of fear. I just got to get through the craziness of what examples I've seen love to be...up to now...well, before I met you. There was a time when I believed that there could be a love like this...then when my Dad walked away from what appeared to be true love, it blew my mind. Do you think he can explain what happened? And I mean own it, don't put it off on my Mom's shortcomings. Because what I see with you, you are here. You've been with me when I've been high as Cootie Brown and confused and when I've tried to get it together.

Maverick: I see something more. I see beyond the surface...baby, I see your potential. And the only way to reach our potential is to have people believe in us. Shane, I believe in you...just live each day and trust that God loves you and wants the best for you.

Now you wonderful hot blooded man, if you asked

me to marry you right now, I'd go buy my ring myself!
I want you so bad I can taste it! Cool it, girl...he might
read your mind. Calm down...cool it.

Maverick: Now...why did you get quiet on me?

If you only knew!

Shane: No reason...just thinking. Where are we
going? To your place?

Maverick: Yes, I need to grab something.
Okay...well, do you want to come in?

Shane: Sure, are you hungry? I want some waffles?

Maverick: Oh baby, that would be nice. I'll put the
coffee on! I think I have some mix around here
somewhere.

Shane: That's cool. I see you like to be in the kitchen
too...that's nice. I love your style.

Maverick: Yeah? I try. Listen, Shane, I know I've
asked you this before, but...will you marry me?

I'm feeling a praise beak coming on ya'll! Woo hoo!

Shane: Uhm...are you sure? Hmm...am I sure?
Uh...yeah! Yes, Maverick, I'd love to be your wife.
Do you promise I won't regret it?

Maverick: Wait...you will? Yes, I do! I promise to
love you in good times and bad! In sickness and in
health...to death do we part! YEAH! Now you're not
saying yes because you're feeling sorry for me?

Shane: What?! Oh no, no, no Maverick. I am saying yes because I want to marry you! That's why I was quiet in the car. I hoped you would ask me today! Hahaha! You are cracking me up!

Maverick: Okay…when? What kind of wedding do you want…the sky is the limit! Come here woman…

Oh yeah, baby! I'm in love with a mighty good man! It feels so good in his arms. I always feel so safe when I'm with him. Listen…this is a really exciting moment and we're going to share a kiss and start dreaming of that special day! So I will see you in the next chapter. I promise, we'll be good! You're funny!

Chapter 36
Confronting the Chaos

Okay, let's get down to business! My girls got to be a part of this wedding! I've got to sit down with them and let them know the deal! I can't wait! And I'm going to break down the virginity thang too! This is the bomb!

RING! RING!

Shane: Hello?

Doc Z: Hello Shane, this is Doc Z. I just wanted to let you know that we are finished with your Dad's tests.

Shane: Okay, hold on a second…Maverick, this is Doc Z, can you talk to him and explain what he's talking about…I'm too scared to deal with this phone call…

Maverick: Sure…hello Z? What's the word?

This is too crazy for me to deal with right now. I want to think happy thoughts right now. I don't want to be in total confusion. I pray he's going to be all right. Oh Lord, I'm so scared. The most wonderful thing I can think of is having my Daddy walk me down the aisle. I pray he will be able to walk again. Uh oh…okay, he's off the phone!

Shane: Okay, what did he say?

Maverick: Um, okay let's relax and take a deep breath.

Shane: Maverick! Is it that bad!?

Maverick: Actually it's not too bad. The infection is responding to the meds, finally! So once it's gone, the healing can begin. Once he's strong enough, they will check his muscles and begin physical therapy. He's looking at a longer stay in the hospital.

Shane: Oh that's good to hear! Let me call Sean real quick!

Maverick: It's wonderful to see you smile, baby.

You're wonderful! So fine and so mine!

Shane: Uh Sean? Hi Big Brotha! Did you hear about Daddy? Yeah, I went to see him this morning. Yeah, you're right, it wasn't as easy as I thought it would be. Okay, so anyway I just heard that he's doing okay. The infection is finally under control and once it's all out, they are going to start him on physical therapy. I know, I know…Mmhm he's going to be in there for a couple more weeks. A captive audience? Hahah! Yeah.

Sean, Mom called me this morning in total trip mode. Yeah, she's looking for you too! Why…because! She's mad because we didn't tell her that we saw him. Yep, we blew it. You'll figure something out. Anyway, she's totally ticked-off. She'll listen to you better than me. Oh yes she will! Sean can you call her, please? Huh? Now! Yeah! Better now than later. Get her calmed down so she doesn't hurt something or someone…named Sam! I'm not getting around her for a while. You nut, this is straight serious! Okay Big Brotha…it's on you. Thanks Sean…Ciao. Love you too.

Shane: Okay, he's on the job! Pressures off of me for now.

Maverick: Good, good. Now, let's eat.

Shane: Sounds good to me. After we eat I want to go talk to my Dad. Cool?

Maverick: Mmhm! Just give him a few hours to clear his head and sleep. He's been through a lot.

That's fine. These waffles are insane! So delicious! He can cook too? What's a girl to do? MARRY HIM! Hah!

BACK TO THE HOSPITAL

Shane: How's my Dad doing?

Nurse: He's doing really well, he's resting comfortably. Would you like to go in and see him?

Shane: Yes.

KNOCK! KNOCK!

Nurse: Sam? You have visitors.

Sam: C'mon.

Shane: Hi…how are you feeling?

This will be about the hardest conversation I've ever had in all my life. Jesus, I need Your help with this right here. I need answers and closure.

Sam: Shane? You came back. Hi, baby girl. Come

on and have a seat. Wow, how beautiful you are.
We've got a lot of catching up to do. Might as well get
it all out in the open. I know you're mad at me.

**More than I realized, Daddy. But we'll get through
this.**

Shane: Yeah. I'd like to start with you leaving us.

Sam: I uh…well…I don't know where to begin.

Shane: At the beginning of our end as a family.

Sam: Maverick…do you mind.

Shane: No Daddy. I'd like Maverick to stay. He's
started picking up the pieces right after you left.

Sam: You were a little girl. Uhm…well, all right.
Shane, I don't want to go into the personal part of me
and your Mom's relationship, but I want to tell you
where I missed it with you. I missed the fact that there
were two beautiful children that needed a Daddy and
how much I needed them. Here I am right now fighting
for my life and my feet. I never could have believed
that my children would be here at my side, after all I've
done.

Shane: Please don't think standing by you is easy for
us. I'm not too good trying to hold back my anger and I
have lots of it toward you, Daddy. I'm not here for
show, I want some real answers.

Sam: It's hard to hear you talk to me like that. Girl,
I'm still your Dad.

Shane: If you're talking about respect...let's establish some right now. You'll get what you give. I'm not a child anymore.

Sam: I know I threw any respect you, Sean and your Mom had for me away the day I walked out. I wasn't a man to be respected at that time in my life. I was selfish, arrogant, and thought I was Slick Rick.

Shane: Why did you leave us?! Why did you leave us, Daddy? Did you know Sean was drowning in a bottle of booze for years?! Did you?! Did you know that only until recently, have I been able to have a healthy relationship?! You left us with broken hearts and broken pieces of our lives that didn't fit. We didn't know how to make them fit. And Mom just about lost her mind! Did you know that, Daddy?!

I was hoping I wouldn't cry, but here comes the waterworks! It's better than slapping him, I guess.

Sam: Shane...back then I didn't have a heart. I was closer to the devil sitting in the church pew, than out at the bars. Your Mom and I were having some struggles and I, with my stupid self, decided to trust in a "so-called" Christian woman to pray with me about my marriage problems. She had all the right answers and said all the right things. While she was saying one thing, she acted another way and I knew it. I should have pulled back and I could have, but I didn't. Your Mom seen that demon coming after me, but I just wouldn't listen. I was a selfish bastard and I wanted what I thought I wanted.

Here I am now. I've been used up, discarded like used toilet paper, and homeless. Fighting for my life and the use of my feet. And thank God, I have a fighting chance for my family. All I can ask, Shane, is that you take each day with me. I need your forgiveness. Give me a chance to redeem myself.

Mom: Redemption!?

Shane: Mom?!

Mom: Redemption?! It won't be so easy, Sam. You tugging on that sympathy card don't mean a thing. At least with your jacked up feet you can't WALK out of their lives as easily as you did the first time!

Doc Z: Okay everyone. Sam's monitors are going crazy right now. He's under too much stress. Please ladies I have to ask you to leave. Maverick, help me out.

Maverick: Shane?

Shane: Okay...Mom, come on, please. You'll have another time to talk to Daddy. This isn't the time for...

Sam: Sharmane, when I'm better, I'm going to get it all out with you. You deserve this much. You...

Doc Z: That's enough for now...really.

Mom: I'm sorry, Doctor. Shane, I'll talk with you later.

Shane: Mom. Maverick, somethings wrong with her.

She did not look right in her eyes. Has she been drinking or crying? Or both.

Maverick: She came with Sean, baby, she'll be fine.

Shane: Bye Daddy. I'll check on you later…

Doc Z: Sam…you can't have this kind of interaction while you're in this condition…it can set you back.

Sam: Doc…I tore my family up when I walked out. It's time I answer questions they've been waiting a long time to ask.

Doc Z: That's fine. I get it, but let's wait a while until your body can handle it. I need to sedate you and you'll be watched throughout the night. All of your calls will be sent to the nurse's station.

Sam: Fine…fine, I'm pretty tired anyway. But I thank God I got to talk to my baby girl. She and Sean were the hardest ones to leave.

Doc Z: Shh…let this sedative work, Sam. Be quiet for now. Everyone wants you healthy.

Sam: Mmhm.

My mind is spinning. I want to faint!

Maverick: Shane…are you okay?

Shane: Mmhm.

Maverick: I'll keep a line of communication open with Z to make sure your Dad's cool.

Shane: Thank you Maverick.

Maverick: I'm here.

Thank God Maverick's here. And thank God for
holding me together. Things are moving at warp
speed, huh. Have you been keeping up? Hang on.
It's got to get better, it sure can't get any
worse...right? Uhm...it just might get worse before it
gets better. We still have to deal with my Mom.

Buckle up and grab your helmet!

Chapter 37
From Chaos to Meltdown

Hey look who I'm trying to talk with...my Mom. And she's in rare form. I can't remember the last time she was so angry.

Shane: So, Mom, I think it would be in your best interest not to see Daddy right now...it's just making you too upset.

Mom: Shane, I've been waiting for years to rip that man's head off! Why don't you understand?!

Shane: I get it, I really do. But Mom, you moved on with your life...didn't you? You've remarried and...

Mom: And what?! This is something I feel I need to do, Shane! He broke my heart and humiliated me! He left me with three babies to rear alone with nothing but pain. And now he brings his nasty tail around looking for sympathy. I'm glad he's sick! I'm glad she dogged him and left him flat on his behind! I'm glad he's feeling pain! He deserved everything that's happened to him! Now that he's back, Mister is worrying me. I hate Sam!

Oh, Lord, please help us. She's crying and screaming. This pain and anger goes so much deeper than I ever realized.

Shane: Wow, Mom. I can't handle the things you're saying. He's still my Dad, just like you're my Mom. No matter what, I love you both...but this is too much for me. I have to go now.

Mom: Shane?! Shane?! Don't go...please don't get off the phone! Please!

Wow, she's crying so hard. She's making me cry too.

Shane: I'm here Mommy. Are you going to be okay?

Mom: Can you come by, baby? Please... can you come and be with me right now? I don't feel so good....

Shane: Yes Ma'am...okay! Can I bring Maverick?

Mom: Mhm...that's fine. Please...hurry Shane...

CLICK!

Shane: I'm on my way! Mom hold on, everything will be okay! Hello? Mom, hello?!

Oh God...keep her safe from herself! She's going off the deep end and I can only guess why! Jesus, please keep her safe. I've got to get there...I'm scared Lord. I'm scared of what she might do. I've never heard her lose it like this before. Lord, can You go to her and help her?! Can You do this for me? I don't want nothing crazy jumping off...I don't think I could take another thing!

RING! RING!

Maverick: Hello, baby!

Shane: Meet me at my Mom's house right now! Maverick she's going nuts! Please hurry!

Maverick: I'm on my way…actually I'm around the corner from her. What's going on?

Shane: Just stay on the phone with me so I know what's going on!

Maverick: Okay…okay! Calm down Shane! Take a deep breath, baby. She'll be fine. No matter what she's going through, God is keeping her…He's keeping her.

Shane: I hope so! I don't know what happened! She lost it Maverick! When she seen my Dad there was this look in her eyes!

Maverick: Okay…I'm pulling up to the curb. The front door is open.

Shane: Maverick…just blow the horn first and stay by the car to be sure she's…

Maverick: Hello Ms. Sharmane…..

Mom: Where's my Shane?

Maverick: She's on the phone with me and she's about 5 minutes away. Are you okay?

Shane: How does she look?

Maverick: Well, she looks a little wild eyed, Shane.

Mom: Maverick…I…don't…feel too good. Tell Shane to hurry up!

Shane: Maverick, I'm calling the ambulance to get them on their way.

CLICK!

Maverick: Okay…Ms. Sharmane, let me help you.

Mom: Maverick, he left me with three babies…I couldn't take care of three babies by myself. I couldn't do that alone. He left me alone with no money. Nothing…he left me hurting and alone. Mister is gone too. I don't know where he went. I don't know what to do Maverick. Where's Shane?

I can't go through this again. My Mom always seems to fall apart when anything comes up about my Dad. When it gets to be too much she crumbles. Okay, I'm here. Now I need to get to her as fast as I can!

Shane: Mommy…Mommy…I'm here now.

Mom: Shane, he left me with the three of you…I couldn't do it…I just couldn't do it.

Shane: Three? No Mommy, it was just me and Sean.

Mom: No, Shane…there were three of you! There was three of…

Shane: Mommy! Wake up! WHERE ARE THEY? OH GOD, DON'T LET HER DIE!

Maverick: She still has a heartbeat. The ambulance is here now. I'll move stuff out the way for them to get to her.

Shane: MOMMY! MOMMY! CAN YOU HEAR ME, MOMMY?!

250

Medic: Did someone call a… Let us take it from here. Ma'am can you hear me? She's not responding. She has a pulse. Is this how you found her?

Shane: Not at first. She called me and I sent my boyfriend over. He said she was acting strange and when I got here, she was slurring and then she passed out! Is she going to be okay?

Medic: Her pulse is slowing down. We need to get her to the emergency room fast! Get prepared to follow us to Med Cross Hospital.

Maverick: Okay…we're right behind you! Come on Shane.

Shane: Let me get her keys and lock the door. What's this? What are these pills? Oh God Mommy took these pills!

Medic: Bring those with you. This could be an overdose. She smells like alcohol too…let's go!

AT THE EMERGENCY ROOM

Doc Z: Shane…Sean I need to let you know where we're at with your Mom. She has overdosed on sleeping pills and alcohol. This combination has brought her very close to death. We were able to sustain her…but…she's in an induced coma right now. She's breathing on her own…so there's no need for anything artificial to sustain her at this point. We're trying to flush her system right now. Until we can clean her body out, this will help ease her discomfort.

Sean: Where the hell is her husband? Where is he Shane?

Shane: I called him…he's on his way.

Sean: Man…what the heck happened!? Why would she do this?!

Shane: Sean…she said Daddy left her with three babies. Do you know what she meant?

Sean: Oh God…no…no…NO!

Oh no. Sean is starting to cry now. I'm about dried out. I don't know if I can cry anymore.

Shane: Wait…what? WHAT!?

Sean: Shane, this is something we need to talk about away from here. Far away…come on.

Maverick: Listen, I can stay here until Mister comes. I'll just wait right here for you to get back.

Sean: Maverick…Shane is going to need you more than she ever did. Can you handle this?

Maverick: I'm committed to the end of my life with Shane. I'm in, Sean, I'm here.

Sean: Okay, we'll be right back. Let's go somewhere quiet, Shane.

Shane: I don't understand…

I don't want to hear anything else! Why is everything so crazy?!

Sean: You will. Don't look so sad Shane, it's going to be okay. This isn't easy to tell you, but Aunt Sheryl wanted me to keep quiet about this. The only thing is sometimes these dag on family secrets can really jack us up!

Shane: Family secrets? What secrets, Sean? Three? Do we have another sibling or something? Who are they? Where are they?

Sean: Shane…what I'm sharing with you isn't a topic of conversation you need to have with either one of our parents right now, do you understand?! This is something they have to work out themselves…for real, baby girl! When they're ready to talk to us, they will.

Shane: I don't know if I can do that. I hate secrets Sean! Plus, Mom was trying to tell me.

Sean: This is hard on everyone, but it's between Mom and Dad. I can't tell you unless you can promise me to keep your mouth shut! I mean it Shane, I really mean this! We can't step in, we really can't do anything but show the love of Christ. This here is the ultimate test…are we really saved?!

Shane: My God, Sean! Okay…I promise I won't say anything. But if Mommy wants to talk, at least I'll be prepared…right?!

Sean: Yeah…she might need to clear the air. Okay…this is the story. When we were kids, Mommy sent you to Camp Genesis and sent me to Aunt Sheryl and Uncle Glenn's house...do you remember?

Shane: Yeah...you were too old to go to camp that year. I never felt so alone...

Sean: I know Sis. Well, Mommy was pregnant when Dad left her. She was about three months at that time. Barely showing.

Shane: Wait a minute, let me get this straight. Mom was pregnant? How do you know this?

Sean: Let's sit down, Shane...just take deep breaths. Are you okay, Sis?

Shane: Mmhm...go ahead.

My mind is spinning so fast right now.

Sean: When Dad left, Mom about lost her mind...and her nerves got the best of her and she ended up losing the baby. Shane, the reason I didn't say anything was I found out by sneaking around and listening to Aunt Sheryl's phone calls with Mom's doctor.

Shane: Oh, now I remember something! When I came home, she was happy to see me but she cried a lot. It was kind of different I thought, because she kept me close. It was what I needed, but I thought she did it because I was so sad missing Daddy.

Sean: I'm sure it was both. She was like that when I finally came home too. But...man, he did a job on our family.

Shane: Did he know she was pregnant?

Sean: I don't know Shane. I really don't know…he stayed away from the house a lot during that time, and eventually he just never came back. Oh…Lord, help us! How evil can a man be?! I'm ashamed to be his son sometimes, Shane! That's why I wanted to pound him for so many years. Finally, I just broke, and started drinking to numb out!

Shane: We both reacted in crazy ways, Sean. But we're different now. Jesus saved us.

Sean: Yeah…to the bone. When I saw him at the B&B that was enough for me.

Shane: What do you mean?

Sean: When you end up at the B&B, you have been broken down and as low as you can go. Believe me, God dealt with him…we didn't have to do anything. God simply lifted His hand off of him for a time. I'm thankful God still stayed close by, or he wouldn't be here today.

Shane: Yeah…I see what you mean. Do you think he's repented to God?

Sean: There's a good chance…after all he's repented to us. It seems to me he's come to himself. Kind of like the prodigal son.

Shane: Yeah…well, Sean, I think we should pray for Mommy and Daddy. They both really need Jesus in a deeper way. This can't be easy for either one of them. It's all pretty devastating. I think I get Mom now.

Sean: Right. Let's pray. Father God…

Our time of prayer was really simple, yet powerful. Sean left to make a call. Oh...my soul aches for my Mom. How she made it this far is a mystery to me! So there is a little brother or little sister waiting for me in Heaven. Waiting for us. Lord, kiss them for me and tell them I love them. I can't stop crying. Can you imagine living with this kind of pain? If it were you, how would you handle this? If this is something that's happened to you, I'm really sorry. I guess this is a time to learn, not only about the love of Jesus, but also His forgiveness. Mommy won't be able to move on and heal until she can forgive Daddy. The inability to forgive can do some incredible damage to one's mind. I'm watching this happen again...but this time I understand the "why". No wonder folks get killed over relationships...rage is a powerful emotion. But murder isn't the way out, neither is suicide. Only Jesus Christ can pull us out of those dark pits of life! Only Jesus.

Maverick: Shane...your brother told me you needed me. Baby, let me hold you. I know it's been a real hard time for you. It's all right, let it out.

Shane: Oh...why? Why can't this pain stop? All of this...this STUFF! All of these secrets!

Maverick: I'm here for you Shane. When you're ready then we'll go. Your Mom is in good hands and so are you.

Chapter 38
Defining Your Truth

Well, it's been a wild journey so far, hasn't it?! So much is happening in my life! Mom is still in the hospital...it's been a couple of weeks now. They brought her out of the coma after a few days. She seemed so disoriented. It's weird...for the first time I see my Mom as a woman, a woman who has been hurt down deep in her soul. She really loved my Daddy. Even though she physically "moved on", she really didn't in her heart. The pain was pushed down, but it was never dealt with. Now she's been in counseling and seems to be doing a little better. At least she's speaking her truth, no matter how ugly it is. Speaking her truth...

Now my Daddy is searching for his truth. Personally I think he found it the day that trick left him. He broke down and realized all of what he lost. It wasn't her, because he never had her heart...he only had ours. And I found out he'd been back in town for a while, but was too ashamed to knock on our doors. When he ran out of money he ended up on the streets. Thank God Maverick's Dad happened to see him.

Daddy should be getting out of the hospital in a day or two. He's been sneaking a peek at Mommy when he takes his walks. I think she knows it. Poor Mister feels like he's on the outside looking in right now, because this seems to be a story without an ending with my parents. I know he's hanging to see where he fits into all of this. But he was there to pick up the pieces. For that, I respect his love for my Mom. I hope he'll hold on through this. He's a good man. He reminds me of Maverick. That's got to be painful though. You can see it all on his face. I don't know what to say to him. I try to keep it light.

Sean and Carol are partners proclaiming Jesus Christ! They are something else! Their work at the B&B has been amazing. Mavericks' parents let them take over one night a week, so they can spend some time together. They have done it two weeks so far, and you can see a difference in his parents...they seem more relaxed and loving.

You know, I'm starting to realize as I watch my parents going through this that life is too short to miss love when it comes and stares in your dog gone face! I have to find the good in the midst of all this pain. Like...like Daddy's back to walk me down the aisle. Remember, it's what I prayed for! He will need a cane, but he's back in my life! I just simply love me some Maverick! He's an amazing man. He's stood by my side through some crazy stuff and he's still treating me good...I wouldn't have it any other way.

What have I learned about life on this journey...since you've been with me? Well, let me tell you! Pain can walk right up to you and slap you straight across the face! It has no mercy! It brings in fear, confusion, un-forgiveness and destruction. But I've learned that God has not given us the spirit of fear, but the Spirit of power, and of love and a sound mind! God ain't no joke...do you hear me?! He's all that and a bag of chips...with some drank and some onion dip! Are you digging me?! Hahaha! Oh yeah!

And when we realize that there is a Greater Love whose name happens to be Jesus Christ that was willing to die for us. Things can look a whole lot better...because we're not alone. Jesus didn't stay dead! He loved us enough to come right back and be a part of our lives...every moment of each day. And all the pain that we deal with can be dealt a blow with His power and love, and we get a sound mind while the dust settles!

Unfortunately, the devil is real with his stanky self! And he hates every human being in this world, because God gave this world to us. Adam and Eve gave up the rights through wicked deception...but Jesus took it back and returned it to the rightful owners! That's you and me! For God so loved the world that He gave His only begotten son, that whosoever believed in Him would not perish but have everlasting life! That's John 3:16!

In order to be a part of this party, you have to give your life to Jesus Christ! Let go of all that mess you're doing right now. You know what I'm talking about, and you know it ain't right too! Yeah...that stuff. It's dangerous dancing too close to the fire!

Tell Jesus you're tired of playing with fire! Hell's fire! And that you want Him to come into your heart and take over your life! Don't play around with it...mean it with all of your heart! And He'll step right on in and take over. And you'll notice that your situation may still be the same, but He'll give you peace while you're in it and show you a way out! One step at a time! Isn't that just too cool?!

There is still a lot going on in my life! This is just a little breakdown thus far. So, I hope you'll continue to hang out with me. I'm hoping my Mom and Dad work things out. That sure would put my mind at ease.

AT THE HOSPITAL

Mom: Well Dr. Z, thank you for stopping in. Maverick is such a sweet heart to have you check in on me. He's going to be a great son-in-law.

Doc Z: Yes ma'am, he's a good man. And your daughter is good for him.

Mom: Yeah, Shane's needed a good man for a long time. I've always prayed someone special would find her. She's been through some fools in the past. This is the first time in a long time that I've seen her really happy. I pray he don't ever hurt her and take that joy away like Sam did to me.

Knock! Knock!

Mom: It must be the nurse. Yes? Come in.

Sam: Sharmane? Can I talk to you?

Mom: Sam?! Why? You've done and said enough…

Doc Z: Sam, can you step out for a minute, please.

Sam: Doc, I just need to make things right with her, I

don't want to upset her.

Doc Z: Let me make sure she is physically and emotionally able to talk with you. She's getting better, but I don't know how ready she is to deal with you. It's been hard on her, Sam. I'll be right back. Mrs. Douglas, do you want to talk with Sam? I know you've come a long way in your counseling. But, it's up to you.

Mom: What do you think Dr. Z? Will this help me get out of here?

Doc Z: It depends on you. The greatest part of your healing will come from forgiveness. The inability to forgive causes a lot of emotional and physical damage. It doesn't hurt the one we don't forgive, it just hurts us.

Mom: You sound like Shane! I thought she said that because she wants us to get back together.

Doc Z: No, I don't think that's it at all. She's learning that forgiveness is a healthy way of living. She's forgiven her Dad, and from what you and Maverick have said, it's taken a weight off of her...Sean too.

Mom: Sean?! Okay, okay, I'll talk to him. Sean is the greater proof between the two of learning how to forgive. Did you know my son WAS an all-out alcoholic? Not anymore! He's a Jesus freak now and I love it! Okay.

Doc Z: No Ma'am. Wow, that explains a lot. So, can I tell Sam he can come in?

Mom: Yeah, let me get this over with. Thank you.

Doc Z: Sam, you can come in. Please keep the conversation controlled. Not too much at one time. Okay?

Sam: Yes sir! Thank you so much Doc! Uh…Sharmane, can I come in.

Mom: Come on in Sam. Have a seat.

Sam: Sharmane…uh…Sharmane, how are you doing?

Mom: I'm getting better, Sam. How are you feeling?

Sam: Well, I'm getting better. I'll be getting out in the next day or two.

Mom: Oh really?

Sam: Yeah…as you can see I'm able to get around. I got strength in my legs. My feet aren't as tender as they were. Enough about me… I came to tell you that I was wrong to leave you and the kids! And that I am so very sorry from the bottom of my soul for hurting you.

Mom: Do you really know all of what you walked away from, Sam?

Sam: I left you and the kids. I left a good woman and two beautiful children.

Mom: Two? You didn't leave two children, Sam. You left three.

Chapter 39
The Truth Hurts and Heals

Sam: Three? What do you mean, Sharmane?

Mom: I was three months pregnant when you walked out that door!

Sam: I never heard about that. You never mentioned it when I called. Why didn't you say something?

Mom: Because I didn't want you to come back for the baby. I wanted you to come back to ME! You left the marriage, Sam, OUR marriage!

Sam: Oh my God Sharmane...I...I'm so sorry! Where is this child? How come I haven't heard the kids talking about...?

Mom: I lost the baby, Sam.

Sam: Oh no...no. (Weeping) I am so sorry, Sharmane. Now I understand...why...oh God...I am sorry, so sorry.

Mom: (Weeping) I didn't have enough strength in my body to hold on. When you left me...it broke my heart, Sam. I never thought I would get over it...and then when I lost the baby...it was too much for me to bear. This isn't the first time I've ended up here.

Sam: Sharmane...this will be the last time. I have let you down for the last time. I need to know...I need to know what can I do to make things right?

Mom: You can be a Father to our kids. It's too late for us as far as our marriage goes. I love my husband. He picked up my broken pieces after you left, he's a real good man. You need to visit the grave...you and the kids. I haven't told them yet. I want you to be here when I do.

Sam: Okay...anything. Before we tell them, please let me go by myself, Sharmane. I need to do this one thing.

Mom: Fine. Listen, she's at the Praying Hands Cemetery on Main Court Street under the oldest oak tree, next to my Mother. Her name is Shayla Vanity.

Sam: Oh my sweet little Shayla. Okay...like I said, I'll be out in the next day or two and I'll go. Sharmane, I have one last question for you. Can you forgive me for what I've done? I felt like I was in some crazy fog when I got with that lady. I was wrong for giving her the time of day. You were right the whole time. I can't change what's done, but I want to put it past us. You don't have to answer me now...but I want you to forgive me, because I'm sorry. I'm really so sorry.

Mom: Sam, let me know when you've visited her, and we'll go from there. I'm tired and I want to rest now. I'll talk to you then.

Sam: Uh...okay Sharmane. I'll let you know. Thank you for seeing me.

Mom: Mmhm.

Sean: Dad?

Sam: Hi Sean, I'm just leaving. How are you son?

Sean: Good...is everything okay with Mom? Is she okay?

Sam: Yes. Your Mom finally let me step in and talk with her for a while. She wants to rest now.

Sean: Really? So is everything okay?

Sam: Well I think it's gonna be real slow and steady, Sean. It may be tiny steps, but we're trying to move on from the past. Listen, walk me back to my room, I feel a little unsteady.

Sean: Sure. Would you like me to get a wheel chair?

Sam: Nah, if I do that, they'll keep me in here longer. No man, I'm just trying to get out of here as soon as I can.

Sean: Dad, when you do get out, where are you going to stay? They won't release you without knowing your living arrangements.

Sam: I don't know just yet, I'm going to talk to Mr. Grace. Maybe he can help me. I know I need to have an address to get my SSI check. Man, I've been through hell, and I only have myself to blame. I took your Mom through hell too...and I'm so sorry for it. Your Mom is a good woman, Sean. I've always known that, I just was too stupid to know how to treat a good one back then.

Sean: I agree with you there. That takes a lot of courage to admit. Sounds like healing has begun.

Okay, we're at your room. Do you need anything?

Sam: Yeah, a little water, please. I really just want to get my life back together.

Sean: Okay. Here you go. What made you go to Mom's room? Weren't you scared? You know how she can be.

Sam: I want her to get better, Sean. And I need to get better too. I can't live knowing that the only woman I truly loved is sick because of me. All I could think about was asking for forgiveness after I came to my senses, not just for me, but for her. Now I need to work on forgiving myself. But I won't rest until all of ya'll can find it in your hearts to forgive me. I'll never stop asking.

Sean: Well, Dad, cross me off the list. I forgive you. I have experience in knowing how to make a bad decision that affects everyone around me. You're just a man like me. As a matter of fact, because I used to put you in an unrealistic view, I lost hold of reality and got lost in alcohol and drugs. It took years, but I finally figured it out and asked for help.

Sam: Yeah, I heard Sean. I saw you once when I first got back in town. When I saw you like that, I knew I couldn't walk into your life just yet. I sure didn't expect to come by way of the B&B...and there you were serving me, all cleaned up and happy. But...it was good to see that you got set free. I admit I was scared and vulnerable. I wasn't sure if you remembered me, and if you did I wondered if I was safe. So, son, I'm proud of you and I thank God.

Sean: Yeah? Hahaha! Well you're at least safe from me. Thanks, Dad. Well, I'm going to check in on Mom right now…so you rest and I'll let the nurse know you're back in your room. I'll check on you later.

Sam: Okay son…I'll see you later.

Doc Z: Hi Sean, how's your Dad holding up? I'll be checking on him in a bit.

Sean: Okay I guess…he's resting now. He said he was a little off balance…is that normal?

Doc Z: Well, given the visit he just had, it is. We'll keep a close eye on him. I'll have the nurse check his vitals and make sure he's resting comfortably for the evening. So, how are you doing with all of this? Both parents in the hospital at one time…are you holding up all right?

Sean: Yeah man. For sure this is keeping me on my knees and away from the booze! There ain't anything left for me in my old life, man! I have real good support around me. And to be honest Doc, this might be the only time I think I'll see them in the same building at one time.

Doc Z: I checked in on your Mom after Sam left. She's doing really well. Your Mom is determined to walk out of here in record time. She's getting stronger.

Sean: That's good to hear…I'm on my way to see her.

Doc Z: That's fine. She might be asleep. I gave her something to relax.

Sean: No matter…I'll just quietly sit and watch her. I just want to look at her beautiful face.

Doc Z: No problem. Let me know if you need me for anything, I'm here for your family, Sean.

Sean: Thanks Doc. We appreciate all you've done.

Chapter 40

Sipping on that Hater-aide

AT THE SISTA'S MEETING

Hey! Where have you been?! I've missed you flipping my pages! Hah! There's a lot going on, right? I guess I've got to get the right head space to deal with it all. It's good to talk to you again. So, I'm about to hang out with my sistas and catch up with them and let them catch up with me. It's been a long time since we've hung out. I hope they get the new and improved me! That's all they get from here on out. After all of this I hope the love is still there and they don't push me away.

Shane: Hello Ladies!

Essence: Shane...girl, what's up!

D.J.: My girl!

Lynn: Shane, Shane, Shane! What's up!

Shane: Sistas, can you believe why we are meeting?! Oh my goodness! Ladies this is all about love!

D.J.: Yeah, yeah...let's get to the business at hand. First, I'd like to say I'm jealous as hell! But other than that, I'm really happy for you!

Shane: Nothing like being honest? Thanks, D.J.

Essence: So, Shane, how did you guys go from "I'm

moving away forever" to "we're talking about getting married"?

Shane: Wow, okay. I give the credit to Jesus.

Lynn: What do you mean Jesus? Translate because I don't get it.

Shane: Well, ya'll…you know I've stopped my extracurriculars and I've given my heart to…

Lynn: Really? Shane, please stop!

D.J.: No. Shane keep talking, let the word be heard! It's about time we do something more than just go out all the time. I just have one question. How can we expect us party at your wedding when you're not partying anymore?

Essence: Yeah, Shane, do you expect us to get saved today? Are we dressing like Nuns for wedding? Hahaha!

Wow, this isn't going as I expected. I'm starting to feel a little knock on my heart's door from the old Shane and she's ready to rise up and conquer this nonsense. Not good.

D.J.: Probably not today, but every single one of us has been in church at some time in our lives! We have seen some of the most jacked up hypocrites there than anywhere in the city! That's why we've been in the clubs, instead of church. Can this sista get a amen?

Shane: No, DJ, you don't get no amen? Listen, everyone isn't the same. You do remember my

Grandma, right?

Lynn: Whatever! Speak for yourself. You don't have a clue about my journey.

Essence: Amen! D.J.'s right about that. I haven't been comfortable yet in church. So Shane, go ahead and lay it out, girl!

Lynn: I'm really not feeling this ya'll. I'm going to sit right here and sip on my drink. You have 5 minutes.

Talk about being put on a spot...okay sistas. Sigh...tough crowd.

Shane: Well, all I can tell you is what happened to me. You know Maverick had a big part, because he accepted me as I was and prayed for me. He believed God that I would get set free from the extra extracurriculars. Ladies, you know good and dog on well that this diva wasn't looking to give up no party any time soon. I wasn't worried about that. Hah!

But then Carol got saved, then my brotha got saved. They stopped all of what they were strung out on. Crack and alcohol! Carol is beautifully saved, ya'll. She is so full of Jesus it splashes out all over the place! Then one night, she was talking about how Jesus can clean you up and set you straight. How He can give you peace and a love no one can take away. I thought about everyone around me that had gotten saved, and realized they were totally chillin'! So I knew it was time for me to give it all to Jesus...because I needed all of Him. So I went all the way! And I feel so good! I'm happier than I've ever been and...

Lynn: BEEP! Your time is up my dear! And girl, it sounds promising, it really does and I'm happy for you. So just pray for me, Shane. I'd love to have what you have...someday. You seem more chill than before. I'll drink to that. Cheers! I could really use a joint right now.

Shane: Okay Lynn, I don't know if you're playing me or nah! Anyway, when the party runs out...there is nothing left. Jesus is eternal...He ain't going nowhere! It's really cool! If you have any more questions I'd love to talk to you more about Him? So...I really want to talk about colors and dresses right now, I don't have a lot of time! Cool?!

Lynn: Okay, Shane. We get it. You got it! Just don't shove it. You blow through here, drop all this and we're supposed to be happy. I'm happy, but I feel some kind of way. Are you too good to hang out with us anymore or something?

Shane: No, Lynn. There's just a lot going on in my family and I wanted to be with ya'll to get my mind off...

I wasn't expecting this kind of vibe. What's she sipping on, hater-aid? Geez! I'm out. Too much already going on.

Essence: See Lynn, you're so selfish! Don't leave, Shane. We want to be here for you. So let's just step past all the jokes and drama and look through these books. I'm really happy for you. Did you pick out a dress yet?

D.J.: Cool! Let's look through this book first!

Lynn: Guess who I saw the other day, Shane? Your boy, Leo. He said he seen you when you were out of town. Mav know anything about it?

Shane: That's nice and none of your business. All right, Lynn. I don't know what's up your crawl, but I'm not about to deal with your snide remarks right now. I can't today. I'll see ya'll later. Thanks for meeting me out. I've got to go.

Lynn: Okay, Shane. Okay. I was just having a moment. He just asked about you. He didn't seem too happy, that's all. I'll stay out of your business. You don't have to leave, I will. Sorry to…make things worse for you. Sorry. I'm out.

Shane: Oh no…you stay right there and finish your hater-aid. I've already said my good-byes. You can stay right there, Lynn. Whoever wants to be bothered with me can call me.

Essence: We blew it, ya'll. She didn't deserve that…

Well that sucked! Not at all what I expected. Sigh… They can keep their lame jokes to themselves, I don't need it! How can you make fun of someone making better life choices? Jealousy? I used to be on the other side of that coin…now I see how ugly I treated folks. Lord, forgive me. But that Lynn is up to something, she sure was acting a bit smug. I was hoping this wouldn't happen, but Leo is her cousin. He knows good and well, there's nothing left between us. Oh, he tried to see me after he found out Mav left early. At that time, it was kind of hard to resist…but I just couldn't do that to Maverick. So I sent him on his

way. I haven't mentioned it to Mav though. He might take it the wrong way, so...I better clear the air before some stanking lies get out there. Enough! I don't want to think about that right now.

Anyway, I can tell they're at that wait and see thing, that's why they weren't taking me serious. Oh well, maybe in time they will see I'm really serious about my relationship with Christ and Mav. Until then I'll just pray. Especially for Lynn to keep her big mouth shut and to get a grip. Don't judge me. Anyway, I've got things to do. I'll see you in a flip of the page.

Chapter 41
The Business of Forgiveness

I need to call Sean. He went to see Mom and Dad today. I hope everything is okay. Lord knows I need good news for a change.

RING! RING!

Sean: Hello?

Shane: Hi Sean. What's up? How are they doing?

Sean: Hey Sis! Everything's going good. Actually better than expected. Hold on to your wig, can you believe they actually talked today?

Shane: Huh, you mean to each other? Any fists swinging? No way! Who initiated this?

Sean: I know right! Haha! When I was going to Mom's room, he was coming out. Shocked me! He looked a little flushed though. He said he asked Mom for forgiveness.

Shane: Wait, you said he came out of her room looking flushed. Uh oh! You sure she didn't smack him upside his head? Wow! So, did she?

Sean: Well, he didn't say she did. Probably not, but he's hopeful. What about you, Sis? Have you forgiven him? He's really going hard on cleaning up the damage. He's changed.

Shane: Uh yeah, a while ago, I guess. I haven't said

the words to him, but…you know, I feel sorry for him one day. But there are days I get really mad. I don't know.

Geez, I really need to have some serious conversations, don't I?

Sean: Go by and say the words to him. He needs to hear the words, Sis.

Shane: Uhm, when I'm in the right head space I'll call him. Are you with him? How's Mom?

Sean: No, I'm on my way to Carols. She's fixing me dinner tonight. Mom's good, she didn't say much.

Shane: Ooh! That sounds good to me. When are you two getting hitched? Ya'll go to counseling together, you see each other every day, and you work side-by-side. Give me a date of proposal, Bro!

Sean: We're talking about it. I don't want to rain on your parade, so we'll wait until you're married and folks can save up for our gifts! Hahaha!

Shane: Hold on now! We'll see about that. That is too funny! If I do, do you think Daddy will be able to walk me down the aisle?

Sean: I'm sure he will in time. If he can't, you know I'm right there! All you got to do is ask!

Shane: Yeah…that's cool to know Sean. I sure do love you! Well, my brotha, I'm going to call my honey and see what's up with him.

Sean: All right, Sis. I'll talk to you later. I love you! Make sure you call Daddy too!

Shane: I am, I promise. Bye!

I love my Daddy. Maybe I can get Maverick to take me to the hospital for a little while tonight. I need to be in the right mood to do it though. I'm not sure if I'm ready to...

RING! RING!

Maverick: Hello Sweet Thang!

Shane: Hi, baby! I was just about to call you. What are you up to?

Maverick: I'm at the B&B finishing up the chapel. Shane, it looks really nice! When are you coming by to see it?

Shane: Well...I want to come tomorrow after I see my parents. Sean told me that my Dad stopped in to see my Mom. He asked for her forgiveness. Isn't that cool?!

Maverick: Yes! Did she?

Shane: We don't know. But Sean told me I needed to tell my Dad that I forgive him. I wanted to go tonight, but I don't want to go alone. Then I'm not even sure if I want to talk about all this right now.

Maverick: Well, baby, I'm finished with what I'm doing, but I need to take a shower first. We can go anytime Z will let us in.

Shane: Okay. I'll just relax and wait for you to get here.

Maverick: Okay, baby. See you in about 45 minutes.

Shane: Ciao!

I guess you're wondering where me and Maverick stand in the lovey dovey department! Well, we still haven't crossed that line, though we've come close a time or two! I'm really proud of us! It's not like we haven't wanted too! I'd jump that man's bones with a quickness! But we are working hard at waiting! I know it will be worth it! We just try to stay busy and around family and friends.

RING! RING!

Shane: Hello?

Maverick: Shane, I just called Z. He said they both are resting comfortably and it would be better if we waited until the morning. Is that okay with you?

Shane: Wow, okay. They must have had a pretty deep conversation today. So if they are sleeping, what do you want to do?

I think it's time I talk to him about Leo. I have a feeling if I don't I'll have problems with Lynn. I don't know what Leo said, so I better get this out in the open and shame the devil.

Maverick: That's what he said. You want to go to a movie or something?

Shane: Uhm, yeah, that sounds fun. I get to pick the movie though. But, I'd like to talk to you about something later, if that's okay.

Maverick: That's fine. I really need to stop working so much and court you better. Ole Peg told me I needed to stop being so scared to be around you. Haha! I'm not scared of you. I love being with you.

Shane: Mother knows best. If she only knew! I'll put you under my love slave spell! Hahaha!

Maverick: See, don't start that kind of talk, Shane. I'll be taking another cold shower. This can't be healthy! Hahaha!

Shane: Maverick, the last thing I want to do is turn you into shaved ice. Gosh, you would think I had some unnatural seductive powers!

Maverick: No comment. Well, the movie starts at 9 p.m. It's about 5:30. So, I'll be there at 7:30…cool?

Shane: Yep that's fine. I need to change into something more comfortable. I just might wear my flooding sweat pants, a t-shirt, and house shoes!

Maverick: What?! Shane you can be so fashionable! So if you do, I'm wearing flip flops with tube socks AND some polyester plaid shorts! I got to make sure everyone understands my fashion statement!

Shane: Hahaha! You crack me up! But for real though, don't you come looking like that, because I will pull off my house numbers and you'll never find where I live again! Hahaha!

Maverick: Hahaha! Wow. Bye, Shane!.

Shane: Ciao!

Okay...sorry about that. We finally ended our nerdy phone call! It can get worse, believe me! We have so much fun now. If you wear the stuff we were laughing about, don't sweat it! It's funny to us...and we're just characters in a book! Right?!

I'm going to relax and unwind for a bit, change, and enjoy my evening with Mav! I'll catch you when we get back here.

Chapter 42
Transparency is Healing Me

AFTER THE MOVIE

Maverick: Well, baby, I had a great evening with you.

Shane: Me too! Thank you for not wearing that ensemble you teased me about! I don't think I could have kept my hands to myself. Way too sexy for me to handle. Hahaha!

Maverick: Yeah? Thanks for not wearing your Miss Moo the Cow house shoes. I would have wanted milk all night. Got some milk?

Wow, he just got real serious on me. Is milk that sexy? Oh...sigh. Too funny. I've got to redirect right now. I love this corny man.

Shane: Yes, I've got some in the fridge. I love you Mav.

Maverick: I love you too, baby. Let me hold you. Mmm, you feel so good, Shane.

Shane: Yeah...it's nice in your arms. Maverick, uh...

Okay, he just planted a kiss on me that made me dizzy AND my toes curled. Wait a minute here! That was a deep one. Mmm and I loved it! Oh no...we've done really well up until now. I want him so bad! Oh Lord, help me! I'm for real!

Maverick: Shane, maybe we could just…

Shane: Oh no, Maverick! No! It's time for you to go! Bye!

Maverick: Do you really want me to go? I thought you wanted to talk. We can talk, okay.

Shane: No comment! We're too close, we can hold off a little longer! Bye!

Maverick: Shane…I want you so bad. Can't I please…?

Shane: No Maverick! No! Please don't do this to me. I've finally come to peace with myself…I don't want any more shame! You've got to go! Bye!

Maverick: Aw, baby, I'm sorry! I'm so sorry Shane. I promise I'll behave. What did you need to talk about?

Okay, he's tripping tonight. What on Earth?! It's going to make this conversation even harder…I think. It just might cool his jets though.

Shane: Well, I see we're going to have to stick to G rated movies! At least until we get married!

Maverick: I didn't think about it…but you're right. That one scene was…

Shane: I don't want to go there! The devil is a liar! And I'm not risking God's blessing for one night! **(Of unwedded bliss! I'm sure of it!)** I've waited this long! I can't do this.

Maverick: You're right, Shane! How about we kick the devil in the mouth tonight! I have a great idea, let's talk first, then go downtown and witness to folks wandering around at the park.

Shane: Hmm, sounds okay. We'll see.

Maverick: Okay, you sound serious. What did you want to talk about? Seems like something's been on your mind all evening.

Okay, girl! Here's your chance to come clean and put the devil to shame. Am I ready to unveil my back-up plan I've had all these years. Once Leo's out the bag, I'll be completely vulnerable. Maybe I should wait. Leo's called me a few times, wanting to see me, since I've been back from the trip. The last time we spoke, he wasn't too happy with my choice for my future. I chose Mav. Okay, here goes true commitment. If he turns me away, I'll have to deal with it. Lord, please help me say the words and help him to love me anyway. Breath in, blow it out. Okay.

Shane: Well, you know I've been taking things slow with you. Just wanting to make sure everything was right within myself. I've done some soul-searching and stuff. I know we've talked about getting married someday. When...I don't know. We haven't made it official with the ring and everything, but we've been exclusive.

Maverick: Oh, I...

Shane: Let me finish, please. There's something I haven't told you about my trip. I should have told you the truth a long time ago. There's a guy that I've known for many years. He's someone I've always thought would be "that" guy. The one I'd end up with. Never knowing there was a man like you out here.

Maverick: So, did you go there to see him? I thought it was for a job interview.

Shane: It was. It's just that he happened to be there too. I didn't know it until you had flowers delivered to me. Uhm, he owns the flower shop. He seen my name and delivered them to me personally.

Maverick: Oh, so that was him that walked pass me on my way to your room, right? You told me he delivered the flowers, but you left all of this out. Wow, Shane.

Shane: I didn't want to spoil our moment talking about him. The flowers were beautiful and you were so charming and loving. I really didn't have anything to say because I sent him on his way. What I'm trying to say is that I shut him down. I told him I'd made my choice and that he couldn't come in and out of my life anymore.

Maverick: So...so what else? There's got to be more to this story, right? Did he talk his way back in when I left? Did you have...listen...this sounds all too familiar. I just can't go through this again, Shane. I can't. Is there any good news in all of this? What are you saying? I want to believe you, but...

Shane: Like I said, Maverick, I shut it down. If there would have been any moment that I would have thrown caution to the wind, it would have happened then. But I didn't. That's when I realized you meant so much more to me and that I deserved to be loved fulltime. A part-time relationship isn't what I wanted in the first place. But that's all he offered and I thought that must be what I'm worth. Then you come into my life and showed me I deserved something so much better.

Maverick: So this was an emotional and sexual relationship, huh? For you to take so long to tell me makes me wonder why. Why was this something you didn't want to tell me right away? There's real feelings involved here.

Now, I'm not about to go there. Nope. I'm going to wrap this up and put a bow on it. His eyes are welling up. There's no way...there's nothing else to say. It's done. It's over. Don't ask me if it was good, because I will be nominated and win the award for a Leading Actress in a Fiction Novel. Don't go there. He'll never know.

Shane: When you met me I was broken. Not really in or out of that relationship. I should have been clearer, but I didn't feel like... We've gone through all of this already. I never pretended to be perfect. I'm coming clean with you so there's no question of where my loyalty and love lies. If you're serious about me, I'm here. I'm not in any rush. I know it gets hard sometimes because we're refraining from something we really want. I'm willing to wait for as long as it takes to do it right. I just wanted to put it all out there. I know that I love you and only you.

Maverick: I hear you. I appreciate you for being honest with me. I thought he looked familiar. I've seen you with him in the past, before I got the nerve up to speak to you. It's going to take me a minute to gather my thoughts. I just wasn't expecting this tonight. Listen, I...uhm I want to leave right now. Thank you, Shane. Thank you for respecting me enough...I have questions. I'm not ready to ask, but I need time to think right now. I'll talk to you later.

Shane: Okay. Be safe.

Well, I guess I'll have to wait and see what happens. I don't know. This has been one of the hardest days I've endured in a long time. But, this time I'm dealing with it differently. I don't feel like going out and getting high. I don't want to cry. I don't have any tears left even if I wanted to. It's my truth and I stand in it. I've got to love who I see in the mirror. No more playing games with my heart. Numbing and finding another lover isn't healing my soul. Enough of all of that. I'm not trying to party my life away and miss a special man like Mav. There aren't many men out here like him. If he decides I'm not the one for him, I can at least know what kind of man I want. I just don't believe I'll ever love anyone else the way I love him. I'm going to grab my Grandma's Bible and read it for a while. I'll see you in the next chapter.

Chapter 43
Jumping Unforeseen Hurdles

Well Mav called me late last night and we talked. He said he didn't want to break-up, but wanted to move past all of the Leo and Tom stuff. Yep, he figured it out and I confessed. I'm so relieved. We'll see how it goes. He wanted to take me to see my parents today. He's such a special guy.

Shane: Maverick, when we get to the hospital, I'm thinking I want to see Mom first.

Maverick: Are you sure, Shane? Last time your Mom had you upset you took it out on your Dad. If you see him first, you'll be more level headed.

Shane: I don't know. I'm so much closer to my Mom, and he's the one that left her.

Maverick: Exactly. That's why you need to deal with your Dad first. Give him a chance. Are you sure you've forgiven him?

Shane: What do you mean? Of course I've forgiven him.

Maverick: How do you know you have?

Shane: I don't know. I guess I'm not as mad at him as I was. I want him to get better and I want to mend my heart.

Maverick: Shane, do you believe Jesus has forgiven you?

Shane: Yes, I do, Pastor.

Maverick: Now that sounds good! Have you forgiven yourself?

Shane: Yeah, why are you asking me this?

Maverick: Well, do you still look in the mirror and see that girl you let down or can you look in the mirror and smile knowing she's forgiven you and you are now the new forgiven Shane?

Shane: Well, when I look in the mirror, I smile. I know that I'm not anything like I was before. And I'm happy about me. I think about how beautiful, fantastic, and gorgeous I am with this new make-up, cute outfit, and rockin' hairdo. Hey!

Maverick: See, you think I'm playing! I'm very serious about this, Shane.

Shane: Maverick, really...I don't hate who looks back at me. Geez you're so serious. Still upset with me, huh? You mad because I'm happy?

Maverick: No. Okay I am a little. I don't want to get into that right now. So, you said you don't hate "who" looks back at you? What the heck does that mean?

Shane: I mean I don't go through all the negative thoughts anymore. I know I was wrong and that it was up to me to be honest, and walk in my truth. I do. I've learned it was Jesus who could heal my past and set me right. And in the process of healing, I began to learn to love myself. Now I love who I see in the mirror, because I was created in His image. And I know the girl looking back at me, loves her some Shane! Hey!

Maverick: So, what do you see when you see your Dad? The man who walked away years ago or a man made in the image and likeness of God? He is a man whom God loves and is willing to forgive.

Shane: Oh, so you think I don't know that? He deserves a chance. I'm willing to give that to him. I love him.

Why is he trying to burst my happy balloon?

Maverick: Shane, I've asked you a couple questions to think about. I'm not sitting in judgment. Just think about it. When you talk to your Dad, you need to understand how you're really feeling. Do you know what I mean?

Shane: Yeah…I guess I do. Before we go to visit, let's stop and get some breakfast in the cafeteria…your treat. We have a long day ahead.

Maverick: My treat? You're stepping into that wife role rather smoothly. Okay…that sounds good to me!

Shane: Yes darling. Hah!

This man can really make me think. I really need to thoroughly go over how I feel about my Dad. When I think about how upset my Mom was, I get crazy. And to know there's a secret sibling that I never had the pleasure of seeing, I want to cuss him out for leaving! But I know this is between them. There has to be a reason my Mom never told us. What if he didn't

know it? That would change things. I know he walked away, but I can't believe he'd walk away from a baby. But then he walked away from me and Sean. I can't go there. I need to go with what is really in front of me. The order of business is forgiveness. How do I forgive?

The only one I know that I can use as an example of forgiveness is Jesus. After those clowns hung Him on the cross He was still able to pray for their forgiveness to the Father. How amazing is that! He asked for their forgiveness with an explanation as to why our Heavenly Father should forgive them. He said they didn't know what they were doing. It seemed to me they knew exactly what they were doing! Oh, wait I see...they were sinners. A sinner only does what a sinner knows to do...sin. If my Dad would have really been walking with the Lord, this crazy thing couldn't have happened. Somewhere he was just as lost as any other sinner out there. Maybe he didn't know, I mean really know what he was doing. Or should I say he didn't know the consequences of flying so close to that flame that it would torch his behind. He reminds me of the prodigal son...

Maverick: Baby girl, you sure seem deep in thought. Can you come up for air? What's on your mind?

Shane: Yeah...I was just thinking that my Dad reminded me of the prodigal son. He was in the house of his father, safe, but he still ended up leaving with what he thought he needed, to go get what he thought he wanted, and lost it all. It took him being in his funky mess to realize that he blew it. He had to come to himself and decide to make things right with his father.

290

And even though his brother was mad at him, it wasn't the forgiveness of his brother that mattered. It was his father that stood there with open arms waiting to welcome him back home.

Maverick: Yep and his father threw a big party to welcome him home.

Shane: And when his brother started complaining about him, their father reminded him that he always had his love and everything he ever needed. And basically to get over his self and stop pouting. That's what I need to do.

Maverick: What's that?

Shane: Get over myself! If my Father in Heaven can forgive my Daddy, I have to. And I want to, because I do love him, Maverick. I really do.

Maverick: I know you do, Shane.

Shane: I'm ready to go see my Dad.

Maverick: Let's do it!

How about you? Are you holding un-forgiveness in your heart toward someone? Are you complaining to the Father about one of your brothers or sisters in the faith who has taken advantage of God's love? And you don't feel like they deserve to be forgiven by anybody? Think about this, even though you didn't deserve a second, third, fourth or even a seventy-fifth chance, Father God gave it to you anyway. Can you get over yourself to let go of the un-forgiveness and

forgive others, because God wants you too? Set yourself free right now. Go ahead, you'll feel so much better after you do. In order to experience that freedom, you have to make the choice to forgive. I'm working at it and I'm feeling good right now in this moment. I know you will too.

Chapter 44

Today's Word: Liberation

Well we've had our breakfast and now I'm checking on my parents. I'll start with Daddy first, even though I wanted to start with my Mom. I need to speak my truth and let him know I forgive him. Then on to Mommy's room and love on her! It feels like things are going to get better now.

Shane: Hi Daddy.

Sam: Hi Shane, how are you doing?

Shane: I'm doing fine. How are you feeling?

Sam: I'm feeling pretty good. As a matter of fact, I'm ready to get up and get moving! I told Dr. Z if he'd just let me get out of here the healing would be complete! I need to get some fresh air, ya know!

Shane: Yeah…well, he knows what's best, right?

Sam: I guess. Have you seen your Mom yet?

Shane: No, I wanted to stop and see you first. I heard you stopped by to see her yesterday, how'd that go?

Sam: I guess it went okay. I really didn't know how devastated ya'll were when I left. You're looking at the biggest fool in this world, Shane! I'm really sorry, baby girl! I'll be living the rest of my life, no matter how short or long it may be, making it up to all of you!

Shane: Daddy, it took me a minute to get used to the

fact that you're back in town. And I wanted to forgive you right away and move on, but it just wasn't that easy. It took some soul searching and I can say with my whole heart...I forgive you.

Sam: Oh, Shane! Oh thank you, baby girl! Thank you! I'm so happy to hear it. I really needed to hear that. Can I get a hug now?

Shane: I really needed to say it. I love you Daddy.

Sam: Come here and give me a hug...

Shane: Okay.

This hug feels SO good! I almost forgot what it felt like to be in my Daddy's arms! Our cheeks are wet with tears.

Sam: I'm so proud of you Shane. Really, I am! Stick with Maverick. He'll be good to you.

Shane: Yeah...he better be or he's going down.

Sam: Oh Lord! Going down is a terrible thing. He's a better man than me.

Shane: Well, God has given you a second chance to make things right, Daddy. Just don't blow it.

Sam: A second chance. I guess you can say that...I sure hope so.

Shane: Well, I need to stop and see Mom. I'll be checking back in on you before I leave. Okay?

Sam: Yes, please. Here Shane, take this note to her.

Shane: Okay, I will. Must be important, you got it in an envelope, all sealed up AND with tape, geez! Are you sure you don't want security to take it to her. Are you sure you trust me to deliver this? Haha! I'll see you later.

Sam: Girl, you still silly. It's good to see that hasn't changed. Mav, she got into so much trouble clowning. You better watch her, she loves an audience.

Maverick and Sean were on point. He did need to hear me say the words. Will he still be humble and accessible when he gets back on his feet? I wonder! Only a foolish man would miss this opportunity to bring his life full circle and blow it. I think I would punch him in his throat if he did something else to jack us up. Maybe the best way to deal with this is to leave it in God's hands. Yeah...Lord, I give my Daddy to you and all the worry that goes with our relationship. All I ask is that You help him keep himself together to walk me down the aisle. In Jesus Name! Amen! I'm sorry if that seemed a little selfish. Don't judge me. Hah!

Maverick: Shane...I just spoke with Dr. Z. He said your Dad wants to talk to me. I'll meet up with you somewhere between your Mom and Dad's rooms, okay?

Shane: That's fine. What did Dr. Z say?

Maverick: That's it. I'll talk to you when I'm done. Go see your Mom, tell her I said hello and I send my love. I'll try to say it myself, but just in case…

Shane: Okay, baby.

That man is straight fine! Fine I tell you! God has blessed me! Our honeymoon will have to be at least a month! Okay, let me get my mind back on track! Mom, Mom, Mom! I pray she's doing well today.

KNOCK! KNOCK!

Mom: Who is it?

Shane: Your beautiful daughter! May I grace you with my presence?

Mom: Oh, come on in Princess Shane. Your Queen awaits! Hahaha! You're so crazy!

Shane: Hello Mom. How are you doing today?!

Mom: I'm doing pretty good. I've been doing a lot of thinking and making peace with myself.

Shane: Peace with yourself, huh? That sounds liberating!

Mom: Exactly! That's a good word…liberating! Shane, I decided to forgive myself. Your Dad messed up, but my focus was on what he did to me. I needed to deal with the way I responded. I blew my stack and broke down. Oh baby, there is a lot that you kids don't know. And I'm going to sit you and your brother down and tell you everything as soon as I'm able.

Shane: Okay…so how are you feeling Mom? When

will you be going home?

Mom: I'm getting better, Shane. I really am. I meet with my doctor in about an hour or so. Once I have this conversation with him, I can give you a better idea when I'll get out of here. I think he's been waiting for me to get to this point. Now my healing begins...I hope!

Shane: Liberation is the first step as far as I'm concerned. It seems if you can set yourself free, you can conquer everything else.

Mom: Yeah, baby! The word for today is liberation! Liberation! It sounds wonderful!

Shane: Yes! Liberation! I love it, Mom!

KNOCK! KNOCK!

Nurse: Hi Ms. Sharmane, I'm here to check your vitals and prepare you for your appointment with your doctor. Are you ready?

Mom: Can you give us a couple more minutes. My daughter is with me right now.

Nurse: Sure, I'll give you about 10 minutes and then we have to take care of you and get you on your way.

Mom: Thank you! I've got some really nice nurses.

Shane: That's good! I better not hear about any of them tripping or telling all of our business. Or they are going down!

Mom: I know that's right! Hey!

Shane: Oh, before I forget! Daddy gave me this note to give to you. He sealed it all tight so no one can peek in. Should I leave the room?

Mom: Oh...he did?

Shane: Yes, here you go. And Maverick sends his love to you!

Mom: That Maverick is a sweetie! That's a son-in-law I look forward to having!

Shane: Aww Mom! I'll be sure to let him know!

Mom: Mmhm...that Sam is something else. It seems like he came back to his senses. Too bad he waited too long to make a difference.

Shane: What do you mean, too late? As long as we have breath in our lungs, there is always a chance to make things right!

Mom: Yeah, I didn't mean he's facing a brick wall with me. It's just that...well Shane, I loved your Daddy with everything I had within in me! I loved me some Sam. I guess a part of me still does a little. At least I love the man I married all those years ago. The man that walked out that door was someone else...someone I didn't even know. It's almost like the Sam I knew died. The doctor tells me that I went through a grieving period of someone experiencing a sudden death. I just had a hard time getting over it. As a matter of fact, I'm just now getting over it. That's why I'm here...learning how to live with who I am today...to step forward from the woman who was abandoned all those years ago. I'm not her anymore.

Shane: Liberation?

Mom: Yes! Liberation! Well, baby girl, I need to let this nurse do what she needs to do and get ready to see my doctor. I'm going to put on something I like to wear today. I need to get out of this hospital get up. I've been mooning everybody I pass.

Shane: Uh oh, Mom over hear serving up some moon pie! Haha! Did Mister get that pretty matching robe and gown set over there? He's a good man! How's he doing? I know it's a lot for him.

Mom: Yes he did! And that's exactly what I'm wearing. He's doing well and he's been coming to some of my counseling sessions too. It's been helping him to help me. Oh Shane, I feel so good today! I really do!

Knock! Knock!

Mom: Come in!

Nurse: Are you ready?!

Mom: Yes I am! And I want to change too!

Nurse: Oh isn't that pretty! Well, let's get started.

Shane: Give me some sugar, Mom! I will be talking to you later today! I love you Mom! Tell Mister I said hi and I send my love.

Mom: I love you too, Shane! I will. Remember, liberation is the word for today!

Shane: Liberation!

Liberation! Wow, Mom is on her way to healing and restoration! If we can't forgive ourselves we're trapped! Her eyes sparkled! Especially when she read what my Dad wrote! I wonder what he said in that letter! Oh well, she's remarried and I don't want to be a part of any of that. If her and Dad can get along after all that's happened that's a miracle in itself! I think I'm going to look for my good looking father of our future children. I'll catch up with you in the next chapter! Ciao for now!

Chapter 45
Secret Visit to the Old Oak Tree

AT THE CEMETARY

Sam: Maverick, I appreciate you and Doc Z getting me out here! Where is that old oak tree at?

Maverick: There it is...let's drive in a little further. I want to get you as close as possible so you won't have to walk too far.

Sam: Now you know you can't tell Shane anything about this!

Maverick: Don't worry about it, she's at work right now.

Sam: Good. The nurse station is taking my calls until I get back. This is really hard for me.

Maverick: Yeah. Everything will be all right! Okay, let me walk with you, it's kind of hard walking in the grass.

Sam: Okay, get the teddy bear and the flowers out of the bag for me.

Maverick: Yes sir.

Sam: Okay...let's see...there she is! Help me put these on the headstone. Thank you for bringing me a folding chair. Man, you're a special cat. If you treat my daughter as well as you've treated me, she's going to be happy. Just keep her happy. Okay, thank you.

Now uhm let me be alone for a while. I'll wave you over when I need you.

Maverick: Yes sir.

Sam: Thank you Maverick. Thank you. Oh Lord…Oh Lord…

Maverick: Are you okay?

Sam: Yes…I just can't believe what I'm seeing!

Maverick: I'll be very close by. Let me know when you're ready.

Sam: Mmhm. (Openly weeps)

Maverick: *Wow, this is overwhelming! I don't know what I would do if I lost a child. If Sam can get through this okay, he can restart his life. If not, this can break him down. Lord, I pray that You give Sam the strength and peace he needs. Lord, I pray that You hold him in Your arms and breathe healing into him. Father, only You can heal the broken places in our lives and that You are faithful and true. I thank You for Your peace that passes all understanding and by Your stripes this family is healed. In Jesus' Name, Amen.*

The only way I can help Shane and her family through this is with love and prayer. I'll talk to Dad and Mom so we can pray for their family too. We've already started, but it's time to take our prayer up a notch. I want to help Sam get it back together. The B&B isn't a permanent residence, so he'll need some type of living arrangement.

302

Sam: Maverick?

Maverick: Yes sir, here I come.

Sam: Can you adjust the flowers and bear for me. They fell over.

Maverick: Yes sir. How is that?

Sam: Good. Thank you. Maverick, I'm not sure where to go from here. My heart is broken in a thousand pieces. Can an old man like me put his life back together when there are so many shattered pieces?

Maverick: I believe that with God you can do all things. You're not alone. You never were. All you can do is hold on to God's hand tighter. Just don't let go.

Sam: Don't let go...okay. I'm ready to go now. Soon as I get back, I want to see Doc Z.

Maverick: I'll call him on our way, so that he'll be waiting for you when we get there. Does that sound okay?

Sam: Good...Maverick. That sounds fine, son. Promise me you'll never let the devil slip in between you and my baby girl. Promise me.

Maverick: I promise, Sam. I promise.

Sam: Good.

Maverick: Hey Z, we're on our way back. Sam asked me to call you and make sure you're there when he arrives. Huh? He seems pretty exhausted. This was a real emotional visit. Sam how do you feel?

Sam: I'm tired, really tired. I want him to check my heart out when I get there.

Maverick: He said he wants you to check his heart out when he gets there. He's pretty tired. This visit took a lot out of him. Good, we're about ten minutes away now. Okay, as fast as I can. Thanks, man!

Sam: Maverick…I'll be glad to get back in my bed. I didn't think my body would give me such a struggle. It's like God played a joke on us. When you're young and strong you grab the biggest sharpest crayon in the box, but you constantly color outside the lines. Then when you get old, there's not much crayon left, but you finally figure out how to color within the lines.

Man, I have a lot on my mind. The one thing that's most important to me is that my children know that I love them. Even the one I didn't know about until now. I told Shane's Mama I was going to come here. Once I'm checked back in and settled, I'll let her know.

Maverick: What will you say?

Sam: Uh, I really don't know. I guess I'll tell her I'm sorry again and again. It's a beautiful headstone. Sigh…I don't know.

Maverick: Sam, I know you carry the burden of guilt for what happened. Do you realize that your healing will begin when you can forgive yourself?

Sam: I tore my family apart, Mav! I have to fix it!

Maverick: You're a man, not God. Yeah, you let your family down, but making a mistake isn't a lifetime sentence when God is willing to forgive you. It's only a lifetime sentence when you refuse to forgive yourself. And it comes in time and with a revelation of God's grace. You've already served your time. Please, promise me that you'll think about what I've said.

Sam: Forgive myself, huh? I ain't never heard of that, Maverick! Shane said something like that too.

Maverick: Do you believe God forgave you when you received Jesus in your heart?

Sam: Yeah...I did and I do! Sometimes I feel like the prodigal son. I'm so ashamed and I'm scared to death, but all I really want and need is the Father to take me back.

Maverick: His arms are open wide. Is it so crazy to take the next step of the process and forgive yourself? You are the only one who can set yourself free! From there you can be a better man to your family.

Sam: Hmm...you gave me something to think about. Boy, where did you get all of that wisdom from?

Maverick: My parents and God. I love you Mr. Sam and I want to see your family healed and whole. After all, I'll be a part of it real soon!

Sam: Yes, you will! I'm glad you will. I love you too, Maverick. There is Doc Z. I'm feeling better since we talked. Stay with me until I get settled.

Maverick: Yes sir!

Doc Z: Hello Sam, how are you feeling?

Sam: Better, thanks to Maverick. This boy is something else.

Doc Z: Yeah, he is. Well, let's get you back in your room and settled. Maverick, we'll meet you back in his room in a couple minutes, okay! Come on Sam, your Chariot of Wheels await...have a seat.

Maverick: Sure...I'll be there.

Chapter 46

A New Start with a New Heart

RING! RING!

Shane: Hello handsome!

Maverick: Hi, baby! How's your day going?

Shane: Good…you sound funny. Is everything okay?

Maverick: Yeah, everything is okay. I'm at the hospital checking in on your folks.

Shane: Yeah…I was trying to get through to my Dads room, but I kept getting the nurses station. What's that about?

Maverick: I'm not sure, I'll find out when I get to his room. I'll have him call you, okay?

Shane: Thanks Honey! Well, it's crazy here at work today, I'll talk with you in a little while! I love you! Bye!

Maverick: I love you too. Bye.

Now I know Maverick well enough to know that everything isn't all right when he sounds like that. I'm going to trust that he's got things under control and get to the bottom of it later. I've got to meet my deadlines today, I'll get another promotion if I can put this together just right! More money means a better wedding! I can't wait until we get to that

honeymoon! He's going to surprise me! I hope it's a warm climate where we can be on dry land and look at the water! I can't do any cruise ships! That just ain't happening! Maybe I need to stress that one more time, so he doesn't forget! Okay, enough fantasizing! Back to work, girl!

BACK AT THE HOSPITAL

Sean: Hey Maverick, man, what's going on?

Maverick: Hi Sean, all is well, man. How's it going?

Sean: Good! I just stopped in to see my Mom. She's doing really good today! I'm surprised she asked about my Dad!

Maverick: Oh yeah?

Sean: Yeah! So, I'm here to see how he's doing. His door is closed and the nurses station wants all visitors to check in with them first. Come on, man, let's see what's going on.

Maverick: Cool.

Sean: Excuse me, I'd like to see Sam Vanity. I'm his son.

Nurse: Hi, let me see if he's ready for visitors.

Sean: Ready for visitors? Why is something wrong?

Nurse: No, no…he's just resting. Just a minute….hi Mr. Vanity, your son is here. Yes sir. Yes sir. Okay I'll send them both back.

Sean: Well?

Nurse: Mr. Vanity would like both of you to go to his room.

Sean: How did he know you were here, Mav?

Maverick: I seen him earlier and he asked me to hang around!

Sean: Oh…

KNOCK! KNOCK!

Sam: Come on!

Sean: Hi Dad, how are you feeling?

Sam: Pretty good. I just needed a little break…I feel a whole lot better.

Sean: That's cool. I just saw Mom. She's up and at 'em. She's in a real good mood today.

Sam: Yeah?

Sean: Yup! She asked about you!

Sam: Yeah? What did she say?

Sean: She asked if you were getting enough rest. I got the impression she wants to hear from you real soon.

Sam: Yeah?

Sean: Yeah! You're funny Dad. Hmm, who laid your

clothes out? Did you go out or something?

Sam: Well…uhm. Maverick, have you talked to Shane?

Maverick: Yes sir. She's doing fine. She's pretty busy at work, so I'll have to talk with her later on. I'm sure she'd love to talk to you once she's off work.

Sam: That's good. Well, Sean, I want to talk to your Mom. Can you dial her room for me?

Sean: Sure, I can do that.

Maverick: So, Sam, are you comfortable?

Sam: Yeah, I'm okay. They checked me out real good. I held up real well. Thanks again Maverick. You are all right with me!

Sean: Okay Mom, here's Dad.

Sam: Hello there. How are you doing today? That's good. You sound real good. Uh, hold on. Guys I want to talk in private. Can ya catch up with me later on today? I want to talk with your Mom and then I'm going to nap for a while. Sean I love you, thanks for stopping by! And you too, Maverick!

Sean: Okay, I have to be getting back to the B&B.

Maverick: Me too. See ya!

Sam: Bye…okay I'm back. Yeah Sean and Maverick just left. Guess where I went today. I saw…I uh went…to the cemetery today. I left a teddy bear and flowers… Oh Lord, I'm sorry Shar, I'm so sorry! Will you ever find it in your heart to forgive me? I just didn't know and my heart is breaking in a million pieces. Seeing it makes it more real… I wish you would have said something to me… Huh? I was a fool Sharmane! Mmhm. Do you think that we can visit the grave together once we both get out? Will Mister mind? I'm not trying to come between you. Well, I just want to bring closure to the pain of the past, as much as we can. I just want to start from this place in our lives with the kids and be a better man. Huh? Yeah Doc Z checked me out…I'm okay, just tired. It's time for my nap, too. Okay, thanks I'll talk to you later.

SAM'S PRAYER:

Lord have mercy on my soul! I messed up real bad! I don't think I want to live if I can't make things right with my kids! I ain't a coward! I know You love me even if everyone else walks away. But I need the love of my kids. Lord, I do care for my children. I don't want to live by myself anymore. I don't want to be on the outside looking in! Lord, help me be the man You can be proud of. Help me be the man my kids can be proud of! Help me be the man that Sharmane can forgive without regretting it! She's a good woman, Lord. And it's time she stops hurting and start living…my kids too. Maybe even me too. Oh and Lord, help me forgive myself. In the Precious name of your Holy Son, Amen.

Chapter 47
Closing the Door and Letting Go

Well, Mom and Dad are finally getting out today. Can you believe it? Of course you can. How that worked out I'll never know! She asked me and Sean to come and get them both. That's different. I wonder how they worked that out with Mister.

Anyway, they want to stop somewhere on the way home. Daddy is going to live at B&B until his apartment is secured. I can't wait to help him decorate. That's cool. If he needs any help, they have medical staff onsite to help him out. This is feeling really weird! I haven't been with both my parents in one place in decades. I hope I can handle it, and not break down. I still can't believe that we've come this far after all that has happened. Liberation! Freedom from our past and dashing toward our future!

Sean: Shane, you ready?

Shane: Yeah, let me grab my purse! So where do you think Mom and Daddy want to go when they get out?

Sean: You really don't know? Think about it.

Shane: To a nice restaurant to get some real food? Hospital food isn't all that great you know. Blah.

Sean: Okay, Sis. Either that or maybe we'll talk about the whole family situation. Opening the vault to our big family secret.

Shane: I don't know if I'm ready for the "baby talk", Sean. That's such a painful topic.

Sean: It is, but it's probably been the one thing that's made Mom so sick. They've been having these private conversations...she's seemed to start getting better. Shane, I think Daddy went out the other day with Maverick.

Shane: Really? He didn't tell me anything about it. When...oh, I wonder if it was the day when Daddy was hard to reach? I kept getting the Nurses Station. Mav never mentioned it. They're kind of close.

Sean: Yeah, when I got there Daddy's clothes were lying out on the chair and he seemed real evasive when I asked about it. His shoes had some dirt and grass on them. And Maverick's did too.

Look at my bro with his I'm A Spy capabilities! He sure did call my butt out on a few things growing up! Big tattle tell! Hahaha! Still the best guy I know!

Shane: Maverick was a little off that day. I was wondering what the deal was. That explains it. If he was tripping with another woman, he would be getting the Vanity Smack Down. He already knows.

Sean: Another woman? Maverick? I just couldn't see him doing that, he loves you too much. More than that, he respects you, Shane. Stop tripping! Anyway, since we know about the baby that helps us not freak out real bad. So we need to act shocked, but not overdo it. Sis, please be quiet and let them talk. You know how you are.

Shane: Why wouldn't I? Sean, look this is serious. Up until now it's hearsay. I guess it's more than that because Mommy said it too and you explained it. Now my nerves are on edge just thinking about it.

Yep, okay, I'll be quiet. I'm having trouble right now holding it together. He knows me all too well.

Sean: I'm just saying…when you get nervous you tend to talk too much. Like now. So take deep breaths when you feel that coming on and force your mouth shut, all right?

Shane: Oh Sean! I've got it together a little better now. I'm not the same girl from yesterday, I did evolve in the last 24 hours! Didn't you?

Sean: Girl, don't you start none, won't be none.

Shane: Whatever. Come on let's go inside…there they are. My love for life is here too! Hi, baby!

Maverick: Hi Sweetheart! I wanted to see your parents off and talk with Z. But more importantly, I wanted to see my baby! Come and give me a hug!

Shane: Aww, what a surprise!

Maverick: Yeah, I like to keep you guessing.

Shane: Sounds good to me. Just don't get crazy with it. Hi Mom!

Mom: Hi Shane, you look so pretty! Do I look alright?

Shane: You always look good. Gorgeous as usual!

Mom: That's my girl. You're not just saying that? Don't have me looking crazy, Shane!

Shane: Oh no, Mom! Really, you look…beautiful and liberated! It's in your eyes! You look like a new woman with power and fight! Something I don't know if I've ever seen in you.

Mom: Wow! That sounds terrific! I feel different…better than ever. I've tied up some loose ends in my past and now I'm ready to step into my future. Sometimes you have to lose your balance to appreciate God's strong hand.

Shane: Yeah, that's what I'm talking about! Hi Daddy!

Sam: Hey, baby girl, I'm finally, out the door! Maverick is going to be a wonderful addition to our family!

Shane: Yeah, I'm starting to see that in a deeper way! You and my honey are getting close, huh? Ya'll even have some secrets, huh?

Sam: Shane? What kind of question is that? Haha! Don't you know men are men and women are women? Haha!

Shane: Mommy, where is Mister at?

Mom: He's getting my final paperwork in order. He'll be here in a minute.

Shane: How does he feel about all this? Is he okay with you leaving with us and Daddy?

Mom: Shane, this is something I have to do for me. Mister knows he'll reap the benefits when I can close the door to my painful past. And today, I got my hand on the door handle. I just have to do one more thing and it involves you and your brother. Besides, he's coming too.

Shane: Uh…okay, Mommy. Is this going to hurt us?

Mom: The past can't hurt us unless we hold on to it while we're trying to go forward. Have you ever tried to go through a door and not let go of the handle? You can only go so far, if you don't let go. No matter how much you move, it will just swing you back and forth, but you still ain't going anywhere. When you close that door and lock it, then let that handle go and walk away…you know that it's secure and you can move on freely. Liberation! It's all about liberation, Shane!

Shane: Liberation. Wow, Mom. You've come a long way and I'm so proud of you!

Mom: That's right! Mister, come here.

Mister: Yeah Shar? How you doing, Shane.

Shane: Hi, Mister. I'm fine.

Mom: Thank you honey for supporting through all of this. I love you, baby!

Mister: Shar, I'll be here clear through to eternity… you know that! I'm not going anywhere.

Mom: You know, Mister, today I believe you for the first time. Now I can see your love for me.

Mister: Good, good! I'll see you later! Sam, Sean, Shane…ya'll take care of her! Maverick, you take care. I'll see ya'll real soon.

Mom: Wait, you're not coming?

Mister: I think it's better that you all do this without me. I've gone with you before and you know I'm here when you're done. Your kids got you, you'll be okay. I'll be waiting with open arms when you come home. I love you Sharmane.

Mom: Oh, Mister I love you. I'll be home soon.

Sam: Mister, thanks man!

Mister: Uh huh! You just better appreciate this opportunity 'cause it's all you're getting. I ain't nobody's fool, this is all for Sharmane!

So Mister got some bass in that voice and it's strong! He's all right with me. You can tell he's an old school big brawler. Kind of quiet, but he don't play.

Doc Z: You all take care! If you need me, you know where to find me. And I'm looking to get that home cooked meal real soon, Ms. Sharmane!

Mom: Yeah, yeah…it will be soon, Doc Z. Soon as I get to the grocery store.

Doc Z: Yes Ma'am! Mav, call me later, all right?!

Maverick: Yeah. Come on let's get my future in-loves in the limo!

Shane: Yeah, that's what I'm talking about!

Sean: Where are we going, Dad?

Sam: You'll see.

Sean just gave me that look. Today's the day. Oh, Lord. Here we go. Please help me hold it together.

Chapter 48
Tell the Truth and Shame the devil

AT THE PRAYING HANDS CEMETARY

Well, Sean was right. Now it feels like we're going to the cemetery after a funeral service, but we didn't have one. It's pretty strange and I'm really scared.

Sam: Listen, me and your Mom brought you here for a special reason.

Shane: Why?

Mom: Well, I guess the only way to say this is to just say it. Back when your Dad left, I didn't handle it well and ended up in the hospital. Do ya'll remember? Shane, I sent you to camp and Sean went to my sister's house for a couple weeks.

Sean: Uh…yes ma'am.

Shane: Yes ma'am. **Wow…this is for real, huh?**

Mom: Yes well, while I was in the hospital, they were trying to stabilize me, because I was also pregnant. The sad news is my body couldn't hold her anymore and I had a miscarriage.

Oh my God! I don't know if I can handle this! I feel like I'm in a crazy dream! Even though Sean told me, it's still crazy to me!

Shane: Oh Mommy…I'm so sorry.

Mom: Yes, baby. Please forgive me for taking so long to tell you. You too Sean…

Sean: Dad…how does this make you feel? Did you know she was pregnant when you left?

Sam: No, no I didn't, Sean. And I regret ever leaving! Shane, Sean you have to know I didn't know! This sweet little baby is...oh God.

Shane: I'm really trying to take this all in right now!

Mom: Your little sister's name is Shayla. Her grave is over by that tree, next to Grandma.

We're all weeping over our sweet baby Shayla and holding one another...like family. It's real and it hurts. As we walk toward the tree holding hands, my heart feels like a hard rock breaking away into little pieces, but there's something glowing inside. We're mourning a past we could have had. But this is where we are right now, in this moment...grieving as a family.

Humanity can be such a trip! Sometimes we live like there is no one else in this world. There are children affected by our decisions, family members all around us watching and hurting, even our friends. But we keep on going on our rampage of selfishness and we leave this path of casualties with regret and brokenness. I can barely see through my tears now. Mommy and Daddy are weeping. I never seen them like this before. Sean is crying. Maverick is leaning on the limo crying too. He must know the story. He and my Dad have been spending a lot of time together. Oh look at that...the teddy bear is wrapped in plastic. Daddy is putting fresh flowers on her grave and Mom's putting fresh flowers on Grandma's grave. This is tearing me up. All I can do is fall to my knees and weep. I miss my Grandma so much! She must have been with Mom through all of this. I'm going to look through her Bible later.

Our little sister is next to Grandma. I know she's taking care of her until we can see them in Heaven. I wonder what she looks like. Wow. I'm feeling some kind of way. All I can do is weep for what could have been. But today is the first day of our new beginning, together, as a healing family.

I'll get back to you after we're done here.

Before you go...

Well, I believe the healing has begun in our family. I can't remember how long it's been since I last saw my Mom and Dad hold one another. There is a life beyond this pain and I'm aiming for it. I think we all are. We're on the right track now. Man that was rough! My eyes are still swollen from crying.

I've learned a lot about myself and I realize I can't handle this life without Christ. I've been a mess trying to do things my way. I hope you caught the vibe about liberation. We blow it sometimes. We blow it real big and have to deal with the consequences of our actions. But if we really want to get it together, we need others to help us, to pray for us, and to guide us through. God will send them.

The truth of the matter is this: This world is full of hurting people and we have to do our part to take the time and let them know they matter, because they do. You matter! That's why this book was written. And you need to know that you can face tomorrow, because tomorrow holds great promise of a better day. Each day takes us away from the past and closer to our better days! We just got to close those doors, lock them, and let the knobs go.

Thanks for riding this thing out with me. I'll be around and I look forward to spending some more time with you in the future. You'll see me walking past, in a stranger's face, even in your family and friends. My kind of story is everywhere. Just make sure you take the time to reach out to them, like Maverick, his parents, and Carol did to us. Or give people a chance to share the love of Jesus with you.

Until then my friend keep working out your salvation. You know it's a lifestyle, right? It all begins and ends with Jesus. His love is better than anything in the whole wide world! His love is like fire down in my bones!

What? So do you want to know what Shane's Fire is really all about? Shall I summarize it for you? So in the beginning was me and the big party, right? There circling like a sexy hot shark was Maverick. God sent that little nerdy chubby boy to my rescue, but he didn't strike me as much at the time. Hahaha! Some girls dream of a knight in shining armor, but let me tell you, no mere man will ever come close to Jesus. Through the journey of prayer, transparency, and mirror reflection, I began to see how God seen me. I witnessed the miracle of my brother, his love for life Carol, and my Dad go through the darkest places in their lives and show up at the door of the B&B. Grace met them and set them on a course toward the Light of the world. Now enters car wrecks, miracles, and family secrets from the past, and it was a doozy! But Jesus was right there healing broken hearts, broken promises, and mending and rebuilding broken bridges. Did you know Jesus has mad carpentry skills too? For real though! Hey!

He always spoke life through his servants to help us along the way. But the devil tried it, but his dastardly plans didn't succeed. My Sistas still don't know what exactly happened to me. Their bad jokes at my expense and Lynn's "I got a secret" jabs didn't thrill me, you know, so I kept to myself until I get a better footing on my salvation. Old Shane ain't completely snuffed out just yet! Hah! It's gonna be all right though. I still love them, I've just started on my path to Heaven, I guess. Things change, people change for the better. Lord knows I'm not comparing. It doesn't make me better than them, just better than my former self. I'm the only one who can measure that change.

Well things are good with me and Mav! He officially asked my dad for my hand and dropped to that knee with the juicy diamond ring in the company of my friends and haters. Hahaha! It was absolutely BEAUTIFUL! He better stop playing with me. Hah! Seriously, I'm not trying to knock the church door down to get married just yet. I believe we can take it slow and learn more about one another and grow in Christ. Plus, it gives me time to plan my wedding and Mav time to save up for that amazing honeymoon! I'll be sure to send you an invitation. You've come this far with me, so I hope you'll attend.
My truth is this...as amazing as Maverick is, Jesus really is my Ultimate Fire. Looking back, I now see He was with me every step of the way. He's always been there when everyone else left me hanging. He uses the people who hear His voice. Jesus is my Lord and Savior, my Secret Keeper, my Healer...He's my ride or die! He already died and rose, so now we're just riding! Hey! I pray you'll let Him light your fire too! ♥

Thank you for selecting my book for your reading pleasure. I pray this fiction made you smile, gave you some positive things to think about, and a better sense of God's love and grace.

God bless you!
Kat

9 781093 237948